The Devil's Halo

The Devil's Halo

Rhys Hughes

With a Foreword by A.A. Attanasio

Elsewhen Press

The Devil's Halo

First published in Great Britain by Elsewhen Press, 2025
An imprint of Alnpete Limited

Quote in chapter two is from 'A Dream Within a Dream' by Edgar Allan Poe, first published in *The Works of the Late Edgar Allan Poe*, ed. R.W.Griswold, New York: J.S.Redfield,1850.

Elsewhen Press, PO Box 757, Dartford, Kent DA2 7TQ
www.elsewhen.press

British Library Cataloguing in Publication Data.
A catalogue record for this book is available from the British Library.

ISBN 978-1-915304-60-5 Print edition
ISBN 978-1-915304-70-4 eBook edition

Designed and formatted by Elsewhen Press

This book is a work of fiction. All names, characters, places, institutions, and events are either a product of the author's fertile imagination or are used fictitiously. Any resemblance to actual events, organisations, states, places or people (living, dead, or in limbo) is purely coincidental.

Singer is a trademark of Singer Sourcing Limited LLC. Use of trademarks has not been authorised, sponsored, or otherwise approved by the trademark owners.

This devilish novel is dedicated to
my heavenly wife, Maithreyi

Foreword

"Reading is a mesmeric experience, and
The Devil's Halo is one hypnotic
horizon after another!"

The Devil's Halo is an impressive literary achievement: a
nested story sequence of voices and perspectives as
kaleidoscopic as Chaucer, metaphysical as Dante, defiant
as Milton, and uniquely Hughes: thoroughly po-mo,
simultaneously structured and chaotic, darkly humorous,
absurd and macabre in cheerfully inventive ways and,
above all, entertaining.

In this novel, the Devil is certainly in the details!
Playful language, puns, and ironic twists rappel the reader
over the edge of the ordinary into the deeper chambers of
the heart. There, in the purgatorial Waiting Room of Hell,
where the living meet themselves dead and time opens to
eternity, we finally get to listen, to hear the stories
defining us all, elaborating our humanity.

I admire the way Montgomery Zubris, true to his name
and full of anthropic pride, cleaves fiercely to his wit and
resilience. He holds his own with the Devil. What valor
he displays, maneuvering the Waiting Room and relating
with resourceful curiosity to "Don't Drink and Drive"
Aaron and "Armchair" Aaron. We all feel his frustration
with the mechanical afterlife where souls are sorted
alphabetically and angels enforce arbitrary seating rules
with flaming swords! Too weirdly familiar!

The infinite nature of the Waiting Room "makes room"
for every absurdity – and I delighted in reading about
Bartholomew's tragic obsession with the fiery Alberto
Whom – and the romantic folly of the rocketeering Star-
Crossed Lovers. Zubris' inventive efforts to accelerate his
judgment with various contraptions celebrate his
ingenuity while hammering home the futility of it all – a
tension that generates a current throughout the novel,

which lights up the filamentary stories of the souls and casts their illumination into the infinite regress of the Waiting Room, eternity's mirror reflecting both the inevitable and the unknown. Even a run-on like that can't catch up with the rush of marvels and insights in this book. Finishing it, I feel invigorated by the energy of the writing and the drama of existential uncertainty that permeate the novel, a grand thought-experiment about morality, meaning, and storytelling itself.

A uniquely irreverent and philosophical novel, *The Devil's Halo* invites us to laugh at the absurdity of existence while contemplating the deeper implications of our own moral and existential choices.

A.A. Attanasio
November 2024

ONE

The Devil said, "Look here, old chap, we are still going through your paperwork and it's more complicated than you suppose. There are very few clear cut cases when it comes to judging a person's life. You assume there is only one question to be asked. Was he good or bad?"

"Isn't that what it boils down to?" I asked.

The Devil winced. "I wouldn't make any references to boiling yet. And no, it can't be reduced to such a simple question. Just using 'good' and 'bad' as the only two variables in the equation isn't a workable approach. No, it's not. There isn't even an equation, not really."

"I am astonished to learn this," I answered.

"People who come here often are. And it's the same in the other place. Lots of deliberation is necessary. Listen, I enjoy mathematics but this is morality, not calculus. The issues at stake are intricate. There are many philosophical aspects in any consideration of how an individual is morally rated. Investigations must be thorough and you appear to be a fellow of ambiguous character. For every act of grace, you have a malign one."

"What am I supposed to do now?" I cried.

"Wait," came the crisp reply, "in the Waiting Room that has been prepared for cases such as yours." Then the Devil's voice became less formal again. With a nudge of his elbow in my ribs, he added, "The Waiting Room isn't so awful. It is certainly better than Hell itself."

"How long do you think my case will take?"

He shrugged. "Twenty-four."

"Hours?" I was alarmed that a whole day would pass in whatever limbo lay in wait for me behind those doors.

He shook his horned head and I gasped, "Days?" but he kept shaking and a horrible prospect opened up before me. "Weeks? Months? Years?" I felt hot and cold at the same time. "Centuries?"

"Aeons," he said. And then he yawned. I blinked. His forked beard was so oily it gleamed in the dim light of the cavern. He took me by the arm, and while his tail lashed from side to side, he guided me to the double doors that appeared to be made from pocked granite.

"Just through here," he said, as he propelled me with a little push. I lost my balance and tumbled into the igneous doors. They swung open to admit me and I rolled on the floor. Before they shut again, I heard him add, "Plenty of waiting chaps inside you can make friends with. The millennia will seem to fly by, trust me. No restrictions on amusements."

I wasn't reassured by his words, which were abruptly cut off by the closing of the granite portals. I knew they wouldn't open from this side. I was bruised a little on my elbows and knees. But I stood and regarded my surroundings. I was in a chamber so vast there was no visible end to it. There were chairs, sofas and divans of all kinds arranged haphazardly. Some of them were occupied. I licked my lips and took a few paces forward.

"Newcomer, huh?" said a man on a rocking chair.

I nodded. "That's right."

"What else could you be? Pointless question. But I *asked it anyway*. That's how I pass the time. Infinity," he added after a pause, "is the heaviest weight on the shoulders of a dead soul."

"You have been here for a long time?"

"Not really. One hundred years, a century. A grain of sand on the shifting dunes of Forever. But I am getting used to it. Tedium can be stimulating if you don't take it too seriously and–"

"There are better amusements here," said another voice, more strident, low in register, and I turned to see a fellow frowning at me from a very comfortable armchair. He was dressed smartly and my intuition told me that he was one of those minor sinners, an embezzler or fraudster, someone who would probably be consigned to a less painful Circle of Hell. Once his paperwork was done, that is. His frown continued. I asked:

"Such as?" and I realised my voice was a croak.

"Telling stories," he said.

2

He leaned forward, although in the luxurious depths of his particular chair he looked just as stuck as when he was sprawled almost horizontal. "Let me say that I prefer short tales, the briefer the better. Thrills without frills. Long stories annoy me. I seem to lack patience."

"A major disadvantage in a place like this," commented the first man, then he chuckled and the shaking of his body made his rocking chair oscillate. With a sigh, the second man continued:

"I have only been here for a few months. I am still in full possession of my senses. The decay of my mind hasn't begun. I will tell you a story and I suggest you tell me one in return."

At a loss for words, I simply stood there, and my failure to respond quickly enough seemed to irritate him.

"It doesn't have to be a major epic," he snapped.

"But my mind is blank."

He threw up his hands, exasperated. "Then you ought to clear off. It's far better to be where you belong."

"Wherever that might be," said the first man.

"Not near here, I hope," snarled the man in the armchair, and he scratched his head with unwarranted ferocity. "Well, I don't care if I don't get any story in exchange. I intend to tell *mine*."

I found this rather mystifying and was about to say so, but he was clearing his throat and preparing to speak. The first man was still chuckling and rocking, but more quietly and less vigorously, and soon he settled back into quietude. At the same moment, the smartly dressed fellow fixed me with his piercing eyes, a gaze too intense for such a casual moment, and then a stream of words came out of his mouth. I was vaguely alarmed.

Sewing

My mother told me that she had started sewing as a hobby. It was something she had never been good at. I assumed she didn't want to be good at it. It had been a long time since I last visited her. Maybe I was feeling a little guilty, but life had been busy. I called on her one day unexpectedly. She invited me in and that was when she told me about her sewing.

"You are skilled at it now, I suppose?" I said.

"Sew-sew," she joked.

That was another surprise. I never imagined her as a comedian, and despite the fact it was a poor witticism, I nodded in lieu of a laugh and said, "Buttons on shirt fronts and cuffs. Hems also?"

"Not just those. I do advanced stuff now," she confided, tapping the side of her nose like a fictional villain.

Then she winked and cried, "Patchwork dolls."

I twisted my mouth.

She offered to show them to me and I wanted to decline, but I had already disappointed her many times, so I warped the twist in my mouth into the shape of a smile and nodded. She said:

"I don't sew them by hand, you know."

"You use a sewing machine?" I asked, but she had turned and was stepping along a corridor and didn't hear.

I called louder, "A Singer? You have a Singer?"

"Oh yes," she answered.

She reached a door and one wrinkled hand reached out for the handle. With a little chuckle, she looked over her shoulder at me. I was close behind now. Her neck made a screeching noise as her head swivelled, as if it needed oiling. Then she said, "In here. It's my room."

"But every room in this house is yours."

"I don't mean that, silly."

No, clearly she didn't. She opened the door. This was her special room, the chamber where those grotesque oddities known as patchwork dolls were created and stored and allowed to blaspheme the universe from the shelves on the walls. In the exact centre of this space stood something unusual, but I didn't notice it at first. I was too distracted by the array of dolls, an insane collection, a mishmash of colours and patterns and grins.

Even the supposedly cute dolls looked evil.

Then I lowered my gaze.

The object in the middle of the chamber was a man. A very rotund fellow. He was dressed formally, in a dinner jacket with tails, silk trousers, shoes with such a perfect polish on them that they reflected mad dolls' faces, a frilled shirt and a floppy bow tie. He had slicked black hair and a trimmed moustache with waxed ends. A kiss curl was plastered to his forehead. He was engrossed in his task, which was sewing a new doll.

My mother moved to the wall, took down a baton that was hanging from a nail by a loop. She gripped it by the handle and swung it, narrowly missing me. I had guessed the twist to this little adventure but it wasn't a conductor's baton. It was more like a club and the bulbous end was festooned with little spikes and barbs. She approached the stranger.

But he wasn't a stranger to her, of course, only to me. She delivered a hard blow to his buttocks and he yelped.

"Too slow! You are slacking. Faster, faster!"

He accelerated his pace.

I was mortified. Somehow she had abducted this fellow and was exploiting him, using him as a slave: a machine.

"Yes, he's a Singer, just as you guessed. From the opera." She slapped him again for good measure, with less force, then leaned on the long baton, wearied by her viciousness. "He's a baritone."

"The opera," I said, but I had nothing more to add.

We left that appalling room.

I sat with her for another half hour, drinking her tea, before leaving. It was many months before I visited her again, and I never asked her about her sewing. It was none of my business. Five years later I died and came here. I suppose she went straight to Hell without needing her sins to be graded. Certainly I haven't had the dubious pleasure of meeting her in the afterlife. But I wouldn't feel any astonishment if that opera singer happened to be among us. Just because he was a victim doesn't mean he was good.

—o0o—

The brief tale was over. I didn't applaud or shout my appreciation. I would have felt very foolish. Instead I muttered something about mothers being strange. The ensuing silence was painful. At last, the narrator of the story collapsed back into the fathomless depths of his armchair.

The first man, the one in the rocking chair, said, "What is your name? That is the most important question here."

"My name?" I cried.

"Your surname. Your first name is less significant."

"Zubris," I told him.

"It sounds a lot like Hubris."

"But it isn't that. It is Zubris. I am Montgomery Zubris. I died of thirst in a faulty elevator. I was trapped for four days and nobody came to my rescue. That was unpleasant, but it's done now."

"I am Aaron," he said.

"Me too," snarled the man in the armchair.

"Related?" I inquired.

"Not that we know of. We just have the same surname. People in this room are arranged in alphabetical order."

"I wasn't told that."

"The Devil isn't too forthcoming with information. But that's the system in place. Alphabetical order of surnames. The letter 'A' is near the front, right here, and the letter 'Z' is at the back."

"How far back? How long is this room?"

The first Aaron looked at the second, who arched his eyebrows and sighed and said slowly, "We don't know."

The man in the armchair added, "It wouldn't even be right to guess. But if you wish, I'll make an estimate anyway." Without waiting for me to respond to his peculiar generosity, he said, "I was a statistician when I was alive, therefore I suppose I am still one now. About 117 billion humans have ever been born on Earth in total. Let's say that half of those have gone to Heaven. That leaves 58.5 billion who were sent to Hell."

"A very rough estimate," observed the other Aaron.

"Better than nothing!"

I wasn't sure about that, but I kept quiet. The man in the armchair counted on his fingers, though these silent quantities were unrelated to the sums that he shouted at me. "Of all those sent down to Hell, I seem to recall the Devil saying that two-thirds were cases that needed to be scrutinised in order to determine the appropriate Circle of Punishment."

"In other words, souls in this Waiting Room."

"Right. Spot on. Us."

He beamed at me, a savage grin.

"So what does that mean? Two-thirds of 58.5 billion is 38.7 billion. That's how many individuals are in this room. Every seat, whether chair, sofa, stool, divan, is spaced about two and a half metres apart from the next. The width of the hall means that a maximum of eight seats can be fitted laterally, but as an average we ought to claim six."

"Six *columns*, in other words," said the first Aaron.

"Yes. So how many rows?"

I heard myself saying, "38.7 billion divided by six is 6.45 billion, a number that, if multiplied by the average distance between each seat, namely 2.5, gives a total of 16.125 billion metres."

The man in the armchair seemed pleased by the fluidity of my arithmetic. I felt he was warming towards me.

"Sixteen million, one hundred and twenty five thousand kilometres, which is 10,019,610 miles. Call it ten million. You have a journey of ten million miles ahead of you. There is no method of transport here other than walking. What is the average walking pace of a man? Three miles per hour. That is three million, three hundred and thirty-three thousand, three hundred and thirty-three hours of walking. 138,888 days, which equates to 380.5 years. And that's non-stop. You had better start immediately."

And he laughed at his own poor joke.

The first Aaron rocked his rocking chair to vent some of his frustration and then he said, "Before you go?"

I waited for him to explain himself.

"My tale can be told too," he said, and he glanced

sheepishly at the second Aaron, who hadn't forgotten his earlier disparagement of storytelling, but there was no objection from that quarter.

"Go ahead," I said. What else could I say?

And that's what he did.

Driving

I was in a city on the edge of the desert. I had business to conduct there and with very little fuss I conducted it. Now before I continue any further with this rather sober and sombre narrative, I need to make you aware that I'm very law-abiding and always have been. I follow rules. My business was over and I took a taxi to the airport to fly home. But the airport was closed. There had been a fire and all flights were suspended. I was told I could find a flight from another airport but that other airport was in a different city.

It occurred to me that maybe this was an opportunity for an adventure. The bus would have conveyed me to that other city at a reasonable cost, and the taxi driver was willing to take me there in greater comfort for a rather larger sum. It was a journey of a hundred miles or so.

But what if I left the country overland? Instead of going to that other city's airport and taking a plane back home, what if I drove all the way over the desert to the border of the next country? I could hire a car to do that. When I reached the border I felt sure I would find someone to drive the car for a fee and return it to the hire company. Then I would seek some other method of transportation to continue my journey. The result would be an opportunity to experience the vast desert, the landscape of rolling dunes and weird rock formations, to pass ancient ruins and meteorite craters and dead volcanoes. To understand a little of what a truly harsh environment really means.

I told the taxi driver to return me to my hotel and I paid for another night's stay. The following morning I visited the offices of a car hire company, where a helpful man called Hector Gonzales listened to my plan and nodded his head frequently as he did so. Yes, my trip was feasible. He had contacts at the border town, drivers who would agree to return the car. It was an unusual request but nothing beyond his capabilities. He would arrange everything. He mentioned the fact that it was a challenging desert to drive across and asked if I had the relevant experience. I told him yes, though I was stretching the truth, and he required no further proof of my competence. And that was that.

Hector gave me the keys to a car and advised me to take plenty of supplies. A breakdown in the desert was a serious matter, even if I stuck to the highway, which saw very little traffic. I drove off and stopped at a shop to purchase food in the form of packets of nuts and a large container of water. That was enough, I felt. The petrol tank was full. I was ready. I set off and soon left the city behind me. I entered the timeless zone, a region of sandstorms and accelerated sunsets and vistas too colossal to comprehend.

As I drove along, a final roadsign warned me in simple terms not to drink and drive. It said: Don't Drink and Drive. How can a message be clearer than that? As I have already said, I'm a very law-abiding individual and always have been. I follow rules. I would not drink anything while driving. Of course, thirst soon began to irritate my throat and my lips started itching. I glanced back at the container of water on the seat behind me.

But no, I wouldn't touch it. No drinking and driving. It occurred to me that I could stop the car on the side of the highway and take a drink, because then I wouldn't be driving it, but on second thoughts what if a policeman came along? He would be sure to ask, "Is this the car you are driving?" and I would have to say yes, it was, which means that on some technical level I was still driving the vehicle even while it was parked on the verge. I didn't want to risk breaking any rule and so I refrained from drinking.

It was a long day and a very long drive and my thirst steadily grew worse and worse and my tongue swelled in my mouth. I recall how a person who was called 'a swell' in the old days was regarded as somebody special, but now the term seemed unpleasant rather than elegant. My vision blurred too. The sweat poured down my face and I felt I was burning up from inside. I was in desperate need of water, no doubt about that, but I remembered the sign and how I always follow the rules. No drinking and driving. Drinking was fine, driving too, but in combination they were simply banned.

At this point, ten hours after I set off from the city, I saw mirages far away, imaginary oases and inner seas, floating gardens and vineyards, and I gibbered with anticipation at the thought I was driving towards them. But I never reached any of them. They were phantoms, some of them created by shimmering air and others by my feverish imagination. I even thought I saw Hector on the side of the road with his thumb raised, a hitchhiker.

At some point in the next few hours a violent weariness that had nothing to do with normal tiredness came over me. I shuddered and shook as I yawned and I felt chills dancing on my flesh. I had stopped sweating. My eyelids were heavy and swollen and kept shutting with an audible creak, like the doors of an antique wardrobe full of pieces of a shattered statue. A statue of whom? Myself, I guess. My senses were disordered and I slept.

I slept for a few seconds at a time, jerking awake again as if some doctor or dentist was lancing me in the neck or the mouth. I had come off the road. I was driving through the desert, bouncing along over the uneven ground, and when I turned my head the highway was nowhere to be seen. My wheels skidded on the loose sand, jumped over the sharp rocks, and fine grains of powdered sandstone covered my windshield. I croaked, unable to articulate proper words. I was now aware that I was trapped in deep sand.

The spinning wheels served only to dig a deeper and

deeper hole. Then the engine died and I found myself at the base of a self-made crater. I gazed for the last time at the container of water and wished I had travelled by mule, bicycle, on foot, or even walking on my hands.

The next thing I knew was that I had died. The Devil was telling me that I was going to be a complicated case to review. I had to take my place with all the other souls in the Waiting Room. There were plenty of people in there who also had died of thirst but I probably wouldn't meet them because my surname was very near the start of the alphabet, thus my assigned place was near the door he was about to push me through. I wouldn't get a chance to stroll the length of the room, chatting to souls as I went past.

And so here I am, sitting on a rocking chair.

—oOo—

He rocked himself with greater urgency just to prove the truth of this statement. His death seemed ludicrous. But there was something else about his story that bothered me. And so I said:

"That's all very well, but if you are as law-abiding as you claim to be, why are you down here? Good people go straight to Heaven. Very wicked people go straight to Hell. The moderately evil linger in this room, waiting to be assigned a Circle and a Punishment."

"He's a dissembler," said Aaron in the armchair, but he smiled as he made this claim. The other Aaron smiled too. "I don't mean you can't trust any of his words, but he doesn't seem to care about things that don't add up. His tales are full of contradictions and continuity errors and claims that defy logic. I suppose he has been a bad man but not too bad, just like us. But I do believe that he died of thirst. He drinks as much liquid as he can get now and that says something. I am amazed at how he guzzles it."

Aaron in the rocking chair said, "Listen, you care about things that add up because you were a statistician."

"You can't wriggle out of it that way, my friend."

"Well, let me just try."

They were about to begin a good-natured argument, but

there were things I wanted to know. "You say he drinks as much as he can down here? Where does it come from in this room?"

They both looked at me and blinked.

I think they had temporarily forgotten I knew nothing about the system the Devil had put in place. They both cleared their throats, but it was the Aaron in the armchair who answered:

"From hatches in the ceiling. They slide open and silver trays are lowered on cords and on those trays are jugs of water, often fruit juice, sometimes beer or cider, occasionally shandy, bottles of wine, and also platters of food, all of it vegetarian, most of it delicious."

"At rare intervals," added the other Aaron, "it is overcooked or underdone but generally it is perfect, soups and curries in tureens, tagines, pasta dishes and couscous, salads too and fruit, cheese and desserts, puddings and ice cream. But you never know what you'll get."

"It's fairly random and I mean that literally. I've been keeping track, trying to discern a pattern, for that's my nature. I love statistics. Trays are lowered and we indulge ourselves and the trays are hauled back up. If we don't eat the food, the trays are pulled up anyway. We are given an hour. It's difficult to go hungry in the Waiting Room of Hell."

"Personally I prefer the drink to the food. I pour as much as possible down my throat whenever I get a chance. I often give my portions of food away. Even here it is possible to trade items. I swap cakes for ale. My companion here ends up with plenty of extra nibbles."

The armchair Aaron licked his lips.

"The hatches open along the entire length of the room. At least that seems to be the case. Otherwise hungry souls would come from the depths of the room and help themselves to our supplies. But they don't. Nobody comes back. They keep going forward or else they take up residence in the zone assigned to them. I think we can safely assume there is nourishment for all. No need to fear thirst or starvation in the afterlife."

"At least not yet," said his companion.

I was reassured by these words. "Why don't I just stay around here? I see plenty of chairs going spare. There's no need for me to trek all that distance to the 'Z' sector. Free food and drink can be obtained anywhere. I reckon I should take up residence next to you."

The armchair Aaron shook his head slowly. "That would be a grave error. If you don't occupy your assigned spot, angels will come to harass you. They'll slash you with burning swords and jab you with spears and do other things that I prefer not to describe in detail."

"Angels, not demons? How can this be?"

"The demons are too busy working in Hell. They have no time for souls in the Waiting Room. If you sit down in an empty chair outside your proper zone, you might get away with it for a few days or a week, maybe even a month. But angels do appear unexpectedly."

"Through panels in the walls," added the rocking chair Aaron, "and that reminds me of another thing, which is that the bathrooms can be found behind doors that cover alcoves in the walls. The doors are painted in bright colours and can't be easily confused with the panels that the angels come out of. But I suppose someone has made such an error at some point. Who knows? It surely wasn't a very pleasant mistake."

I was about to wonder aloud what mistakes *were* pleasant but I decided to keep my mouth shut. The two Aarons were losing interest in me. I guess I was rather a boring newcomer compared with so many they had encountered. They must have had conversations with uncountable numbers of dashing individuals. But possibly the statistician had made a tally of the souls that passed him and so they weren't uncountable after all.

I said, "Well, it was nice meeting you, but I think I'll push on. I have far to go and only legs to carry me there. From what you have told me, we won't meet again, unless we end up consigned to the same Circle when a decision about our cases is reached. Farewell to both."

Aaron in the rocking chair nodded at me, his sartorial

comrade in the more comfortable seat didn't bother to swivel his eyes in my direction, and then I was rapidly walking away from them, striding down the immense room, my journey properly begun at last. Most of the chairs I passed were empty, but several were occupied. No one attempted to speak to me. I was walking too fast and I wore a rather hostile expression on my face.

But as the hours passed, my annoyance faded and my pace slowed. I kept reminding myself that hatches meant food, doors meant bathrooms and panels meant angry angels. I was growing tired and decided to sit down and wait for a meal to appear. There was an empty sofa on my left. It faced another sofa with a solitary occupant. I lowered myself onto the cushion and I leaned against one of the padded arms. It was rather a luxury.

The man opposite was reading a book and holding it in such a way that it was easy to read the title on the cover. It was a textbook on applied mathematics and I wanted to ask him if books could be obtained down here as well as food and drink. So I wasn't averse to engaging in conversation with him. I wondered how to initiate contact. I cleared my throat. Slowly he lowered the book, gazed at me with forlorn eyes and nodded.

I opened my mouth to ask my question but he spoke first. It turned out he wanted to tell me a story, a story about his own life. His surname was Abbot, he said and he had been killed very violently indeed. It was an accident but a really spectacular one and he was proud of the intensity of his doom. He was a little miserable too, but that was for quite a different reason. I was unable to interrupt him. He was already in full flow.

His story concerned homemade rockets.

Star-Crossed

I was always baffled by the famous phrase, 'star-crossed lovers', and for the life of me I couldn't understand what it meant. I know now that it refers to astrology and how two incompatible horoscopes can sabotage a relationship.

At least, that is my present understanding. I am happy to be put right on such matters. But for most of my life I had no interest in astrology. It seemed a lot of nonsense, some superstitious parody of real astronomy.

There was a woman I loved, and she loved me. And because we were both dreamers, when the idea came to me, I shared it with her without hesitation. She wouldn't mock me for it, I knew that.

And I was right on that score. She thought it was a marvellous idea. We sat under the stars and I told her that we were like a romantic couple from some old story and then I used the words 'star-crossed lovers' and admitted they seemed a little strange to me. Stars are points of light. They don't move, at least not as far as the naked human eye is concerned.

I know that everything in the universe is in motion. Planets orbit suns and suns orbit galaxies and galaxies orbit clusters. It's very complicated. The stars in the sky above us have proper and apparent motion and there is axial precession and who knows what else? But the point I am trying to make is that to the minds of normal human beings on the Earth's surface, the stars seem fixed in place in specific constellations. They don't go wandering about the firmament. And she and I were perfectly ordinary people.

Well, perhaps we were different from the general mass of humanity in the sense that we were both more emotional, impractical, idealistic. But our attitude to the stars was the standard one. The stars were up there and they didn't move. They were like sequins on the velvet dome of the heavens. Meteors flashed past and occasionally comets appeared and it can be said that they left visible trails behind them that looked like threads. And if *they* had crossed each other then I would have said that the words now made sense. But all the same, meteors and comets aren't stars, nor have I ever seen them cross each other's paths, not once in thousands of brilliant night skies.

Stars are required. And they are fixed, they don't have

tails, they don't cut visible lines into the celestial dome. So how can they cross? They can't, that is clear, but if they can't, how can 'star-crossed lovers' exist? It's impossible and I don't like to think that the old poets were wrong. I was missing something, the meaning of the phrase must be different to what I was assuming, but I couldn't work it out. And the love of my life felt the same way. She also was bewildered by those curious words.

"But your wonderful idea will solve the problem."

She said that to me. I replied:

"I thank you for your confidence in me, dearest."

"You are a genius," she said.

And I was acutely aware that I was nothing of the sort, but that mattered to no degree at all, she was besotted with me, and I with her, and that was the key to everything. I ought to reveal my idea to you too, the listener of this tale, and I will. There's nothing complex about it. I had suggested constructing two rockets and naming one of them for her and the other for me. The largest rockets that a private individual might be reasonably expected to construct. Then they would be launched at exactly the same time.

That's correct. They would take off at night, trailing thrust flames, exhaust fumes and vapour trails behind them. Two needles dragging silver threads into the sky. And these rockets would glow like stars. Then they would cross over in graceful ballistic arcs. Sure, they wouldn't be real stars, but would the old poets who coined the phrase know any better if they were alive today? Star-crossed lovers! That was the crucial point. I said to Juliet, for that really was her name, but I'm only *a* Romeo, not *the* Romeo, I said, "Ideally, the two rockets must be launched from separate locations."

"To reduce the chances of a collision?"

"Yes, but also for symbolic reasons. We were apart before we met, living in different towns, and then we came together. I will construct my rocket and call it by my own name and launch it from the town in which I grew up. You shall do the same thing in your hometown."

Did I forget to mention that we were both amateur engineers? Hobbyists of great skill and persistence. She was as good as I was, perhaps better. She caught a train the following morning to the town where she once lived, and I went back to the town where I had lived. We both rented workshops and began fabricating our rockets. We followed the same design, which we prepared together, talking about the details over the telephone.

The rockets took shape. They were the same length as the workshop rooms and when they were completed and named we hired men to drag them out and set them upright. All the calculations had been double-checked. There were no problems with the fuel lines. The guidance systems were rudimentary but good enough for our purpose. The specified night came, the clock ticked onwards, it was the great moment at long last...

The countdown started. The excitement mounted. We remained connected and coordinated by our telephones. We took it in turns to bellow, "Ten! Nine! Eight! Seven!" and so on. The liftoff on my side went without a hitch, and she told me the same was true for her.

The rocket had blasted off from the yard at the back of the workshop. Out I ran with a deckchair in my hands. I put it down and sat among the charred brick walls and blasted concrete floor of the yard. I gazed up. No need for binoculars. This sight was more lovely with the naked eye. In the blackness, my rocket was a bright streak and it was gliding skywards like an arrow of love, which is what it truly was, with only a slight deviation from the vertical. This deviation was a part of the plan, of course. The rockets had to cross each other and to do that it was correct for them to fly in curves. And then I thought of Juliet's own curves and she thought of mine, erotically.

I saw her rocket rising in the distance. It grew brighter, both the star that it had become and the silver thread dragging behind it, while my rocket fled from me. There was not long to wait. The two missiles passed each other, the flames of thrust and the exhaust fumes and vapour trails crossing sublimely. And then I applauded and

17

laughed, for we were finally star-crossed lovers, Juliet and I! The happiest instant of my life. The next day I would take the first train back to the city in which we dwelled and so would she. United as before, but now with the knowledge that we were poetical.

Much to my dismay, I never had the chance to catch any train anywhere. It was our oversight, of course. We had calculated the flight paths of our rockets as far as the point where the trails crossed over. We never bothered with what came next. But the rockets were insufficiently powerful to achieve orbit. They had to land somewhere. And as luck would have it, or maybe not luck but destiny or an act of divine manipulation, I can't say which, her rocket struck the workshop I'd rented to construct my own rocket.

My demise wasn't instant. I had backed away from the launch site and so I avoided complete obliteration. But I was riddled with shrapnel from the broken building. I blacked out and was taken to hospital, where I lay delirious for a few days before succumbing to my injuries. I then found myself outside the doors of this Waiting Room and the Devil gave me details of my death. He also informed me that Juliet had died before me. My own rocket had landed on *her* workshop, which she was occupying at the time.

Her death had been instantaneous and she had been shown into the Waiting Room within seconds of the accidental rocket strike. She had a headstart on me. I ran through the doors, hoping to find her, but I never did. I suppose she is still making her way to her assigned zone. I am here without her and the journey to be reunited with her is too daunting. Her surname is Jones. But there's another reason I haven't set off to find her. What if she resents me for what happened? The rockets were my idea. I find the notion she no longer loves me unbearable. I would prefer never to know. And that's my story.

—oOo—

He grinned at me when he finished, but his eyes were

melancholy. I felt unable to offer him any words of comfort. After entering the Waiting Room, why hadn't Juliet lingered in his zone or nearby? It was a bad sign that she had instantly set off for her own zone. But even that was assuming too much. Maybe those nasty angels had forced her to move on.

I said, "Not everyone can stomach long journeys. But I believe that I can. Your name is Abbot, so I must be making good progress already, considering I only started to walk earlier today."

His grin faded and he shook his head.

"Unfortunately for you, that's not my real surname," he confessed and then he sighed, "but it's my first name, and there was a bureaucratic mixup when I arrived and I ended up in this zone."

"What is your surname?" I asked in trepidation.

"Aaron. I am Abbot Aaron."

My shoulders slumped. This was an atrocious thing for me to hear. After five or six hours of tramping through the room, I had barely made any progress at all. I was still on the Aarons, at the low end of the Aarons in fact. I stood and thanked the rocket hobbyist.

"The sooner I set off, the sooner I will arrive, even though my journey is going to take several centuries."

He said, "Wait, I am an engineer. I can help you increase your speed. To travel on foot is inefficient."

I was amazed. "Is that a serious offer?"

He nodded vigorously.

Then he described what he had in mind. It wasn't another rocket, much to my relief, but a vehicle like a bicycle made from chairs fitted with castors. The power source would be the only tricky part, but he was confident he had enough skill to find a workable solution. I decided to give him a chance and so I settled deeper into my sofa. At that very moment, one of the hatches above me opened and a tray descended on a silk cord.

"Help yourself," he said, gesturing at the tray.

"What about you?"

"I don't have a sweet tooth. I much prefer savouries.

The dishes and bowls on the tray today are full of cakes and puddings. What's in that jug? Fruit juice? I might have a sip or two of that."

He drank it gingerly, and in fact it had grated ginger in it but was chiefly a blend of apple and grapefruit juice, while I gorged myself on croissants, trifles, tiramisu and mignardises. This was the first food I had eaten since my death. In fact it was the first sustenance I had received into my body, dead *or* alive, since I entered that faulty elevator almost five days previously. I smacked my lips in appreciation and wiped my chin.

"I will begin work on your vehicle today. The first requirement is for me to think about it, turn the thing over in my mind, model it in my imagination while considering it from all angles. That's how I always work," he explained, "and I have learned from experience it's the best way to accomplish my desire. Then I will sketch designs on paper. Once I have a feasible design, I will collect all the components necessary for the device. Half an armchair, half a bicycle. I reckon we should call it a *fauteuil-rapide*. That's French," he added, after a pause, "for a fast chair with upholstered arms."

I shrugged. "I leave it all in your hands. I will linger around here until you have finished. But what if the bad angels come to chase me away first? All the work you do on it will be wasted."

"That's the risk we must take. Even the afterlife contains risks. People who say that the dead have no more troubles are talking nonsense. There are worries down here too, lots of them. Worries are one of the fundamental constants of the universe, just as photons and neutrinos are. Too bad. Now let me concentrate on the project. No more conversation!"

He retreated into a world of his own, closing his eyes and letting his brain toy with options for the design of the craft that would carry me to my ultimate destination with efficient comfort.

But that wasn't really my ultimate destination, was it? No, it was only one more temporary resting place before I was consigned to an appropriate Circle of Hell. That Circle was my true home and would remain so for eternity. I shivered when I pondered this awful truth.

I shouldn't deceive myself any longer. I was a damned soul, one judged to be worthy of the neverending flames that the Devil tended, and the only reason I wasn't burning right now was because no decision had yet been made as to the intensity of the horrors I deserved.

Personally I thought that even the mildest punishment to be found in Hell, whatever it happened to be, was too harsh for me. But my opinion didn't count for much. The Devil would decide. I had no influence over him. I did my best to distract myself from such notions.

I picked up the book on applied mathematics that Abbot had been reading and I browsed through it. Most of it made no sense to me, but I persisted. What else was there to do? I finished browsing and turned to the first page. Within a few days I had read it properly, from cover to cover, and a couple of weeks later I had even read it backwards and upside-down, and that is when I began to think of myself as reasonably competent at matrix multiplication, fluid mechanics and even combinatorial optimisation.

Would any of this knowledge assist me in any way? There was no help for me, so the question was redundant.

Finally, the design of my vehicle was ready.

TWO

The weeks turned into months, as they always tend to do, but it was impossible to calculate exactly how *many* weeks had passed, despite my newfound talents in the field of mathematics, because there was no obvious way of marking time down here in the Waiting Room. There were no clocks, no windows allowing a sun to peep through, no strict routines.

Souls ate and slept when they felt like it, and nobody came to berate them for greed or indolence or irregularity.

And I continued to trundle on my transportation device. Note that I don't refer to it as a *fauteuil-rapide*. Abbot had come out of his trance and made the unfortunate announcement that an armchair vehicle would be too cumbersome to work well. He had gone over all the variations in his mind and come to the conclusion that the most efficient design featured a stool. Less comfortable, of course, but luxury is only a frippery. I'm not sure what he wanted to suggest by such a tautology but I was acquiescent.

The Waiting Room has the power to make fatalists of us all. Why struggle too much against the way things happen to be? Futility is an abomination. That is what I believe anyway. This doesn't mean I was meek and passive. I just did the best with whatever was on offer.

It's a sensible behaviour to demonstrate.

So let me reveal to you with a straight face that my vehicle was a barstool from some underground jazz club in some monochrome decade. I don't know how else to describe it. The seat was very high but it had a rung between its legs for my feet to rest on. However, I only rested my feet there when it was coasting on the remnants of its momentum.

Most of the time I had to work the pedals, which were on either side of the wooden legs. The gearing mechanism was located directly under the seat and connected by cords to an axle that turned the castors fitted to the underside of the legs. The stool itself had been found easily enough, just an easy stroll from our sofas and still in the Abbot zone. The castors came from a few empty armchairs. The gears were fashioned from the metal trays that came down from the ceiling. The cords were the cords that lowered those trays. These weren't as good as chains but chains were unavailable. Abbot had done the best job possible with what he could acquire.

I was grateful to him in spite of the way I groaned as I pedalled the thing. I was out of condition at first but my muscles grew stronger with the rigours of the exercise and then I found it easier. My speed was perhaps three times that of my walking pace. This was pleasing. It meant my journey would take only about 127 years instead of 380.5 years. I was so cheered by the notion that I rode with a straight back and a contented expression that probably looked haughty and I caught the attention of a fellow who jumped out of his seat, which was facing me, and stood to bar my way.

There were no brakes on my contraption and although I stopped pedalling at once, I careered straight into him. We tumbled together and rolled and with a dismal splintering sound, both pedals were torn off the vehicle. I sat in a dazed condition and rubbed my aching head.

"That wasn't very nice," I said to my assailant.

"Wasn't meant to be," he replied.

He was no less bruised than I was. We took our time clambering back to our feet, but we helped each other when we did so. There is no point bearing a grudge when you are destined for Hell anyway. That was my opinion. He felt the same way. I told him my name was Zubris and he introduced himself as Bartholomew. I grinned when he said this.

In the Waiting Room only surnames were used when meeting strangers. I had learned this custom on my journey so far. I hadn't learned much else, to be honest. People wanted to be helpful, despite the fact that the atmosphere of the place tended to make them a little melancholy, but the majority of them had no insights to offer. We were a tribe of bewildered dead souls stuck in the system, equals in ignorance, generally speaking.

"Well, at least I have moved up a letter," I remarked, "It's certainly good to find myself in the 'B' zone already."

"Don't be deceived," he said. "Not all these zones are of equal size. Some are much larger than others. The 'Q' zone, for instance, is rather small. The 'B' zone is one of the very large ones. It's still going to take you a long time to get to your destination, even on that thing."

"That thing has been destroyed," I remarked.

"Well, nothing lasts forever."

"Not even eternal suffering in Hell?"

"Apart from that," he conceded and he laughed sourly. I gazed sadly at the wreck on the floor. There was no way I would be able to fix the pedals without assistance. I am not at all competent at working with my hands. Even changing a lightbulb is a dreadful challenge for me.

"I can't hang a picture on the wall straight. I can barely tie my shoelaces properly," I muttered, but this was more of a joke, a self-deprecating remark that served to reduce tensions further.

Not that it was strictly needed. He was in a good mood now. I said, "See how the pedals have not only fallen off but shattered? I don't know why you blocked my way. It's out of order."

"I can repair your vehicle. In fact, I can make it better than before. Such an uncomfortable contraption was scarcely worthy of you. Don't fret. You'll learn that our collision was fortunate."

"You are an engineer?"

"No. I was a fireman, one of those guys who hold hoses and spray water on flames. I died in a fire. Can you tell?"

He blinked to draw attention to his sooty eyelids.

"But you have mechanical aptitude?" I persisted and he blinked faster, as if he was racing each eyelid against the other, but neither won. He limped to the nearest chair, which wasn't the one he had originally been sitting on, and with a groan sank into it. Then he said:

"You rode on that contraption like a statue. You had the bearing of a piece of monumental sculpture. A marble demeanour. That's what I found annoying. I simply couldn't bear it. I jumped up to urge you to change your posture and expression. Like a pompous statue on a pedestal, you were." He thought for a moment and added, "Or rather, on a *pedal-stool*." Then he laughed at his joke uproariously and repeated, "A pedal-stool, yes!"

I admitted that this was quite witty, indeed that I should have adopted that name for the improvised vehicle, but it was too late now. He shook his head. I waited for him to cease laughing.

Finally he calmed down and observed, "It's never too late. I will fix it but you'll have to invent another name for it because it won't need pedals any more. You'll see. I'll begin working on it after I have told you a story. You do want to hear a story? Everyone in this place loves stories. We exchange them the same way monkeys trade nuts. That's an assumption, as I don't really know much about monkeys. But I love beasts of all kinds. Anyway, here's my tale."

The Fire

Fire is alive, it's a living creature, it grows and breathes oxygen and reproduces with sparks, and I wondered if it might make a good pet. We think nothing is odd if people keep dogs and cats and parrots in their homes. We just accept it as normal. Those animals belong to a different species. Fire isn't just a different species but a different life form altogether.

Yet I felt sure it was sentient, maybe sapient too, and I decided there could be no harm in investigating the idea and coming to some firm conclusion about the true status of flames. My conscience was bothering me, to tell the truth. I put fires out, that was my job, my calling in life, and when it finally occurred to me that fire was *alive*, I started to brood.

Did this mean I was a killer? The notion was awful. I'd always imagined I was one of the champions, a hero risking his life and health to run into burning buildings and climb ladders with a hose. Could it be that I had committed some unrecognised form of genocide by extinguishing all those blazes? The bad guys never recognise themselves as villains.

I yearned to redeem myself, but I doubted that I would be able to do so. Dampening an inferno, as I had done many times, might be akin to killing a whale with a harpoon. An obscenity, in other words. Yet I couldn't resign my job because I needed the money to survive. I began taking long walks in my free time, musing on the paradoxes of existence. At least I think that's what they were. Maybe they were tribulations. I tend to get easily confused between an unsolvable paradox and an unbearable tribulation. My walks took me far out of the city in which I lived and worked.

On a patch of waste ground one evening in winter, the sky already dark and heavy clouds threatening rain, I found a small circle of tiny stones with glowing embers within. Some homeless wanderer had tried to kindle a fire and failed to produce a blaze and so had moved on. But a hidden spark must have remained after his efforts and it had slowly grown. This wasn't a viable fire yet, but on an impulse I resolved to adopt it, care for it, turn it into a steady blaze, a real fire, and give it a chance to thrive.

I had a metal flask with me and I unscrewed the lid and pressed some dry moss into it and carefully scooped up the embers and put them on the moss. In fact the moss wasn't very dry at all, but it was the driest that could be found. I now happen to think that was an advantage because if the embers had flared up the fire would have burned itself out.

As it happens, I managed to carry the embers safely to my apartment, and I prepared a clay pot as a bed for the baby fire. I would feed this little fellow in the most sensible way, little and often, allow it to grow slowly until it was a fierce adult blaze, which I would then set free in the wilderness. This was my chance to partly redeem myself for all the fires I had murdered over many years. Bits of paper and shavings of wood would do for the first weeks of its existence. It was important not to rush the process.

I still went to work, of course, but my heart wasn't in it and my comrades noticed my increasing reluctance. One afternoon, the fire chief took me aside and said, "How?" and when I asked, "How what?" he shook his head and with a twisted mouth snapped, "I am the fire chief. 'How' is what chiefs say, isn't it? And I am saying it to you. But I have something else to mention, which is your poor recent performance. You seem reluctant to turn merry blazes into smoking ash piles. Why is that, Bartholomew?"

I wasn't able to answer him convincingly. I stuttered and my excuses were spontaneous and peculiar. I believe that at one point I said, "Because, sir, there are triangles whose internal angles add up to *more* than one hundred and eighty degrees." And his sneer of contempt burned me more painfully than any ember from a collapsing edifice or drop of molten lead from a superheated roof. Then I knew my days were numbered. But it was always a joy to return home and be greeted by the welcoming snap and crackle of my pet fire, which I had moved from the clay pot to a large metal tub.

You are surely wondering if I gave my fire a name? I can reveal without embarrassment that I did. I called it Alberto Whom. A curious name, you are thinking, but the truth is that it's an anagram of my own name. Six months had passed since my fateful walk on that patch of waste ground and I considered it time to show Alberto the greater world beyond the walls of my apartment. So I constructed a trolley on which the tub could be placed and I tied a leash to this trolley and very soon we were going for walks together after sunset. At such a late hour, there were very few children who would come up and ask questions about my pet, but homeless wanderers would sometimes warm their hands on the leaping yellow and red of his fur.

I lost my job, naturally enough, and the fire chief refused to give me any severance pay or even a good reference. I was in trouble. But I had Alberto and we were now almost inseparable. I took him for walks more and more frequently and for longer and longer periods of time. I also transferred him to a wider and deeper vessel because he had outgrown the small tub. Now he flickered from the generous volume of an old oil barrel and pulling him along on a leash was really quite a strenuous task. But I persisted. Nothing was too much effort for my lovely Alberto Whom, my friend.

Without a job, my money dwindled to nothing and I was unable to afford the rent on my apartment and finally I found myself permanently on the streets and trundling the barrel endlessly around and around the same thoroughfares. I felt hunger and thirst but my main concern was Alberto. When it rained, I pulled him into the shelter of a bandstand in a park or under the generous eaves of an old mansion or even covered him with my own scorched body. I fed him on all the best sticks I could find, never on trash, and he remained loyal to me in turn and never reminded me of my original intention to set him free in the wild the moment he became a fully grown adult.

The truth is that I was far too attached to his company. I wanted us to live together for the full span of my life. But I couldn't expect him to be happy out in the open, at the mercy of the weather and troublemakers. Already bad men had lit their cigars from him and one gangster had even made toast against his glowing tresses with bread on the end of a long fork. It was atrocious. I knew what my duty was. To find new accommodation for both of us. And I prowled the more obscure corners of the city in order to do this. One evening I forced my entry into an abandoned warehouse.

It was a very large building and it was full of shadows but in my famished and partly deluded state it seemed an excellent residence for Alberto and myself. I hauled his barrel through the broken main doors and dragged it to the middle of the room in which we found ourselves.

He cast enough light for me to appreciate my surroundings better. It was a cluttered place in fact, despite its size, with wooden boxes piled to the ceiling. It must have been abandoned at least fifty years ago. There was a thick layer of dust on everything. I sneezed directly into Alberto, not having time to turn my head away, and he flared up even higher for a brief instant and I saw that these boxes had words written on their sides.

The words said 'Etimanyd' and I found this bewildering. Was it a foreign language? Maybe Welsh or Turkish? I couldn't be sure. Did it even matter? I reasoned that maybe the boxes had once been full of edibles, but after half a century or more they would have rotted away to nothing. There was no point looking inside them. Alberto settled down and the writing was lost in darkness again. Only the metal screws embedded in the boxes gleamed. I said, "At least we are safe from the rain in here, Alberto."

I struggled to remember anything about the history of this part of the city. Always apart from the residential districts, near the railway line that ran from the docks to the inland mountains. The industries had failed one by one. As a result the city was cleaner but poorer. I am not making a judgement on history by saying that. I see no reason why an urban centre can't be clean and affluent at the same time. I gazed at Alberto with affection. I was out of work because of my love for him and his kind, but I felt it was a sacrifice worth making. There is a limit to what we can morally endure.

I sat near to him and his friendly warmth made me drowsy. I was clearly exhausted after everything I had been through. My body was worn out and I had a troubled mind. But now I was relatively comfortable and my sleep was very deep. I dreamed that the fire chief was standing over me with something in his hand. A fire axe?

I saw that it was a tomahawk and that he was plotting to strike me, but it turned into a bird as he swung it, a phoenix, and it flapped away and left him looking foolish. "How?" he said, and I replied, "Is that just something you feel you ought to say?" and he shook his head. "I really want to know," he said, but it was too late.

I woke up. My eyelids snapped open, the same eyelids you now see are blackened with charcoal, and I realised that I had slept for a long time. Maybe a few days. Thin rays of sunlight slanted through tiny holes in the warehouse walls. I turned to Alberto and to my horror I saw that his flames had vanished. I peered into his barrel. He was only a couple of glowing embers, almost dead. With an awful shriek, I desperately seized the first flammable object I could get my hands on, one of the wooden boxes, and dropped it into the barrel. I guess I just wasn't thinking straight. I didn't even notice how heavy it was. Down into the barrel it went and stuck fast there.

I slumped back and prayed that Alberto would be able to refuel himself on the wood in time. I needn't have worried. The fact of the matter is that I should have worried more about something else. Let me reveal that this warehouse had once been a store for a mining company. The boxes were full of rejected sticks of dynamite. The boxes themselves were rejects. Why were they rejected? Just because the warnings on them had been printed backwards. 'Etimanyd' wasn't a foreign word after all. What a pity!

The dynamite in the box was old and it was defective anyway, but it still knew how to explode. And the explosion set off the other boxes, all of them, copycats that they were. The warehouse was blown to bits and so was Alberto and that is how I died. It's my story. I have often wondered if Alberto can also be found somewhere in this Waiting Room. His surname is Whom, so if he is here, he's closer to the end of the hall. Maybe you'll pass him on your travels. But I fear that fires don't go to Heaven *or* Hell and don't come to this waiting area either and that I will never see him again. People have told me that I will have plenty of opportunities to find another fire to be friends with when my case is decided and I finally go to Hell.

I find small comfort in such words. I was a simple fireman. But I believe I can help *you* to achieve your objective. I ask only that you pass on a message to Alberto if you do happen to meet him. The message is this: dear friend, you burned your identity all the way to the centre of my damp soul. You turned to steam all my doubts about whether fire is truly alive. That steam drifted away and has vanished for good. Thank you.

—oOo—

Bartholomew wiped away a grimy tear but he soon regained control of himself and he shrugged. "That's all I have to say about my time on the surface. It has started to feel more like a dream."

"All that we see or seem is but a dream within a dream," I quoted from a poem by a writer I once adored.

"Just one dream actually," he corrected me.

I said nothing to this.

Eventually he roused himself sufficiently to stand and declare, "Now I'll tell you my initial ideas for your new vehicle. A comfy chair instead of a stool. I would suggest a sofa but it might be too wide to fit between the other seats you'll encounter on your journey."

"A comfy chair sounds very appealing," I said, and I added perhaps just a little ungratefully, "Abbot was incapable of incorporating a comfy chair in *his* design. I appreciate your efforts."

He dismissed my thanks with a wave and began pacing, rubbing his chin in thought. I sat down and watched him. But something was bothering me. At last I had to voice my concern.

"A minor issue. You said that you died in a fire but in fact you expired in an explosion. Weren't your parts scattered over a wide area? How come you are here in one integrated piece?"

He turned to face me with an amazed grin.

"You still know so little about how things work down here? The body is reconstituted whole. There are some stains or marks that serve to reveal how a person died, but generally speaking we are reborn anew." Then he considered his own words. "Maybe reborn isn't the right way of putting it. We become a second edition of ourselves. But this is wasting time and that's never good, no matter how many hours we have."

He resumed pacing, suddenly stopped in his tracks and cried, "No pedals or cords! It will be water powered."

I waited for him to say more, but he had to pace for another five minutes before he did so. Then he erupted: "Listen, it's simple enough. There are many bathrooms in this waiting room, all set into the walls. I am a fireman and water is one thing I understand. I will rip one of the hot water tanks out of one of the bathrooms and fit it inside a chair."

"Will you?" I said, because I couldn't think of a better reply, and staying silent would have seemed dismissive of his enthusiasm. He was throwing his arms high in melodramatic gestures.

"I will fill that tank with water and arrange a nozzle to act as an exhaust. Your weight on the chair will serve to keep the water at a very high pressure and it will squirt in a thin but powerful jet out of the nozzle, propelling you forward just as a rocket engine would. You probably don't think you are heavy enough to compress the water sufficiently?"

"I don't," I admitted.

He nodded. "That's where my ingenuity comes in. As you trundle along on the chair, you will be shifted back and forth a little, bounced up and down. This movement will be almost imperceptible but it will serve to work a pump fixed beneath the cushion you are sitting on. Over time, by tiny increments, the pump will ensure the pressure in the tank becomes massive. When the tank is empty the vehicle will grind to a halt, but you can refill it from one of the bathrooms. I don't foresee any difficulties at all."

"But I will be spraying a lot of water everywhere."

"Who cares about that?"

"Some of the occupants of the seats I pass might."

"But you will be passing them. You will soon be out of range of their fury. Nothing can go wrong. Trust me."

His tone was so persuasive at this point that I decided to put my destiny in his hands. I wouldn't regret it, he assured me. I hung around in this area for the next few days, while he worked on the vehicle, and fortunately no angels came to chase me away. I helped him rip out the hot water tank from a bathroom and carry it over to the selected armchair.

He constructed a cunning device for compressing the water in the tank, a system of gears with ratchets. He had said there would be no pedals or cords. He was right about the pedals but cords proved to be necessary. When the tank ran out of water I would have to drag the chair to the nearest bathroom. Cords were the best way of pulling the thing along.

At last the vehicle was ready and Bartholomew asked me what I wanted to call it. Every cherished object ought to have a name, he said. I thought about it and decided on *Triton* and he nodded.

"Classical references are always good. It would be better if you could hold a trident while sitting on it, but let's not worry about that. I suppose you should be setting off today. The angels have stayed away but I'm sure they'll be turning up before long. Best to get going now."

"One small matter first. How do I stop the chair?"

"Why would you want to do that?"

"In case there's an obstruction ahead of me."

He scowled and I wondered if he was offended. "You haven't been paying attention, have you? As the water level in the tank drops, the chair will decrease speed. When the tank is empty, the vehicle will roll to a stop. That is just basic physics. I am surprised at you, Zubris."

"But all the same–"

He refused to hear any more words from me. I was sitting on the armchair and he bent over and opened a valve on the nozzle. Then he pushed me to start me off properly. The chair jerked forward, picking up speed rapidly. I glanced back over my shoulder and saw him sliding on the film of water I had sprayed over the floor. He was soaked through.

But he waved and I waved in return and laughed.

I felt the joy of velocity.

To be honest, my speed wasn't so great. It was about the same as the pedal stool I had formerly ridden. Three times that of my walking pace. But it was a vastly more agreeable vehicle. A runner could have overtaken me easily, but it seemed that very few people were inclined to run or lope in the Waiting Room. They preferred to lounge and sprawl instead. Whether this was an effect of the environment, or whether it was more sedate kinds of people who ended up here, was a question I was unqualified to answer. I am unqualified to answer the vast majority of questions, as it happens.

My cushions were so soft that I soon fell asleep.

And I had a strange dream.

All dreams tend to be strange, there's nothing weird in that. A dream that isn't strange would be the most peculiar dream of all. But this dream was about my death, a sort of serious documentary concerning the events that had led up to my demise. There was nothing fantastical about it. The scenes didn't jump about or merge into each other. It was all precise and true. I realised that this was a tale I was telling myself because I had no audience. Everyone down here likes to tell stories. Bartholomew had confirmed this. It was clearly my turn. In my dream, I paid close attention to what I was saying.

I didn't disagree with any of it, much to my relief.

The Dream

I am a wine taster. Or perhaps I ought to say I was a wine taster. There are some opportunities to taste wine in the Waiting Room but the situations can't really be compared. A wine taster on the surface tastes wine but doesn't drink it. Down in this place we guzzle it for thirst reasons.

My dream was to emigrate to New Zealand and work as a wine taster there and I did everything in my power to make it happen. That was my dream, I say, but in fact *this* is my dream, the dream I am standing in right now. I was certain that a disaster was coming to Europe, economic or environmental, and I wanted to be out of danger. I wanted to be safe.

But emigrating is no longer as easy as it once was. It hasn't been easy for a long time. When I was a youth it was simplicity itself. Countries welcomed you and there wasn't much paperwork. But now governments are shutting doors and hunkering down. Everyone seems to be expecting a catastrophe of some kind. It is a siege mentality that has gripped nations. Moving abroad has become one of the biggest headaches you can imagine.

New Zealand didn't really want me. What could I offer them? I was a wine taster, hardly an occupation of vital importance, scarcely one in high demand. I was also middle aged, too old for a country still with a youthful demeanour and a fresh attitude on the world stage. I was redundant. But still I yearned to escape my confines and taste wine down south.

It occurred to me that I might increase my chances of being accepted as an immigrant if I became renowned. Being competent at a profession isn't enough, if one's profession is so generally useless, but to be a personality, a celebrity, an authority overrides all other objections.

In order to become renowned, I needed to be noticed, and that required the modification of my current style. I needed to be flamboyant, witty, astonishing, engaging, perhaps gently outrageous, and original. Originality was the real key, I felt. And so I started to compare wines in a manner that none of my colleagues did. Instead of talking about 'hints of chestnut and tinges of vanilla' I would be more inclined to refer to 'tinctures of robot thumbs and essences of pessimistic armadillos'. This turned out to be amusing for others but the joke quickly wore off and then I was held in contempt.

I had to try again. This time I no longer compared wines to anything with my voice. I expressed myself in gestures only. I hopped on one leg, twisted my lips into awful pouts, wiggled my ears, oscillated my eyebrows, undulated my pelvic regions, flapped my hands, in short I twisted my body into knots of an awful complexity, and I suffered accordingly. But this didn't work either. And in fact my employers grew restless.

Fashion seemed to be the key to success. I dyed my shirts in wine, wore a hat that looked like a bunch of grapes and instructed a tailor to twist the sleeves of my jacket into corkscrew shapes.

My colleagues now openly sneered at me and even told me that I wasn't a professional and should resign before I was sacked. I was on the edge of a small version of the disaster I had been expecting all along. New Zealand was further away than ever, despite the fact it hadn't altered its geographical position at all. What should I do? I was desperate.

Well, desperate times require desperate measures. And the best measure is a large quantity of wine. I came up with a plan to attract attention and generate sympathy, a scheme that would endear myself once again to my fellow workers and my employers, and also serve to make headlines in the national newspapers. I was going to become renowned one way or another. I obtained a dozen bottles of wine and I announced that I intended to work from home. Everyone gazed at me with derisive eyes. Some giggled.

My apartment is on the highest floor of an old tower. The elevator is rusty and battered. I entered it and waited for the doors to close. Then I punched all the buttons at the same time. I knew that this would confuse the system. Up the elevator lurched but then it came to a shuddering halt between floors. The thing was stuck and I was trapped within it.

This was my tactic. I would get extremely drunk on

the wine as I waited to be rescued. I would finish all the bottles and be utterly smashed when the doors were forced open and the maintenance men came to help me out. I had no doubt at all that I would be missed and the alarm raised. It never occurred to me that I was so expendable that none of my colleagues would care to make inquiries if I failed to turn up to work the next day.

And nobody in the tower bothered to report the broken elevator. Or maybe they did, but the technicians were slow to respond because our tower wasn't at all important and no individuals lived in it who mattered. This was a lesson that I learned the hard way, the deadly way.

I began drinking the wine. I was in a good mood. When I had finished the first bottle, I started on the second. I was worried I might be rescued too soon. I needed to be drunk when I was found. There had to be a story in my situation, a quirk of circumstance that would enable journalists to have fun with it. I had to become something of an instant hero.

Three bottles, four, five. Before long I had finished all of them. I was too drunk to stand and I curled up on the elevator floor in a state of incredible and possibly dangerous intoxication. I yapped in my semi-sleep, growled, purred. I was scarcely human. I was a massive drunkard, an avatar of Dionysis, the god of wine, an incoherent maelstrom-man.

I woke with a thumping headache perhaps twenty hours later. As another day passed, my hangover slowly wore off, but my thirst and hunger increased. There was nothing left to drink, nothing to eat. I banged on the doors with my fist, shouted at the top of my voice, all to no avail. No one heard. I was racked with chills and shivers at this point. I knew I was doomed. I had no idea what might await me after death. I never suspected that more *waiting* was awaiting me. My tongue swelled in my mouth.

Dying of thirst is a terrible way to go. I went that way after four and a half days. I should have smashed one of the bottles and used a jagged glass edge to end my life more rapidly, but that option never occurred to me. I tasted death at long last and I licked my lips as I did so, exactly as if I was tasting a new wine from some obscure and darkened land.

—o0o—

I woke up. Something was wrong. I blinked my eyes. I was sitting curled up and *Triton* was zooming in the wrong direction. I was going backwards! How had it happened, this atrocious reversal?

I looked over the edge of the chair and I saw that the tank had ruptured. It was spraying two thin jets of water from the front of the chair and these worked against the propulsive force of the single jet behind. Thanks to the dictates of physics I was being pushed backwards.

I gazed around but it was impossible for me to work out exactly where I was. All the zones are remarkably similar in their appearance. I groped for the brake before I remembered that there wasn't one. Could I jump off while the chair was moving? Yes, but I didn't want to risk injuring an ankle. If I did that and the angels moved me along, I would have to limp in great pain. I stayed on the chair while the tank emptied itself.

People I passed on the way shook their heads at me. I don't suppose it was a common sight to see someone heading the wrong way through this room. The Devil would probably be annoyed if he found out. The angels would be furious too. But I was helpless, stuck in my seat.

I quietly cursed Bartholomew, though I was aware it wasn't his fault, not really. I wondered if I would pass him soon. But I had slept for too long. In fact, I had passed him long ago. I was heading back to the 'A' zone. I noticed a slight decrease in my speed and I sighed with relief. But it was many hours before the tank drained itself completely and the armchair rumbled to a halt. I stood with a grimace and inspected my surroundings.

"Good day," said a voice.

A man was sitting on a divan and smiling at me.

He seemed pleasant in tone and feature and so I approached him, shook the hand he offered me, and when he indicated a vacant chair, I sat down. We faced each other across a table on which was piled fruit. This fruit had come from the hatches in the ceiling, of course.

But the way it was arranged was rather curious.

He had constructed a face from it. I mean that he had taken apples, pears, a banana or two, peaches, plums and slices of melon, and made a sculpture. Not quite a sculpture, in fact, but a bas-relief, a likeness of a man in profile, but with fruit for features. I was astonished.

"It's my speciality," he explained, adjusting a plum.

Something stirred in my memory.

I had seen paintings along the same lines, portraits of people made not just from fruit but books and fish. I opened my mouth to ask a question but he knew what I was going to say and answered:

"My name is Arcimboldo. I was an artist."

My shoulders slumped.

So I really was back in the 'A' zone after all!

"You can call me Giuseppe if you prefer, although I am aware that nobody uses first names after death."

"An Italian artist, yes? From the Fifteenth Century?"

"Sixteenth," he corrected me.

"And you have been waiting here since then?"

"Of course! Four hundred and fifty years isn't a very big percentage of the average waiting time in this room. My waiting period has barely begun, if you really think about it. And you?"

"Zubris," I said by way of introduction.

"Ah, then you must be a newcomer, if you are still in the 'A' zone but are travelling to the 'Z' zone. Why were you reversing? That's very unusual. It has been decades since I spoke to anyone else who did that. The angels soon turned him around and chased him away."

I leaned heavily on the armrest of my chair.

"It wasn't intentional in my case. My vehicle malfunctioned. I will have to resume my long journey on foot."

"We'll see about that," he responded.

I gazed at the bas-relief.

"Who does it represent?" I inquired.

"It is the head of a man I met ages ago, a fellow named Vaughan who spent a few days resting here before pushing on to his own zone, and he impressed me a lot with his conversation. I have never forgotten him, though I suppose he has forgotten me. I like his jawline."

"It's a banana," I said, somewhat lamely.

"And rightly so!"

I didn't know what to say next, so I fell silent, but the silence was awkward and I desperately sought for a subject to discuss. I said, "You are Italian but you speak perfect English. That's nice."

He shook his head. "I don't speak English."

"But I can hear you plainly."

"Nobody speaks their former languages in the Waiting Room. We all speak a universal tongue, Esperanto in fact, and that's also the language we think our thoughts in, which is probably why you haven't noticed. The change happens to our brains and vocal cords when we arrive here. The next time you say anything try to concentrate on the sounds."

"Very well, I shall," I said, and those were the words I focussed on. To my amazement I distinctly heard, "Tre bone, mi faros," and Arcimboldo chuckled at my dismay. I began laughing too.

"What did I tell you?" he said, grinning.

"Wonders never cease."

He became abruptly serious. "One day they will."

I lowered my eyes sadly.

It was difficult to maintain a melancholy mood in such convivial company and we soon cheered up. He offered me a cup of wine and I accepted, drinking it in the normal way, not as a wine taster would. It was refreshing. I glanced at my saturated steed, *Triton*, and pursed my lips. I couldn't repair it and I doubted if it was worthwhile asking Arcimboldo to try, or searching for someone else in the vicinity who could manage the task.

None of this mattered for the present anyway, as my host now drained his own cup of wine and said softly, "I have a tale to tell you. We tell tales in this room, as I'm sure you already know."

"Go ahead," I said.

He gestured at the fruit portrait and began.

Fruit Man

When I was at the height of my fame, working in Prague at the court of Rudolf, the Holy Roman Emperor, my whimsical portraits of men made from everyday objects were becoming more popular than my ordinary artworks. For I have to say that originally I had only wanted to be a conventional painter. It came as a surprise to me that my comical grotesqueries were more appreciated than any of my serious studies done in the accepted style. Although many of these pictures of mine, the men made from vegetables or flowers or daggers, depicted nobody in particular, occasionally I would be asked to paint a wealthy sitter in that very strange fashion, and I mostly accepted.

For example, rich merchants would come and commission a portrait from me and when I asked them how they wished to be represented, meaning what outfits they intended to wear, what messages they wished to convey, they would reply, to my amazement, "From clouds," or, "From songbirds," and they would jangle purses of gold coins in front of me to encourage me to nod and take up a paintbrush. I would make a sketch of them on that very day and they would go away and only return when the portrait was finished. Always they were utterly delighted with the result and often they would be incapable of speaking for an hour or more because of their laughter.

Prague during the rule of Rudolf was a peculiar place with an atmosphere of brooding menace mixed with an ambience of wild-eyed optimism. I accepted the fact that my bread men and sticks-and-stones men were liked more fiercely than my ordinary portraits. We never choose the effect our creative work has on those who pay for it. That's one of the minor mysteries of art in general. I grew to expect requests for the whimsical portraits and I started to define my vocation as one of strange humour. Bear in mind that this was centuries before the word 'surrealism' had been coined. And talking of coins, one portrait I did showed a man made entirely from hard currency.

But now I am going to arrive at the point of my story, for it's a short tale, and unlike most tales told in the Waiting Room, it doesn't concern my death, an event that occurred in 1593. No, it's just about an ordinary working day when I was in my studio and varnishing some recently finished paintings. There was a knock on the door and I said, "Come in," as I always did, without turning to see who it might be. The unseen visitor cleared his throat, as they generally do, yet it was an unexpected sound, sort of wet, even juicy, rather than the dry rattle of a normal human oesophagus. I responded:

"What do you want?"

"A portrait," came the answer.

"Made up from plants or animals or jewellery, I suppose?"

"No, an ordinary portrait."

"You wish me to paint you exactly as you are?"

"That's correct. As I am."

"With no trickery or strangeness involved?"

"A perfect likeness."

Finally I turned around to see just who I was dealing with. Now let me tell you that I have often been stupefied in my life, shocked even, turned to stone by an unexpected happening. But this was far and away the most extreme thing that had ever come my way. I say 'thing' but it was a man, a real man. It's simply an unfortunate fact that he was made from fruit. Don't misunderstand. It wasn't the case that he was *wearing* fruit. He *was* fruit, his cheeks, forehead, nose, lips and chin, his torso and arms and legs. A fruit man. Almost the same as the figures in my portraits, but solid and alive.

I gingerly approached him and prodded him with a figure, squishing one of his peaches. He bruised very easily, poor soul. 'Gingerly' wasn't the best word choice, I fear. There was no ginger in his composition. He was soft fruit, almost entirely, although his fingers were tamarind pods. He was smiling but there was a sadness in his strawberry eyes.

"I don't know what to say," is what I said.

"Paint me please, sir."

"Certainly. How could I not?"

"Before I go rotten."

"I understand. I will prioritise your commission."

"How much will it cost?"

I rubbed my chin. He was evidently not the wealthiest individual to ask for my services, this was obvious from the quality of his rinds and peel, which were to him what garments are to us.

I made an impulsive decision that I have never regretted.

"For you, it will be free."

Sweet tears, tangerine flavoured, trickled down his rosy grapefruit cheeks and he trembled with barely suppressed passion. I saw he was going to collapse to his knees in gratitude, but I prevented him from doing so by waving my hand in a forbidding manner. Then I had an idea. I wasn't sure how he would greet it but I put it to him anyway. I was fully prepared to paint him exactly as he was, in all his citric splendour, but there seemed to be an even better alternative. My tone of voice was dominant without being stern. I spoke like a veteran lecturer who no longer needs to prove himself.

"If I execute an accurate portrait of you as you are," I said, "do you know what people who see it will say?"

Without waiting for him to reply, I continued, "They will say, 'Oh, look at that. It's another of Arcimboldo's fruit men. Very witty!' and they will chortle, chuckle or even guffaw, and this laughter of theirs will be authentic, but it will soon wear off. Then they will return to their business and forget all about you. I have painted so many fruit men that they are no longer but a novelty. But what if I paint you as a flesh and bone man?"

"What do you mean?"

"I mean only what my words indicate. A flesh and bone man! A real man, in other words, a standard human being. For every plum I will substitute on the canvas a muscle. For every cherry, a tooth. Visible ribs for those bananas there. Kneecaps for those small melons that join your upper and lower legs. And that coconut of a skull of yours? A head!"

He was overcome with emotion, he broke down and it was many minutes before I could get any sense out of him. "That would be wonderful," he gasped, between racking sobs. And so I painted the painting and it remains the strangest of my portraits despite its normality.

—oOo—

I was delighted by Arcimboldo's story because it demonstrated to me that things on the surface could be just as anomalous as they were down here. I found that to be a relief for some reason, perhaps because it implies that the universe was a crazy place in full, rather than only in certain segments, and in turn this meant I didn't have to curse my misfortune at ending up in one of the insane regions. If it was *all* mad, the bad luck was illusory. This sounds like a needlessly complex way of interpreting his simple story.

But it was a way that suited me. I clapped my hands and said, "Bravo! It's the best story I have heard to date."

"There will be millions more before your waiting is over," he replied with a show of modesty, "and I'm sure many of them will be better than mine. But I must stress that mine is true. It's not possible to tell false stories in this Waiting Room. Forces prevent us from lying."

"I wondered what happened to the fruit man?"

"He went off," said Arcimboldo.

"Such a soft life must have been very hard for him. What if crows pecked him as he went by? To say nothing of other fructivorous beasts, including men and women.

That wouldn't be cannibalism, after all. But how I would love to see the portrait you did of him!"

"Not possible. Nothing like that can be brought down here and anyway it was destroyed in a studio fire a year later, just before I left Prague and relocated to Milan. I lost many of my artworks. In the long run it doesn't matter at all. It's possible that he is in this room."

"Do you remember what his name was?"

"He never told me."

"That's a shame," I said, and I sighed.

"Listen," he said.

"To what?" I asked, stirring in my seat.

He shook his head.

"Nothing. I thought I heard one of the panels slide open. I thought an angel was about to emerge. Then you would be goaded out of that chair and forced to walk at a brisk pace towards your designated zone. But it seems I was mistaken. The panels nearest us remain shut."

"I will have to rouse myself to move on soon."

"Abandoning your vehicle?"

"Of course. I don't plan on dragging it behind me now. *Triton* turned out to be a failure. I will use my legs."

"Not so fast. I have an idea. I think it will work."

I waited for him to explain.

He took his time. He stroked his neat beard. He was very urbane, jovial, an engaging presence. I was happy to wait.

Eventually he spoke and his words were as soft as the flesh of the fruit man who had visited him centuries ago.

"I am an artist. I have turned chopsticks and the hair stuffing in some of the plumper armchairs into paintbrushes. The chopsticks sometimes descend from the ceiling hatches when the food is geographically thematic. I have made paints from vegetable juices. There are no canvases down here but I paint on cushions and pillows. I can help you proceed more quickly to your destination than your feet can manage. Yes, I can do this."

"With paint?" I cried.

"With paint," he confirmed, and he winked.

"But how?" I yelled.

"I will paint a demon's face," he said.

"A demon's face?"

"On the back of your chair."

"On the back of *Triton*? What good will that do?"

"Plenty of good," he said.

He paused and then added, "Yes, plenty of good and all of it *bad*. From the hatred of the angels for the demons, you will achieve thrust. That's the point of the concept. Free propulsion!"

In order to digest all that he was telling me, I had to lean forward and hold my head in my hands as the remainder of his explanation cascaded over me. A face on the back of a chair that resembled the visage of a demon would arouse the fury of any angel that saw it. The angels would assume that an intruder from Hell had somehow broken into the Waiting Room. They would chase it out and to do this they would attack it.

"With pikes and whips," he continued.

"I see," I said, not seeing.

He knew that I didn't comprehend his scheme. Patiently he added, "Poking it and prodding it with pikes and lashing it with whips. That will move it along. It will begin to trundle forwards, with you sitting in it. The force that angels can exert when they are annoyed is tremendous. You'll see! It will trundle forwards, increasing its speed. Soon it will be travelling at a remarkable velocity. You will make up for all the time you lost travelling in reverse. *Triton* will become easily the fastest vehicle ever seen in the Waiting Room. But don't worry that there is no limit to the chair's acceleration."

"What is the limit?" I asked nervously.

"With all the poking and whipping, the paint will eventually flake off and then the angels will lose interest."

"Won't they be irritated to have been tricked?"

"Not with you, Zubris."

"They will stop punishing the chair?"

"Yes, they'll simply turn away and return through one of the panels in the wall. You will continue to trundle thanks to inertia, but your speed will decrease until you come to a halt. However, by that time you will be in one of the higher zones, I can't say which one."

"It depends on the durability of the paint?"

"That's correct. Well?"

"I'm willing to try out your idea."

"Good man! Might as well get started immediately. Painting a demon that's lifelike enough to fool an angel might take a few days. But that's fine. And then you'll have to sit in the chair and wait for one to appear. I still think this scheme is a brilliant one. I don't mean to boast. I won't take credit for it. I'll thank only my Muse, who inspires me to paint well. Not that I have a Muse in particular. It seems to me that she's an abstract."

"Talking about abstracts, my personal opinion is that you were on the verge of inventing abstract art with your vegetable men."

"I don't really know what you mean by that, but I can assure you that there is nothing abstract about plants. Organic, yes, but abstract? They are the truest forms that ever existed on Earth."

There was nothing I could say in reply. I nodded. It was at this very instant that a hatch opened in the ceiling.

A tray came down on silver cords and on the tray there was beer, bread and olives, also a little cheese. A good basic meal, hearty and rather old-fashioned. I enjoy beer almost as much as I like wine. This was an interesting brew. I am no infallible scholar when it comes to the grain instead of the grape, but I believe it was Brugse Zot Blond, frothing in very large glasses. I toasted Arcimboldo and he toasted me and then we laughed.

A few days later, his painting was finished.

THREE

My speed was incredible and to tell the truth I was frightened. The walls flowed in a blur and the chairs and sofas and divans barely registered on my retinas as I passed them. I was worried that *Triton* would violently collide with one of them or that my vehicle might overturn.

But why was I so anxious? No accident could be fatal. I was dead already. Yet pain still existed, as I had learned from scalding my hands on hot food and tripping against low coffee tables.

Arcimboldo had painted an incredible demon, a really hideous portrait of a damned monster, with horns and eyes of magma and a forked tongue, prehensile snout and pointed chin. It was disgusting, atrocious, very effective. Then I sat in the armchair for a week. Finally, a panel slid open and an angel emerged. Three angels, in fact, of different types.

One of the angels went off on its own, flying close to the ceiling, departing for some remote region of the Waiting Room. But the others remained and it wasn't long before they noticed the demon. The angel that had flown away was one of the more conventional models, looking like a human being with wings, a radiant and beautiful, if slightly chilly, figure with a trumpet in a scabbard at its waist and a miniature harp hanging from one wrist on a strap. Its wings flapped melodiously and it was like a sweet moth, not quite as colourful as a butterfly, but endearing all the same. Pleasant.

The two remaining angels were intimidating.

One might almost say they were abominable. The first was a circle with a dozen arms protruding from it. There were no wings but it had a rotor on top, a set of alarming blades that span too close to people and things, but without ever striking them. A hovering multi-limbed loop of gold, it carried a pike in two of its arms, a very lengthy pike indeed.

The second was a sphere of eyes and these eyes had iron eyelids that shut with a ponderous clanking and opened again with a high pitched squeak. These eyes were all different colours or shades of the same colour. In place of limbs it had one extremely long bullwhip of iron that jutted from below, as if the angel was a head that had been torn from a body and was trailing its spinal cord. The effect was diabolical, to use an unfortunate term. I wasn't sure which of them I found more scary. I started to gibber.

Arcimboldo shouted at me, "Don't take it to heart."

"Take what to heart?"

"The outer ugliness of these beings. They are authentic angels and possess minds that are the purest riddles."

"Shouldn't the guardians of Heaven be friendly?"

"They are. Like equations."

"Are you suggesting they are mathematical?"

"Chess pieces in a chess problem, Zubris. In the most ingenious and tricky chess problem ever devised. See?"

"I'm sorry to say that I don't. I'm baffled."

"Not enough time, Zubris."

"Not enough time for what?" I bellowed.

"Explanations!" he cried.

And that was true, because a few seconds later the nearest angel attacked. I jerked forwards violently. He had rammed the back of my chair with his pike, and although the blow was cushioned by thick pillows and pillowed by plump cushions, it jarred me and sent ripples of pain up and down my spine. At the time I was appalled at my situation, but now I know I was lucky. If the blade of the pike had been as sharp as it ought to be, it would have punctured the chair and pierced my body. Its bluntness saved me. *Triton* trundled forward. Before it slowed down, the pike jabbed again.

It began to accelerate and now the angel with the whip was close enough to strike. The lash doubled the speed of my chair and already I was moving faster than I had done with the compressed water engine. The angels roared after me, a series of jabbings and lashings doubling my speed again and again. The castors began squealing and I smelled smoke. What if those tiny wheels burst into flame? This was a dangerous game. Why had I allowed Arcimboldo to persuade me to try this method of transportation? Had my brain softened to a sticky mush in this grotesque place?

Certainly, I couldn't have been thinking clearly when I sat in the chair and waited for the angels to catch sight of the painted demon. The impact of a pike and whip on the upholstery was devastating. Scraps of shredded material fell off. It was a chunky armchair but its destruction would be rapid. The painting would be destroyed soon, I hoped, but I hadn't reckoned with the acidic paint seeping through the fabric layers. The image ran deep. What if it had soaked all the way through and I was pressing against it even now? What if there was a demonic face imprinted on my shirt or even on the flesh of my back? I would be jabbed and lashed into oblivion!

Those angels wouldn't see sense, and I doubted if any vocal appeal could be made to them, especially as they seemed to lack ears. They had a task and it was one they approached with single-minded determination. The chair started to wobble alarmingly. I thought I glimpsed Batholomew as I whizzed through the 'B' zone, but I couldn't be sure. He was little more than a smudge of muted colour. I gritted my teeth and tightened my grip on the armrests. I was horrified by my speed, which was still increasing.

The angel with the rotors, in other words the one with the pike, was rather more nimble than the sphere of eyes. He could keep up, but the spherical one dropped back and could no longer reach *Triton* with the tip of the long whip. They say that a problem shared is a problem halved. Does this also mean that a problem halved is a problem shared? If so, who was I sharing it with? With the one angel still in the race, the circle of arms? The removal of the whip from the game was a relief but I was still scared.

The pike kept jabbing, and twisting with each strike,

and every blow was very painful for me, so agonising that I wondered if I had already been judged and consigned to one of the Circles of Hell. But no, that was a foolish fancy. I actually prayed for my ordeal to end, and that's a curious thing to admit, if you bear in mind that I fervently prayed to angels, any angels at all, to protect me from *these* angels. What a twisted system!

I hesitate to estimate my final speed when the painting of the demon was destroyed. It couldn't be faster than two hundred kilometres an hour, but my face was battered by the wind caused by the rush of my passage. And the little wheels were burning merrily. Soon they would fall off and then I would be done for, as the chair came to an abrupt halt, hurled like a stone from a catapult, probably to smash into some table.

Done for in relative terms, I mean. As I stated before, I was already dead. I couldn't die again, at least not logically. But suddenly the jabbing ceased and I twisted my head to look back. The angel with rotors and numerous arms had veered away. The demon's face must have been totally erased, a victory for that celestial guard with his absurd pike, and now it remained only for me to hang on until the armchair rolled to a stop.

It lurched and sagged as the fire started by the friction of the small wheels spread to the underside of the chair. The stuffing burned slowly, emitting dense pungent smoke that threatened to choke me. I leaned forward to cough and that is when the front castors broke and the chair tipped me out. Already half curled up, I pulled myself into a tighter ball and rolled over the floor, bruises hatching one at a time on every part of my body, but without any bones fracturing. With a gasp of relief, I slowed sufficiently to risk stretching myself. Sprawled on the ground, I laughed sourly to myself.

"Angel-powered transport isn't to be recommended."

I had spoken those words.

But I sat up and looked about, as if they had issued from the lips of some other person. I was dizzy, unable to stand on my feet for the next ten minutes. In every joint of my frame, an ache pulsed. The chair was ablaze a hundred metres behind me, belching plumes of smoke, and the anxious inhabitants of the vicinity were throwing jugs of water or fruit juice over it, beverages from the most recent breakfast or supper. The flames hissed but died down after a sufficient quantity of fluid had been dumped on them. Goodbye, *Triton*! I had journeyed far on that ludicrous thing.

"Awful," said a voice.

I blinked. This time the voice wasn't mine.

"Sorry?" I ventured.

"The stupidity of the angels," it continued.

"I see," I answered.

"Any entity of even negligible intelligence ought to know that an armchair isn't a menace to anyone. But they like being unpleasant, those heavenly hosts. They aren't really angelic at all. My name is Collins. That's my introduction. It is always good to get the introductions over with quickly. I can plainly see you won't be going anywhere for a while. You are far too injured to travel. You can stay here for a few days. Lots of comfortable sofas around these parts. Now let me tell you a story about myself."

The Baritone

I was an opera singer. I believe I was a very good one too, a baritone, and yet I found it difficult to make enough money from my art to pay all my bills. This is because despite my skills I wasn't renowned enough to command large sums for performances. I was working my way to the top but I wasn't there yet. We can say that I was halfway up the ladder.

That ladder in the musical business is rather like a scale on a piano. There are twelve notes and the scale sounds good if the piano is in tune and there are strong fingers playing it. But if there's something wrong with the tuning or the fingers, then the scale will sound wrong.

Well, in my case, exterior circumstances were the

piano and they were a little warped, so the piano was out of tune. And I had the fingers but my health wasn't too good, so the fingers were crooked. So now you can see the obstacle I had to surmount. Crooked fingers playing an out-of-tune piano meant that I was never able to move up to the big time. I remained in the small time. Sure, time is an illusion. But it still pains me.

There was one ray of hope in my life, but it was a sordid ray, if that isn't too tortuous a description. We think of rays as pure, clear, illuminating, clean, but this one was degenerate in a minor sort of way. Let me cut to the chase. I was often visited after a show in my dressing room by certain kinds of ladies. I am being coy now. In fact it was one type of lady, those elderly lustful widows who seemed to be my biggest fans.

First they would praise my voice and we would talk about music, about the great opera composers and also about the lesser luminaries who still had a lot to offer the artform. Not everyone can be a Rossini, Verdi, Puccini. There ought to be room for smaller talents too. I love the work of Mercadante, Lalo and Offenbach, all of whom are neglected now. My favourite opera of all is the almost forgotten *Dragon of Wantley* by John Frederick Lampe, and when those lustful grannies asked me to sing something to them in private, I would usually choose a song from that curious epic.

But the music was an excuse and they weren't really that interested in it. As I sang some rousing extract, they would leer at me, sometimes even fondle themselves, and it was all very depraved. But I was sorely in need of money. I wouldn't reject their advances. I couldn't afford to. They would wait patiently for the song to finish and then invite me back to their homes. Nothing formal was ever agreed upon. There were no contracts. But if I pleasured them, there was nearly always a fistful of banknotes waiting for me in the morning. This is shameful to confess. No doubt it's the reason why I find myself in the Waiting Room instead of in Heaven. Too bad!

But one evening, after a performance in which I believe I excelled myself, a woman visited me in my dressing room who proved to be of a much different character. She was malign. I didn't realise it at the time. She seemed similar to all the others, wrinkled but sprightly, grandmotherly but rampant, what I used to think of as a saucy biddy. But let's not be too colloquial here. I can see you understand me perfectly. I was a gigolo of sorts, but a gigolo in tune, and that's how I managed to make financial ends meet. All of us in this room have done stuff to be ashamed of, haven't we?

I know you're not judging me, so maybe I ought to be less defensive, but I feel soiled after contact with that woman. Confession is a sort of wet towel and I can scrub myself with it, but will the stains come off? That woman's name was Mrs Sloper, and her name should have given me a warning, because she was a slippery slope. Also 'Sloper' sounds like 'slops' and also like 'slobber' if you twist the consonants, as she twisted me.

Yes, she twisted me, physically and mentally. I went back to her house and she led me down a corridor and into a room and as soon as I entered I saw that she had soundproofed it with thick drapes on the walls. I felt a sharp pain in one of my buttocks, the left one in fact, and when I turned to confront her, I felt too giddy to stand. She had injected me with some fast-acting agent, and by 'agent' I mean a chemical, not a government spy.

Well, of course I mean a chemical, a solution, but there was no solution to the fix I was now in. And 'fix' is also an appropriate word, for I began to feel high as well as unsure on my feet. I think the chemical was carfentanyl or some similar opioid analgesic, extremely potent. I staggered, presumably collapsed, and slept for many hours. While I was unconscious, evil Mrs Sloper went about arranging things for my future torment.

I awoke with a throbbing head and found myself strapped half-naked to a sewing machine. Mrs Sloper was standing behind me and she was dressed in the most grotesque costume I have ever seen. It was kinky underwear but all made from wool. It was repulsive and absurd and when I laughed, she lifted a spiked baton and beat me on the backside. I was horrified but never suspected that my death would eventually come by this weapon. What do you make of that? The perverted granny is the worst creature!

—oOo—

At this point I stopped him by raising both my hands and shaking my head. For a moment he gaped at me. It simply wasn't good etiquette in the Waiting Room to interrupt a story, especially one about how a person had expired. He glanced from right to left and I had the notion that he was looking for an angel in order to register an official complaint.

"I know the story already," I told him.

"How is that possible?"

"Mrs Sloper's real name was Mrs Aaron."

"What do you mean?"

"I mean what I say. It's simple. I met her son soon after I entered this room and he told me all about her. He wondered why she wasn't in the 'A' zone. And he had searched for her, but he finally decided she wasn't in the Waiting Room at all and had gone straight to Hell. But it seems she changed her surname. She must have remarried without telling him. Maybe she's ahead in the 'S' zone? I will seek her out when I get there."

"Seek her out to do what?" cried Collins.

"Confront her," I said.

"But why?" he muttered nervously.

"To express my utter disgust at the way she treated you," I said, and the baritone was very pleased to hear this.

His disappointment at my truncation of his tale vanished and was replaced with gratitude. "And yet," I added.

He waited patiently for me to explain myself.

"If she's in Hell already, then I won't be able to do that." I sighed. "Not for a long time anyway. Not until I end up there myself, and maybe not even then, because our movements might be limited to our assigned Circles and hers will surely be different from mine."

After a pause to let this sink in, I said, "I never whipped anyone, certainly not while wearing woollen lingerie."

Collins nodded. "But you are injured, and as I said before, you won't want to be travelling until you are better."

"I think I can limp onwards," I answered.

The truth is that I feared his company more than the pain of my bruises and damaged bones. He might drive me mad. I just had that feeling about him, that he would talk endless nonsense, despite his obvious talents as a singer. I suspected he was one of those unfortunate men who create their own problems and wallow in them and actively dislike being rescued from them. As soon as they are out of one slimy pit they rush headlong into the next, blabbering all the time that they are floundering. But I didn't want to hurt his feelings by admitting any of this, so I said reasonably:

"It's reassuring for me to know I am already in the 'C' zone. Now I desire nothing more than to push on until I reach the next zone. I am very keen indeed to arrive at my destination."

"Why?" was all he said in response.

There was no answer to that. The whole thing was foolish. But the angels were an authentic hazard. I had felt the sheer power of their lance thrusts and lashings. I shrugged. He pouted.

He hadn't risen from his seat and now he averted his eyes, humming some aria to himself, probably as proof he didn't need me to hang around. But I could see how his nose twitched like a rabbit's. I gazed back at *Triton*. The flames had been extinguished and the smoke was only trickling up instead of billowing. To name a chair after a mythical being was silly, I decided. From now on, if I ever had occasion to name a chair, or a settee, I would call it something sensible like *Perchville* or *Bumchester*. I don't know, anything that wasn't mythical, a more prosaic and practical cognomen.

I walked away from Collins and my ankles made strange clicking noises as I went. My knees wobbled. My pace was slow and ungainly. But did this matter much? There were comfortable seats on which to rest for the entire journey and there was food and drink and bathrooms. When the discomfort became too great I slumped full-length on a sofa and slept. No angel awakened me. No occupant of the vicinity engaged me in talk.

That first day was tough, but the second was easier, and the third was even easier. My bruises healed. I rested frequently, always choosing the most sparsely populated areas, avoiding conversation as much as I could. People did speak to me, and I was polite enough, but I never permitted them to tell me long stories. Brief anecdotes were acceptable.

By now, I had decided to call my next vehicle, *Galahad*, whether chair or sofa or some other device. It was a name with historical provenance, strong and kind yet with a being of the fantastical running through it. But it wasn't certain I ever would have a vehicle again.

The days passed, the weeks passed. They always do and doubtless you are familiar with the process. I recovered my health perfectly. I wined and dined. I was never assaulted by an angel. Whenever they appeared, which wasn't a very frequent occurrence, I was either already walking, in which case they ignored me, or I was dozing and the humming energy of their approach alerted me. If I jumped up and immediately began moving, they would drift away. Occasionally I would meet people who had been prodded or lashed by those entities. Some of the angels were more conscientious than others. But none were appeasable. The concept of mercy was beyond them.

They were automatons with very simple minds.

It is surely needless for me to add that the weeks became months. And what would the months do next? Then I saw something in the distance that seemed quite different from everything I had seen so far. An object that hung from the ceiling, a frame with outstretched arms.

But as I approached I realised that the arms were wings of fabric.

A glider? Who had constructed a glider down here? It was astonishing and I had to rub my eyes before I could believe it. I increased my pace, fascinated by this contraption and when I stood under it and marvelled at its incongruity, I saw that it was suspended on cords.

This solved the mystery of how it happened to be hovering there without flapping its wings. So engrossed was I in this vision that I failed to notice who was sitting on the nearest chair. He coughed politely to attract my attention and I turned my eyes towards him. He was an old fellow with a long white beard but his complexion was fresh. He said:

"One of my creations."

"It is fantastic. But who might you be?"

"Daedalus," he replied.

"The legendary figure from long ago?"

He laughed at this.

Then he told me his story. This appeared to be a common compulsion in the Waiting Room, an irresistible urge to share tales with new acquaintances as quickly as possible after meeting them for the first time. By this stage, I was expecting nothing else. I listened.

His narrative was the oddest I had yet heard.

The Labyrinth

Yes, I am Daedalus, original designer of the Labyrinth of Knossos in which the Minotaur was housed. That was more than three thousand years ago. I am more famous now for inventing the wings that helped me to escape Crete after I fell afoul of King Minos. My son came with me and died when he flew too high. It is often said the sun melted the wax that held together the feathers of his wings but that isn't true. We know that when we gain altitude the temperature drops. Poor Icarus flew so high that the wax froze and became brittle and the flapping of his arms shattered it. He was unlucky.

My own wings bore me safely to another island. Later, when Icarus' body was washed ashore there, I buried it and named the island after him. Icaria. But I don't like to dwell too much on those events. I prefer to talk about what took place later in my life. You know the tale of Prometheus? He gave the secret of fire to humanity and was punished by being chained to a mountain. Every day an eagle arrived to rip open his flesh and devour his liver. But his liver would regrow so the torture could be repeated.

Prometheus was immortal and unable to die. His torture was supposed to be eternal. But many generations later, the great hero Hercules happened to be wandering in the same mountain range and he encountered Prometheus and he used his phenomenal strength to break the chains. That is one of the greatest rescues in mythology! When the eagle turned up the next day, there wasn't any victim for it to swoop on. It flapped angrily away and pouted for an awfully long time on a remote eyrie. That's another name for the nest of an eagle and has nothing to do with the word 'eerie'.

Yes, there's no need to remind me that we are speaking Esperanto and the pun doesn't work in that language. It wasn't a pun anyway, but an observation, and now I observe that you are bewildered. What on earth does Hercules have to do with me, you are wondering? Well, let me instruct you. I decided to make greater use of my wings and tour the world. I happened to be passing right over the mountain range known as the Caucasus when I spied a figure down below that was chained to a rock. It was him!

Prometheus, none other. I reduced my altitude and saw that he was being attacked by an eagle. So then I knew that the account of Hercules rescuing him was false. Prometheus was still in chains, the eagle was ripping his flesh. But it didn't devour his liver then and there. It grasped it in talons and flew off with it back to its nest, maybe intending to feed some chicks. An idea came to me. My best ideas are always spontaneous. I flapped in pursuit of the eagle and I soon caught it up. My wingspan was wider.

I carried a long pole in my arms that I used to push myself off the ground when I wanted to take off. I now employed this to strike the eagle. It dropped the liver in surprise and I swooped and caught it. Then I flapped away, found a cave and stored the liver inside. The following day I repeated the same action. I kept intercepting that eagle and taking the new liver back to the cave. Because the liver kept regrowing inside Prometheus, I realised it could be exploited as an endless resource. The eagle was destined to keep attacking Prometheus and extracting his liver, so there was no question of me running out of livers. Soon the cave was full of them, all the same liver but multiplied by hundreds. Then I calculated that I had a sufficient quantity.

It took many trips for me to carry the livers back to Crete. Finally the task was done and after resting for a few days I began to construct a new labyrinth from all the perfect copies of the metabolic organ. I mean that I used the livers to make walls. This labyrinth was even more complex in layout than the older one. Working alone was hard, I won't deny that, but it was the only way to be certain the layout wasn't known to anyone else. When it was finished I made my way to the capital city of Crete.

I landed on the roof of the palace and hurried down the stairs to the main throne room and I requested an audience with the king. He was one of the less brutal successors of Minos. I told him who I was and he received me with due respect. He knew all about the earlier labyrinth and the Minotaur and how the hero Theseus had killed the monster.

"I am here to make you an offer," I told him.

My words baffled him.

"Make it from what?" he asked.

Now I was confused.

Then at last I understood. He had assumed an 'offer' was an object and it was clear he had never heard the word before. Not all the successors of Minos were as bright as that vicious ruler had been. That is why they aren't renowned and why you probably don't know their names. I explained the meaning of the term and he nodded appreciatively.

"How much time do you need to make it?"

"I can do so right now."

He was impressed. "Then please do."

I held myself straight, which wasn't so easy, for I was an old man by then. I told him that my original labyrinth had been a prison for both Minotaurs and any human who ventured into it. What was needed was a prison that Minotaurs were unable to escape from but which would present no problems for men and women. At least, not for men and women of that time, with a few exceptions. I will explain this in a few moments.

"Well, that sounds absolutely delightful," he said, "for although we don't have any Minotaurs at the moment, there's no telling when we might acquire a few fresh ones. A place to keep them safe is much needed. But explain to me the theory behind your new prison."

"It's another labyrinth but with walls made from different materials. Stone walls trap monsters and people indiscriminately, but walls made of liver will be impassable to vegetarians like the Minotaur, whereas heroes like Theseus can simply eat their way to freedom in a straight line. No need to grope down dark passages. Just put your face to the wall and chew until you break through into the adjacent corridor, and then immediately start biting your way through the next wall. This is something that a Minotaur, who has the head of a bull, will never attempt, because that head is herbivorous. A labyrinth with liver walls can permanently imprison beings with bulls' heads but it will allow men like Theseus to escape gastronomically."

The king considered my words. He frowned and said, "But I have heard it said that some people, like Pythagoras, are vegetarians too. What about them? I shudder to think of that marvellous mathematician trapped inside it because he is averse in principle to a carnivorous diet. That seems unfair to the man who knows so much about triangles."

"Never fear," I responded to this criticism.

"Why not?" he asked.

"Because we have nothing to fear but fear itself," I said, and this sly and ultimately meaningless answer seemed to reassure him. Then I told him that my new labyrinth was already finished and was standing on a remote part of the remotest peninsula of the island.

"You can buy it from me for one thousand gold coins," I said, and waited for him to try to haggle the price down. But he was rather foolish and declared it was worth two thousand instead!

I didn't argue with that. I gave him the location of the labyrinth, took the money and I tried to fly away with it. But although I am an ingenious fellow I had forgotten that gold is one of the heaviest metals. I managed to get airborne but only flapped erratically for a few minutes before crashing into the side of a mountain. I expired in a splat and now I am here. I have been waiting for ages. I have no idea if any new Minotaur occupied the liver labyrinth. Nor do I know if anyone found the gold coins I spilled when I collided with that rockface. It's all just a memory now, a fading set of images in my mind. You are wondering why the liver didn't go rotten, yes?

It was the liver of Prometheus, remember, and he was immortal, so it was able to constantly refresh itself. That liver would never decay. It could be eaten but it would always reform the following day. Now I can see you are agitated. I think I know why, it's the same reason that everyone I tell this story to pulls an ugly face. You think I was cruel and selfish because I made no attempt to free Prometheus from his chains? Let me correct your ideas on this subject. After I departed Crete for the second time, I intended to stash the gold and then return to the place where he was secured.

I was going to break those chains and do what Hercules should have done and there's no way I would have allowed Prometheus to continue suffering. It is true that I benefited from his appalling situation but I am amoral rather than immoral and I always intended to give him his liberty. But I never had a chance thanks to my fatal crash. Ironic, no?

Maybe my liver labyrinth is still there. I suppose it might be covered now by drifting soil and leaves blown from the trees over the centuries. In another few generations, an archaeologist might discover it and history will have to be rewritten until it is more in accord with mythology. I died and here I am. Yet I am still an inventor. The Devil advised me to give up my hobby but I told him that it was impossible for me to abandon tinkering. It's not a hobby, I said, but my entire reason for existence. And I do exist, don't I? Even though I am dead I still exist. He conceded the point.

How could he not? I am nearly always right.

—oOo—

I puffed out my cheeks and whistled a long low note. His tale had been curious and horrid in many ways. I remarked that I had first read about his escape from Crete with his son Icarus in Ovid's *Metamorphoses*, a book that had been one of my favourites when I was young. I had owned an abridged version produced for children, I explained, but had long intended as an adult to read the full text, an ambition I had surely left too late.

"Oh, I don't know. There might be a copy down here somewhere. This is a very big place, after all." He tapped his nose. "And harder to get out of than any of my labyrinths, believe me."

My mind turned over memories of those adventures. How I had thrilled to read of transformations and renewals. I said, "I regarded Ovid's book as pure literature and it frustrated me when readers treated it like an encyclopaedia of mythology. But now I think it began as light entertainment and Apollo or some other deity turned up and magically changed it into that encyclopaedia. There's no reason why books can't mutate."

"It would be fitting," agreed Daedalus.

"And what next?"

He gestured at the machine hanging above us.

"A new glider," I said.

"Yes, and it's at your disposal if you want it."

"That's very generous."

"Not at all. I require a test pilot."

"Ah, is it unsafe?"

"I don't know yet. A test pilot will find out."

I laughed at this.

He explained how he had made it, the frame from wood taken from tables and the fabric for the wings from luxury chairs. But it wouldn't fly properly. It was a fixed-wing glider and he hadn't solved the problems of instability. Those aerodynamic difficulties were long after his time. He had tried constructing an ornithopter but they always fell apart. He was hampered by a lack of tools and could only do his best, while remaining aware that his best was inadequate. Yet the glider was ready for its maiden voyage. He just needed someone willing to sit in the thing and try flying it.

"The data I collect from the first flight will enable me to refine the design and create a better model," he said.

"How will the report of the pilot reach you if the flight is successful? He will be far away along the hall."

"Word of mouth," answered Daedalus.

I said nothing to this.

He expanded on his reply. "It's the same way I constructed the zip wire on which the glider is suspended. It's not really a glider, you see, but slides along a great many cords that have been connected together into one line. The line is strung under the ceiling. This system was established recently. It required the assistance of many volunteers."

"The cords belonged to the trays that descend through the hatches? Then you cut them off to re-use them?"

"I had the idea. I stood on the table and when a tray descended I sawed at the cord with the edge of a cutlery knife. I had a good length of string. Then I walked a few steps ahead to my nearest neighbour and told him what I'd done. I asked him to do the same thing and also to tell *his* nearest neighbour. And so on. Word of mouth is a marvellous thing. I secured one end of the string to the ceiling using several forks and passed the other end to my neighbour, who tied it to his own length of purloined cord. Once he had done that, he passed it to the next fellow along, and so on."

"How far does the line go now?" I asked.

"I don't know," he said.

"But the first person to pilot your craft will find out. And you want me to be that daredevil? Are you sure?"

"Yes," he admitted. He lowered his voice. "Not long after arriving here I noticed something. The floor isn't flat. It slopes at a very small gradient. But it keeps going down. If you drop a ball it will start rolling and never stop unless it strikes a chair or table. The gradient is so gradual it hardly impinges itself on our consciousness, but it is real."

"I hadn't noticed," I confessed, and he said:

"Few fellows ever do."

"What is the relevance of this to us?"

"If the floor slopes, then the ceiling slopes too, which means the line that the glider is suspended from also slopes. If the glider is given a push, it should keep going without any further input of energy. It will continue thanks to those laws of physics I adore so much."

"Gravity will power your vehicle. I can understand that. It seems to be an ingenious apparatus and I am willing to try it out. What is the point of being cautious now I am dead?"

"That's one way of looking at it."

"I accept your offer."

"Whatever happens to you, the news will eventually reach me. You can't go further than the line is long. Everyone you pass over will know about this project of mine. They will report back to their neighbours and all the reports will travel in a reverse direction and eventually reach me. Then I can make a new glider better than this one. Your flight will be a test flight to obtain data. I can work wonders with data."

His absurd proposition appealed to me.

"Let me be the pilot."

He nodded. "The job is yours."

I decided that I had been fortunate to arrive at the right time. This was the best opportunity to travel rapidly that I could ever hope to find in the Waiting Room. How many zones would the zipline take me through? Even if it carried me only to the end of the 'D' zone I would consider that to be great progress. I brashly told Daedalus that I was ready whenever he was. He clapped his hands together and said, "Right now!"

This response dismayed me a little. I was hoping to have something to eat and drink first, perhaps a nap, but if I betrayed any reluctance he might decide I didn't have the right character for the mission. In that case, I would have to trudge onwards with my legs, some other pilot would be chosen, and he or she would whizz over my head while I was tramping and cursing. No, I was wiser than I used to be. I cried eagerly:

"That's tremendous! How do I get inside it?"

"Stand on the table."

I did so and he told me to reach up and grasp the glider, but I lacked the agility to pull myself up and over into the cockpit. He asked me to take all my weight in my arms and lift my legs up. I did this and he took another table and put it down on top of the first table.

Now I straightened my legs and stood much higher and it was relatively easy for me to haul myself into the tiny pilot's compartment of the glider. But I must have looked very ungainly doing this. No matter. Daedalus didn't giggle and that was the main thing. It was a cramped space up there and a very flimsy contraption, but I felt victorious.

"What is the name of this machine?" I cried.

"It doesn't have one."

"I won't be crass and call it *Icarus*."

"That would be bad."

"Because your son died in an accident?"

"No, because flying vehicles are always female and my son was male. It should have a woman's name."

"Like *Aphrodite* or *Artemis*, you mean?"

"Those corny old names! No, no, your aesthetic sense is terrible. I had in mind something more romantic."

"Such as what?"

"*Mavis* or *Ethel*," he said.

I had no intention of opposing him. I smiled. He waved and I waved back and he shouted up that it was time for the inaugural launch of his flying machine but I shook my head at these words, for the vehicle was less like a real glider and more like a breeches buoy, assuming you know what one of those is. Just in case you don't, I'll state briefly that it is an emergency rescue device used to transfer people out of danger and it looks like a squat lifebelt on cables. He was still sitting, resting his chin on his clenched fist, presumably trying to decide on a name for the thing. He sighed.

"I can't do it," he said, "so you ought to."

He reached to his side.

And he tugged at a cord that I hadn't noticed before. This pulled off a sort of improvised peg on the main line that was preventing the glider from moving forward. Immediately I began to slide, very slowly, but my speed increased by tiny amounts until I was moving at the equivalent of a fast walk. Daedalus was soon lost to sight behind me. Occupants of the chairs and sofas directly below shouted encouraging words. These were the volunteers who had strung the line and they had an emotional interest in my progress. Now I was moving at a fast trot. Already I had cramps in my legs.

I wondered what I would do for food. Could I snatch a descending tray in mid flight? A tricky manoeuvre, for certain. And what about bathroom duties? The more I thought about it, the more I realised my situation wasn't a good one and that I was actually in big trouble.

One of the occupants of a chaise-lounge I passed over was a woman with a megaphone, one of those primitive speaking horns that are just cones. It seemed to be made from aluminium. She must have made it herself by rolling up a tray. She was clearly desperate to tell me a story, for she began the moment she saw me approaching and continued until I was out of earshot. She abridged the story as she told it, because of the brevity of my transit. I wondered again at this wild urge to share narratives with strangers.

The Genie

My name is Delilah. That's my surname, so don't think I have cheated and am in the wrong zone. I grew up in the 1920s, when women were supposed to be meek and mild, but I was independent from a young age and I yearned to have adventures in distant lands. I ran away from home when I was seventeen. First I went to Egypt and then I crossed the Red Sea in disguise and wandered through the Hejaz. You can imagine how risky this was! But I loved the excitement and the danger. I picked up Arabic fast. I have always been good at languages. I can imitate local accents accurately too.

To avoid detection, I acted just as I supposed a man would act, and to tell the truth I overdid it. I got up to some pretty unpleasant activities. I became a gun runner and an alcohol smuggler. At last the authorities rumbled me. I was sure to have my head cut off with a scimitar, so I fled into the Rub' al Khali and no one followed me there because that desert is judged to be certain death. It's one of the most inhospitable places known to man, but I was a woman, and so I thought that maybe the perils wouldn't apply to me. I was wrong about that, but it was worth a try. I still believe this.

Wandering in a daze over the endless dunes, dehydrated, hated, sunstruck, moonburned, starcrossed, and who knows what else, I collapsed to my knees. I was about to give myself up into the arms of doom but decided to crawl over the next ridge, just to see what was there.

I reached the summit of the ridge as the sun was setting.

I was facing east and when I stood up, very unsteadily, my shadow was cast into the crater that I found myself gazing down into. Yes, a crater, made from the violent impact of an ancient meteorite. But the crater wasn't empty. Ruins stood within it and I realised that I had stumbled on the lost city of Ubar, also known as Iram of the Lofty Pillars, a place of palaces and towers which had previously only existed as the disbelieved rumour of an almost forgotten memory. I stumbled towards it, hoping I would find fresh water there.

But the wells that had once served its long-dead population had dried up a thousand years earlier. I dug in the sand desperately. With the last remnants of my failing strength I unearthed a brass lamp. What use was this to me? I rubbed it anyway, because that is what one does in such situations, and to my surprise a genie did actually emerge from the spout. He was large and blue, insubstantial, like a cloud of coloured hydrogen gas.

He said to me, "You may have a wish, but only one. I am not one of those irresponsible genies who grant three. There are some rules about what you are permitted. You may not wish for more wishes. Nor may you wish for me to fall in love with you, so that I give you lots of extra wishes voluntarily. Apart from those two restrictions, you can ask for anything. Once you make your wish, I'll grant it and then disappear forever."

My first impulse was to wish for water, but I decided that wasn't cunning enough. I considered the matter. At last I said, "I wish to be rescued from the worst situation I ever find myself in."

He vanished like a burst bubble and I waited for the wish to be granted. It was a great disappointment when nothing seemed to happen. I remained here, in the ruins in the desert, rather than finding myself transported to some nice place and I wondered what had gone wrong.

It finally occurred to me that maybe this *wasn't* the worst situation I would ever find myself in. That is why the spell hadn't been activated, which meant I would survive the ordeal. This cheered me up. I waited a few more hours to be certain and then I gave up waiting and departed the city with more confidence than before. If a worse situation awaited me in the future, a situation the spell would rescue me from, I couldn't die of thirst in the middle of the Rub' al Khali. That is logic. But even though it was night and cooler, I remained abominably thirsty. My tongue swelled in my mouth, my blood became sluggish. To cut my story short, I died one hour before dawn.

And then I found myself immersed in flame, agony coursing through every nerve in my body. The odour of sulphur was abominable. Because I had been a wicked person, an arms dealer and drug pusher, I had been consigned to one of the Circles of Hell. That was obvious. I was unequivocally an evil individual, a sinner of the worst type, and there was no need to judge me carefully. Sentence had been passed in the blink of an eye.

But whose eye? The Devil's eye? I don't know. Yet the agony lasted only a few seconds. Suddenly I found myself outside the Waiting Room, and the Devil very politely opened the doors for me, and I entered. I made my way to the 'D' zone and I have been sitting here ever since. For a long time, I was mystified by what had happened. Then I understood.

That Circle of Hell, to which I rightly belonged, was the *worst situation* I would ever find myself in. So the spell was activated. And I was transported by the genie's magic out of the fiery pit. I don't belong in the Waiting Room but I am here anyway. Will the mistake be noticed? Will I be compelled to vacate my seat and return to Hell? No, because that would violate the terms of the wish. I suspect the way the wish works is by messing up the paperwork concerning my case and creating confusion. If I was sent back to Hell I would instantly return here. That's how I reason it. Anyway, I am Delilah, as I said, and thank you for listening. Have a good and safe journey.

—oOo—

This tale was shouted to me in a fast babble, in order to fit all the words into a short space of time. I was out of range of her megaphone now and travelling at a fair rate. But the cockpit was so tiny and my position so uncomfortable that I doubted I would be able to endure it for much longer. As my speed increased I was torn between two conflicting desires.

I wanted to make as much progress as I could towards the 'Z' zone and I wanted to do this as easily as possible. I abhorred the idea of walking all the way there. At the same time I wanted to be out of that winged capsule. It was vibrating painfully now and jolted me every time the line was secured to the ceiling with salad forks. There was some mechanism that allowed the pulley to disengage and then re-engage, otherwise the glider wouldn't have been able to pass those nodes. I shut my eyes tight.

In the seclusion of darkness a name for the vehicle came to me. I took the words Mavis and Ethel and combined them into one word and then I found an anagram in that word. From the anagram I made a new name and it was one that was both a first name and a surname.

Thelma Ives. Yes, that was nice. It was female and elegant and I think old Daedalus would have approved. But even if he didn't, so what? I was doing him a favour and owed him nothing. Now I was moving at a furious gallop and my knees ached abominably. Shooting pains ran up my shin bones, my teeth rattled in my head. But I didn't shout out.

After a few more hours, my legs were so numb they stopped hurting. This was a worrying development but I was pleased to be free from pain. I was also tired of the cheers of the occupants of the seats below. I ignored them, angling my chin haughtily at the ceiling. Hatches began opening and trays appeared but none of them lay in my path, luckily.

As one tray passed near my head, I lunged for it and managed to snatch a bunch of grapes, but I also knocked a jug of wine over and it drenched a chap on a chair who yelled and shook his fist at me. I crammed the grapes into my mouth, the juice staining my chin. I spat the pips over the side. I made another attempt to shift my weight into a more comfortable position but this swaying action had the unfortunate effect of tipping the glider over. I was upside down and prevented from sliding out of the cockpit only by the fact I was jammed in it. Now I did shout out, to no avail.

Even if someone had wanted to come to my aid, what could they do? My speed was increasing all the time. The blood began to rush to my head. I felt a strange sensation in my face and my thoughts became muddled. I believe that my shouts turned to songs and then mumbles. I blacked out. Some jolt awoke me and I struggled to focus my eyes.

Many hours had passed and one of the wings of *Thelma Ives* was missing. It had been sliced off by the edge of a descending tray, or so I presumed. That was the jolt that had brought me back to consciousness. I stirred sluggishly and saw that there was a break in the line at the limits of my vision. The line continued on the other side of the break, but what use was that to me? No point muttering a prayer, for who would I pray to?

The impact was savage but not quite as horrendous as I was expecting. The glider slid to the point where the line ended. I saw that it wasn't broken. It was just that this section hadn't been completed. *Thelma Ives* came off into thin air and because it only had one wing, it spun slowly, more like a helicopter than an aeroplane. My descent was therefore less precipitous than it might otherwise be and I crashed into the piled cushions of a plump sofa. The chassis of the glider shattered and I was free again, utterly numb, gibbering, red faced and bellowing curses at myself for my foolishness.

Splintered planks of *Thelma Ives* went careering into other chairs, some of them occupied, knocking folks out or causing them to spill their drinks or both, and I knew that I wasn't going to be popular in this region of the

Waiting Room in the immediate future. But I had an answer to this, two answers in fact. Firstly, I wasn't to blame. It was Daedalus' fault. Secondly, everyone down here was an immoral individual, at least to some small extent, and thus deserved some pain now and again. Then my mind sagged.

What I mean by this is that I didn't exactly lose consciousness but my ego retreated into some inner sanctum in my personality and curled up there, hiding from my external environment and the consequences of my actions. I was in a fugue state. I believe that is what medical practitioners call it, though I may be wrong, for I know very little about medicine. I was a wine taster in life, as you already know. Thoughts flickered around the perimeters of my disengaged mind without being able to fully enter inside.

And yet another part of me, separate to the remainder of my identity, was a cool and rational entity. It seemed to be a smaller mind of its own, connected to my larger mind by a silver thread down which occasional feelings were blasted, like cylinders along a pneumatic tube.

This lesser but clearer mind was thinking about Delilah's story. According to her narrative, she had assumed that being stranded in the Rub' al Khali in the dry and barren ruins of Ubar was the worst situation she would ever be in, but in fact going to Hell was worse. She found this out the hard way. But then the spell lifted her out of Hell and transported her to the Waiting Room. She couldn't be returned to Hell because if she was, the spell would activate again and carry her out once more, and so on. She was safe from that fate. That was her assumption. But I saw a loophole in her reasoning.

She could be taken back to Hell but deposited in a Circle that was *slightly* less dreadful. This would no longer be the worst situation she had ever been in, for the simple reason that the other Circle had been worse. But then again, to be trapped *forever* in a slightly less dreadful Circle might be worse than to be stuck in a worse Circle for just a few seconds.

So the spell really would be activated again and she would be rescued yet again, and she was right and I was wrong. I smiled at this. Tying myself into a series of mental knots. I was dimly aware of arms lifting me up and carrying me to a soft divan, where I sprawled with an idiotic smile on my face. I shouted out about how logic was a monster. Then my mouth seized up and refused to work. I was temporarily paralysed and happy.

FOUR

Hot coffee revived me. Cakes enthralled me. I sat up on the divan, blinked and found myself staring at the most hideous person I had ever seen. I shuddered, a wave of revulsion flooded through me. But I controlled myself. This individual was clearly very kind and attentive. I had no wish to offend them. But to gaze on that visage was a genuine ordeal.

"Take it easy," came the voice of this apparition.

"Difficult to do that."

He pondered my words, decided I had intended to make a joke, and with a convulsion of his horrible face he uttered a short laugh. Then he drew back and I breathed deeply and slowly. I needed to calm myself down. My glider was in splinters and the report would be on its way to Daedalus, passed from mouth to mouth via a chain of chair occupants.

"I crashed because a stretch of the line was missing," I said, and the figure with the ghastly countenance nodded.

"That was my fault, I'm afraid," he replied.

"You are afraid?"

Because he could respond that his use of the word was rhetorical, I found myself pointing directly at him.

"I am the one who is afraid!" I yelled.

His shoulders slumped.

"Sorry for my appearance," he said quietly, "but there's nothing I can do to change it. The way I expired was somewhat unusual. My name is Eckhart, let's get that over with first. I have been here for seventy years. This means I am still regarded as a newcomer. Some of my neighbours say that I resemble a skeleton with shreds of flesh hanging off."

"You look like a mangled corpse," I said.

"I won't disagree."

Shivers ran through me. And yet I was delighted to learn that I was already in the 'E' zone, and now it seemed to me that I had been cruel. I said, "But I bet you have a beautiful personality."

"Please, no," he said.

"It was a lovely compliment," I protested.

"My friend," he said, "we are in the Waiting Room of Hell. None of us can be said to be beautiful down here."

"You mean morally, of course?" I babbled.

"The only kind of beauty that matters is moral, yes. But although I wasn't a particularly good person on the surface, I can't say I was a nightmare. That's the reason I am here and not yet in Hell. My case hasn't been determined. And I am cautiously optimistic I will finally be assigned to one of the milder Circles when the paperwork is eventually done."

"One of the shallow lukewarm pits, perhaps?"

He nodded and said:

"Shall I tell you the tale of how I ended up looking like this? It's the tale of my death. After death we should be made whole again, but the system failed in my case. My tale features fruit."

"I already heard a story about fruit."

Ignoring me, he began.

Banana Boat

I am a lazy man. But I was also the captain of a banana boat. Drifter Eckhart, I was called by my men. Despite this, I knew my way around the ocean as if I had a whale in my genetic heritage. Truly, it's remarkable how many seas and island chains I was familiar with. My cargo was always the same. Bananas. I was too lazy to learn how to transport anything else. My hold was stuffed with bananas. On each voyage I would sail to distant ports to unload them. I was lazy but I had a hard-working crew, which explains why my voyages were successful and how I remained in charge of my vessel.

Now there's one thing about bananas you may or may not know, but I shall tell you anyway. Bananas continue to ripen after they have been picked but they produce ethylene gas when they do, a lot of it, a lot more than other fruits do. It speeds up the ripening process, so if you put bananas in a bag, the ethylene will collect in concentrated form and the bananas will ripen very quickly indeed. It's a special concern for a banana boat skipper. Of course, my crew were competent and did all the worrying on my behalf.

My hold was full of bananas and I had to get them to their destination with as little delay as possible. Otherwise they would over-ripen below deck. But let me encourage you to get this mantra into your head. Bananas ripen other things. That's the key phrase here. There were eight men in my crew and they all came from different nations. We were like one big happy family and I was the father, a very indolent father but good-natured and easy-going. I liked to be out on deck and lean over the rail and yawn at the horizon. We would often pass close to an island and monkeys would wave at me.

You ask why monkeys might wave but you never wonder why the waves of the sea monkey around. That's a separate issue, so forget it and allow me to say that there was never any trouble on any of my voyages until the final one. I guess that the trouble was storing itself up in order to be unleashed in one huge deluge of sloppy nastiness. We had left Curaçao and were on our way north to Nova Scotia when we entered a region of dense fog. Visibility was reduced to zero and the sea was absolutely calm.

There wasn't a breath of wind and our sails hung limply, like bedsheets on the morning balcony of a lustful lover. No movement at all. Just as if we were in the Sargasso Sea, which was still hundreds of leagues away. Becalmed. The heat was intense. We sweltered and swore.

Some of us swore first and then sweltered, but whichever order we carried out this procedure in, we ended up slicked with perspiration and with our stock of curse words exhausted. And the bananas in the hold were ripening. There was nothing we could do to prevent this, but I ordered the hatches of the hold to be opened to prevent an accumulation of ethylene gas. This was a mistake but I didn't know that at the time. None of us did. The gas rose up and smothered the deck and we breathed it in. But it was invisible and we didn't know that's what we were doing. We smelled bananas, that's all. Not a bad smell, rather a superb one, if I am going to be perfectly honest.

Now let me explain that my crew was a gang of fruit-eaters, yes it's true, I can hardly blame them. I was one too. What do you expect of the crew of such a vessel as mine? We were carrying ludicrous amounts of bananas. Of course we ate many of them as we went along. Even eating fifty a day each, which makes a total of nine multiplied by fifty, for there were eight crewmen and myself, in other words 450 bananas each day, more than three thousand every week, barely dented our stock. But it did mean that our bodies were rather fruity, more fruity than the bodies of normal people on land.

And as the ethylene gas entered our lungs we started to ripen. When fruit ripens, it becomes softer and then mushy and finally it decays to a sludge. But when humans ripen, they grow older. The hair on the heads of my crew turned grey and then white. Wrinkles spread over their faces and they stooped instead of standing straight. The bananas were ripening them to death. Something had to be done. But what? While I dithered over the question, feeling too indolent to issue direct orders, they decided to act.

They began hurling the crates of bananas over the side into the sea. I tried to stop them, but my efforts were feeble and ineffectual. The bananas were our ballast, you see, and as the hold emptied, the ship became less and less stable. I dreaded what might happen if the wind started blowing strongly again. But the men kept rushing into the hold and coming up with bunches of bananas. When I say 'rushing' I really mean 'hobbling' for some of them were now so ripe they ought to be in bed sipping hot chocolate and listening to the cricket on the radio and complaining about all modernity.

Despite my cries, the hold was eventually emptied and the bananas drifted around us. But now the gas from them started to prematurely age the ship. Rust ate away at the railings and eroded the anchor to black crumbs. The sails soon had huge holes in them. Everything that could decay did so. The ship was now overripe and a danger to all who sailed in her. Then the wind picked up and the sea began heaving and we capsized.

As the deck came up beneath our feet, we were catapulted far into the sea. The hull was full of holes and the empty hold flooded with seawater. The ship rapidly sank. We were almost sucked down with it but luckily we were distant enough now to resist that force. We floated among the bunches of bananas and the men clung to them as if they were buoyancy aids. The navigator even tried to collect many bunches and tie them together with his shoelaces to construct a raft. I instinctively knew this was an unwise idea. Proximity to so many bananas accelerated the ripening of his flesh.

As we drifted among the crescent fruits, which were no longer yellow but black, we aged more rapidly than we might have done. For example, the bosun was only thirty years old but when I looked at him, he seemed to be eighty, even ninety years of age. His flesh was falling off his bones. The navigator was in an even worse condition, so senescent that even his superannuation was outdated. I shuddered to behold him a decrepit mummy, spavined rather than venerable but also desiccated, withered and hideous.

In fact, the navigator was the first to go. He had gathered so many bunches that his exposure to the ripening ethylene gas was enormous. Before our eyes he turned into a skeleton and his bones fell apart and sank under the surface. They lie on the seabed now. I say 'before our eyes' but many of us had become quite myopic thanks to our increased age and didn't witness his doom. "Where is the navigator?" they croaked, and when

I cried, "He went under," they asked me to speak louder, for they were also hard of hearing. We were turning into mush, a crew of human bananas, putrefying.

One by one, my men died of premature old age. The bosun went next, the other six followed shortly after, and soon I was the only one left alive. A speck appeared in the distance. It was a rock protruding above the waves, no wider or higher than a kitchen table. But at least it was solid land. The current was taking me towards it. I decided to make it my final home. I am too lazy to swim with a vigorous stroke. I turned over and gently backstroked my way to that rock. But is that even a real word, 'backstroked'? Or should it be backstruck? Neither has the ring of authenticity about them.

No matter. I reached the rock, mainly with the current's help, and I pulled myself onto it. The banana boat crew had been prematurely ripened into a death ship squad, they had slipped under the turbid blue forevermore, dissolved and broken into chunks and bones, but not the captain. I was alive. I was very old but I was still alive. I climbed to my feet on that tiny square of dry land and I watched as the bananas encircled my sanctuary, knocking against my diminutive shoreline, mocking me with their softening gunk, or so I imagined. But maybe they weren't mocking me. I was confused in my mind, for in effect I was now one hundred years old, a centenarian.

Lots of my flesh had dropped off my bones, which is how you see me, and I probably should have died too. But I was too lazy to do that, so I didn't. That's right, too lazy to expire! Incredible, isn't it? It reminds me of a time I was bitten by a dog and acquired rabies, which is always fatal. But I didn't die. It wasn't that my immune system was somehow stronger than everyone else's. It was just that the symptoms of rabies include fever, hydrophobia, shaking, frothing at the mouth, spasms, and that seemed like a lot of work. I just couldn't be bothered to die that way, and thus I got better, much to the doctors' surprise. I am lazy, very lazy. Drifter Eckhart, they called me.

I have mentioned that already, haven't I? Forgive me

for repeating myself. It's easier than saying new things and I like ease because I am lazy. I was stuck on this small rock, but then something unexpected happened. The rock started rising higher and more exposed land appeared around it. The bananas were the agents responsible for this. They were ripening the natural geological processes of the region. Remember what I said, bananas ripen other things. Not just other fruits and themselves. They can ripen history too. This rock was destined to rise up eventually and turn into an island.

That's how islands are formed. It's one way, at least. The bananas simply accelerated the upthrust, so that it took just minutes instead of millennia. The rock lifted and became a mountain in the sea. And I was perched on the apex and I commanded an amazing view, though the view was just more ocean, as I was still very distant from true land. But all the same! Now the bananas in the water were very far away and I was safe from the ethylene gas. The acceleration stopped and I returned to ageing normally. I was one hundred and twenty years old and I looked like a Halloween ghoul.

So now you know what happened to me. I was ruler of that island. Not as magnificent a position as it sounds. There was no vegetation, no animal life, no human inhabitants, just bare rock and seafoam and the occasional black banana skin that had been washed ashore. But a few days later I spotted a rescue plane in the distance. I removed my ragged shirt and waved it above my rotting head and attracted the pilot's attention.

The plane turned and approached my island. But this was at a time when aeroplanes weren't as reliable or as safe as they are now. The mountain at the centre of the isle must have disturbed the thermals and altered the air currents and created too much turbulence. The pilot lost control and the propeller came off and smashed into one of the wings. Just like your own glider, which landed with an ungainly and awful bump, throwing you out of the cockpit, this plane descended in an erratic fashion. The pilot and his crew were killed in the crash and so was I, when the plane landed on top of me. We all died together. I might be too lazy to die of rabies or old age, but being flattened by an aircraft fuselage is something quite beyond any indolence.

We found ourselves standing outside the entrance to this Waiting Room. I went inside first and the three fellows followed me. They accompanied me to the 'E' zone and then continued to their own zones. They must still be sitting on chairs up ahead. Karlsen, Lopes and Morselli are their names. If you see them on your journey, give them my regards. Anyway, that's all I have to say about how I died. I avoid bananas down here, which occasionally are served on the trays. I have developed a phobia of those fruits.

—oOo—

"I am not surprised," I responded.

"Not even slightly?" he asked, somewhat dismayed. I realised that he had misunderstood my words. I said:

"I am *very* surprised by your story, ultimately astonished, in fact. What I mean is that I am not amazed that you now have a phobia of bananas. That's a perfectly understandable reaction."

"Thank you," he said, smiling awfully.

"I feel unwell," I said.

"That's because of your crash," he replied, and then added, "and it's also one of the effects of looking at me."

"One of the effects? You mean there are others?"

"Well, it's the main one."

"You *are* appallingly grotesque," I admitted.

"True enough." He laughed.

I laughed with him, but my chuckles turned into coughs and then sobs and then into hysterical giggles. He said:

"You don't have to stay in my company for long, you know. In fact, it will be a good idea for you to get going as soon as possible. The folks around here won't be pleased that you clobbered them with the debris from your glider. The community will be against you."

"It's not my fault the thing came off the wire."

"It's *my* fault," he said.

He had already claimed responsibility for this aspect of the accident and I raised my singed eyebrows at him.

But he explained himself convincingly.

"I was too lazy to string the wire up along my section. I agreed to help the project, I thought that Daedalus was attempting something unique, and I swear that I had every intention of making my contribution. But laziness prevented me and I kept postponing the task. I never expected him to find a fool, sorry I mean a willing volunteer, to fly the deathtrap so soon. Not that it's really a deathtrap, because you are already dead and trapped, so how can you be double dead and double trapped? You know what I mean, even if I don't. My neighbours ahead of me and behind me berated me."

"Rightly so," I answered him in a sour tone.

He nodded. "Too bad."

"But you weren't so lazy that when word reached you from Daedalus what he planned to do, that you didn't spread the news to the nearest neighbour ahead of you? There's hope for you yet."

I had intended to be sarcastic but while uttering that statement, my sarcasm dropped off like rotting flesh from an over-ripened cadaver and my tone became gentle. I felt kindly towards him because of his condition and also because I saw how he was actually a nice person. And by 'nice' I mean within limits. If he was perfectly nice, he wouldn't be here.

"Eckhart," I said, "I think I will hobble onwards."

"If you can," he answered.

"I have done something similar already," I replied, remembering *Triton*. If my bruises from that misadventure hadn't faded by now, my new bruises could have kept them company. But the new ones were all that could be found on my battered frame. I waved him farewell.

"Don't do anything I wouldn't do," he advised me.

"Why not?" I frowned.

He shrugged. It was a meaningless warning, and then I stumbled forwards, hoping to vacate the area before the occupants I had knocked unconscious with debris awakened and decided to berate me with words, fists and kicks. After an hour of lurching, I judged it safe to sit down and rest. A hatch opened and a tray descended from the ceiling. Potatoes and peas in a curry with a plate of rotis. I gobbled it all up, despite my sore jaw.

I asked myself again, why was I in such a rush?

The 'Z' zone was very distant.

There was no reason I should arrive there quickly. Some people down here had taken years, decades, centuries to make their way to their proper seats, even though they belonged to one of the early zones, the 'A' or 'B' zones. The zones near the back were aeons away, the Devil had told me that much and despite his reputation, I didn't think he was a liar.

The zipline continued on the other side of Eckhart's personal space, but it didn't continue for long. He wasn't the only lazy one down here. In fact, he had been diligent enough to communicate Daedalus' idea to the neighbour ahead of him, whereas some of these others hadn't even bothered to listen properly to the message as it was passed on, and so in turn they had failed to pass it on, or had passed it on in an oddly garbled form.

But it isn't my position to judge, quite the opposite. We were all here to be judged by a higher authority. I must never forget that simple truth. I wiped my lips with my sleeve after my meal, stood and walked onwards. I walked until I was obliged to visit a bathroom. Then I would emerge, find a comfortable seat and recline on it. I followed this routine every day, not that 'days' are the same here as on the world's surface, indulging in brief conversations with those who called out to me. I never initiated any of these casual contacts. In fact I preferred being an outsider, an observer, listening to others but making no contributions to the discourse myself. It was simpler.

While relaxing in a soft and deep armchair, I overheard a conversation that was being conducted by two nearby occupants of the zone. I reproduce it here for the sake of its baffling nature, which illustrates well the enigmatic quality of so much of our everyday discourse. Our quotidian interactions are often cryptic and absurd, but we are too close to them to realise this fact. I don't think either of the speakers were aware of my presence. One was a man dressed in furs with a club resting in his lap, the other was a woman in a flouncy dress with a bonnet on her head and disapproving lips.

"You know something?" she asked him.

"I do," said the caveman.

"Something specifically strange, I mean."

"Tell me, if you would."

"Well, I heard that Edwards changed the name of his group from 'Mustard on an Aardvark's Elbow', which I always thought was a good name, to 'Rancid Custard Dangles', which strikes me as less poignant. He also altered the privacy settings from 'semi-public' to 'quasi-private'. A big mistake, I reckon. Can you account for such behaviour?"

"Not without my washboard, missus."

"You can sit there and say that, yes you can, but it doesn't convince me in the slightest. What is a washboard compared with a javelin? My aunt owned an obsidian mantlepiece, crammed."

"Yes, they often are, gleaming like olive convexity. Mascots, munitions, a few framed photographs, some depicting scenes of great latitude, and yet there can never be another vibrancy of comparable intensity unless you yourself are inclined to attempt the revival."

"Oh, but my knick knacks are mostly longitudinal."

"Hush now, hush."

I rolled my eyes in dismay.

Perhaps dismay isn't the right word, because it didn't bother me too much that I couldn't understand what they were talking about, but it seemed that there were anachronisms in that exchange. A caveman talking about munitions? That didn't ring true, unless he was referring to flints in a sling and trying to be posh about it, in order to impress the lady. But they might have picked up information from many different centuries while they were waiting here. In fact, the diverse cultures of the Waiting Room were surely in an endless process of blending into a monoculture, as the population was constantly replenished by new arrivals. On the other hand, why did I care what it was or should be? None of this was any of my affair. I was a dead wine taster.

I slept in my chair and when I awoke, I stretched cautiously and continued my journey, passing the caveman and the lady in the bonnet, the grunter and the prissy, as I privately thought of them, who were dozing themselves. I noted they were holding hands. They had vacated their own seats and were plonked side by side on a sofa. His club was nowhere to be seen. He was an extreme example of human hairiness, she was an equally extreme example of pallid smoothness, but so what? My business was elsewhere.

I heard many conversations of a similar nature, baffling, seemingly stuffed with non-sequiturs, mystifying, surreal, often amusing, sometimes frustratingly arcane, pretentious, factually incorrect, grammatically bad, occasionally sincere in tone, pointless, essentially human.

I wondered where all the dead animals were?

And what about the plants?

All the fungi too?

Did they have Heavens and Hells of their own and Waiting Rooms outside paradise or perdition? Or maybe some other system applied to them, rebirth and reincarnation, or transfer to some other planet or dimension. Once again, it was none of my concern. I was a simple soul and my task was to get to the zone that had been assigned to me. No more.

A woman by the name of Eunice hailed me.

The Amoeba

Hey, you! Come here. What's your name? You have a long way to go, but that's true of us all. Some have a long way to go in space and time, others in attitude and understanding. I can tell by the look in your eyes that you are wondering why the only animals down here happen to be human beings. I am perceptive and I can read people like a book.

That's why I no longer read real books, apart from the great difficulty of obtaining them here. But people make better stories. Listen. You don't know me, I don't know you, and that's a useful thing. It keeps our relationship pure. It's impossible to tell lies down here, but even if it wasn't, there would be no reason for me to try to deceive you.

I wouldn't gain anything by it. Let's be quite clear. I'm not a biologist but I know about amoebas and the reason I know about amoebas is because I am one. I'm not really a human female. Well, I am sort of a woman, just enough of one I guess to justify me ending up here.

But when I first arrived the Devil was surprised and troubled by me. "You don't smell human," he said, and he should know, he has been smelling dozens if not thousands of them every single hour for the past two million years. "I am uneasy," he added, his horns glinting.

Doubts afflict every existing creature, even angels and demons. The Devil is no exception to the rule. Finally he decided to let me enter the Waiting Room and that's what I did. My surname is authentic, by the way. Why can't amoebas have names? But you want to know why I don't look like an amoeba. I am too big, for instance, and the wrong shape.

And I can talk intelligently and none of this adds up, does it? You know a little about amoebas, I suppose? I mean, just that they reproduce by splitting in two and then those two halves go off and grow and split in two when their time is right, and so on, and so on. This is common knowledge. So even though you aren't an amoeba, you know about them.

Like I said, I know about amoebas because I am an amoeba. Ages ago in the dim mists of time, only they weren't dim, they shone like the Devil's horns when he said he felt uneasy, there was an amoeba in a pond and something was different about it. That pond had been struck by lightning an hour before. Could that be the reason for what happened?

I don't know. I'm not a physicist any more than I am a biologist. Amoebas reproduce by splitting in two. But let's consider what this means. When the split takes place, the amoeba can be said to have died. The split is the cause of death. Two new amoebas are created but they aren't the original amoeba. And yet they are, because they are identical to the original amoeba. We can say that the first amoeba has died and been *reincarnated*, but doubly reincarnated, reincarnated as itself, but as two of itself. This process will continue indefinitely and always the very first amoeba will be replicated.

But the amoeba in that pond didn't follow the amoebic traditions. Instead of splitting into two when it got large enough, it remained whole and just kept growing. Every time it was due to split, it failed to do so. It grew and grew and eventually it stopped growing because of the constraints of gravity on the gluey gloop that was its essential substance.

It couldn't grow any larger physically, but it could still grow in intelligence and that's exactly what happened. Every so often, when enough time passed, its intelligence doubled. Before long it became as intelligent as a human being. The fact it was also the same size as an average human being meant that there wasn't much left to stop it pretending to be one.

Much easier to function in human society disguised as a woman rather than flowing about in the form of a massive amoeba! And the world is dominated by human civilisation, so I had little choice but to try to integrate myself into urban life. I forced myself to adopt a womanly shape and I wore clothes and I found a job in the import/export department of a shampoo warehouse. And I died when I was knocked down by an experimental motorised tricycle when I took a holiday and went to Marseilles for two weeks.

Will the fact I am an amoeba be discovered by those in

charge? Do I run a risk of being expelled from the Waiting Room? It should be clear from what I told you that amoebas are reincarnated when they die. That should have been my fate too. But for ordinary amoebas, the reincarnation itself is the thing that kills them. Do you see? They don't die and then get reincarnated. They live and continue living *until* they are reincarnated.

So the process for them is different as to how it would be for other entities. It's tedious down here. I want to be back on the surface, reincarnated as myself, even if that means I have to split into two identical women who are tiny but who will grow. I tell my story to everyone down here who will listen because I want word to get back to the authorities that a mistake has been made, that I shouldn't be here. I could have told the Devil all this directly but back then I didn't know what the Waiting Room might be like.

I thought there was a chance it might be wonderful, not quite as grand and soothing as Heaven, but a luxury facility all the same. If you consider the sheer amount of resources the rulers of the cosmos have, it seems reasonable to expect elegance, variety, beauty, serenity, pleasant distractions. What I actually found was drabness and cheapness, the sort of thing you might have encountered back in the 1970s in East Germany. I weep often when I think about this. But I can't shed real salty tears. I am an amoeba.

What was that? You want to know why I am muttering rather than talking in a clear voice? It's because my vocal cords aren't quite the same as yours. I'm not human. I have a human body and face and mind, a human name, and I ended up having a human fate too, but I'm an amoeba from an electrified pond. Where are you going? It's rude to walk away!

—o0o—

I left Eunice to her futile mutterings.

Time passed. We have gone through this already. Time passed. How can I say it in a way that seems fresh? I met many people and I was told many stories but none of them amused me. Strangers shared details of their deaths but even they seemed bored by the narratives.

They had died in their sleep, peacefully or not peacefully, or in car wrecks or train accidents, they had been murdered by spouses or false friends, they had hanged themselves or jumped off bridges. Some of them had taken the wrong kind of medicine by mistake. A few had fought duels. One fellow had been killed by an extremely unusual hailstorm, with hailstones as large as galvanised buckets and nowhere to shelter from them.

One person had been trapped in an elevator, just as I had, and we shared a few sadly jovial remarks about thirst, claustrophobia and despair. But that was the only thing we had in common. I told him about the man killed by hailstones and he said, "Why didn't he use one of the hailstones as a shield to protect his head from the other hailstones?" and I decided this showed a lack of sympathy and I quickly moved away from him.

I met a musician electrocuted by his electric guitar, a writer who wrote so much that his fingers fell off and so he died of gangrene, an artist who painted himself into an abstract corner and couldn't get out until the paint was dry and died of starvation first. I met an accountant who fatally tripped over a duck in a public park, a priest who jumped through a stained glass window for no reason at all, a carpenter who constructed a wardrobe with himself on the inside and no door for him to get out of the thing.

Many people couldn't remember *how* they had died. The whole thing had been a blank to them. They told tales about other aspects of their lives. Some of them told me tales of how they had been killers, not always maliciously, and it seemed a few of them were able to tell tales of the deaths of those individuals who couldn't remember their deaths.

A professional executioner from the Dark Ages was very fond of telling an anecdote about the King he served. He told it six or seven times, even though I only rested near him for about twenty minutes. The anecdote concerned a reply the King had made to him when he went to deliver his report at the end of some battle or other. Apparently he'd said, "Sire! I want you to know, I have executed your enemies with an axe and now they gaze sightlessly down from the tops of sharpened poles," and the King had answered, "Thanks for the heads up," but I had doubts about aspects of that exchange. We were speaking Esperanto at the present moment, but the executioner and the King would have used an entirely different language. It made no sense.

But making sense isn't a deep feature of the universe and the fault actually lies with our expectations, which are at their most unrealistic when we believe them to be reasonable. There *is* an order to the cosmos, we tell ourselves, even if we are incapable of seeing it. That thought comforts us a little and that is all very well. But if it comforts us too much, we grow overconfident, and then we try to discover what that 'order' is. We might even dream of adjusting it when we find it. That's the lethal mistake.

Some of my encounters with random individuals were cut short when one or two panels slid open and angels emerged, typically two or three. They came in a wide variety of designs. One looked like a harp with a face and a thousand tiny feet that enabled it to scuttle faster than a man can run. Another appeared to be made from rusty iron screws and nuts. I might be in the middle of a chinwag with some fellow, but the moment we heard a panel draw back, he or she would call out a warning and I was out of my seat in a flash and striding forwards with my tired arms pumping by my sides.

I was talking to a lighthouse keeper who kept baby lighthouses in a hutch in his back garden when a panel near us slid open and a purple polyhedron flew out at high speed and made straight for me, screaming incoherently in Latin or some other dead language. An instant later I was on my feet, jogging for my life even though I was dead. The angel lost interest as soon as I was moving. But the lighthouse keeper had had a chance to tell me about how the hem of his jacket snagged on the lamp of one of his larger fosterlings and he had been rotated to death over a very long period of time.

A little later I met a lawyer who got drunk at a party and pretended to be a gibbon with such savage enthusiasm that before the night was over he whooped himself to death, and a hotel manager who lost control after too much exposure to rude guests and poked his tongue out at one of them and kept poking it and poking it until finally it dragged out his entrails and he couldn't get them back in. Mundane and peculiar dooms in equal measure. One man tried to swallow a snake whole, in revenge for the fact his uncle had been swallowed whole by a snake, and he had choked on the python. One woman had the idea of jumping on a trampoline while standing on a pogo stick and she had banged her head on the underside of a passing aeroplane.

If some of this seems unlikely or even a little silly, please bear in mind that you haven't really yet questioned the fact I am dead and wandering through the astronomically long Waiting Room of Hell, and if you can accept that, then you should be able to accept anything. But I suppose you might be one of the very few readers who *have* questioned it, in which case I apologise for lumping you in with the rest, with all those who just can't wait for an opportunity to suspend their disbelief. They love that kind of suspension. They really loathe their sense of disbelief and itch to string it up.

Talking about itching, there were no fleas in any of the soft chairs here, no bugs of any kind, and that was a relief. I had lived for too long with cats to be anything other than grateful for a flea-free afterlife. The little wounds covering me had nothing to do with insect bites or scratching away itches. They were the result of vehicular disasters with powered armchairs and zipline gliders. But I am telling you stuff you already know.

One night while I was struggling to fall asleep, an object whooshed over my head but I didn't see what it was. Just a vague shape. Not an angel. It had missed me by a few inches, but so what?

I got up and resumed walking. I wasn't tired at all. Time passed and I lost track of it. Time is a bizarre phenomenon. But is the converse true, are bizarre phenomena timely? I just don't know. I don't want to know. Time passed and at last I entered the 'F' zone, very foot sore.

A fellow I made friends with told me his tale. His name was Frampton and he was an unfortunate seismologist.

The Seismograph

I worked for an international organisation that was devoted to detecting seismic activity and issuing earthquake warnings in good time for the governments of the countries affected to take as many measures as possible before the worst of the catastrophe occurred. Even just a few hours' warning could save thousands of lives, giving the authorities time to evacuate populations from areas at risk. It was a moral job, though I can't say I was entirely an ethical man. I enjoyed too many vices for that, especially marijuana and prostitutes. I also liked gambling my wages away on cards and roulette.

But I was well-liked by my employers. "Frampton," my line manager said to me one day, "you are a regular sport," and by this he meant I was a good guy and not that I was some sort of anthropomorphic version of cricket or football. I did my work diligently. It was a calling as well as a career. I detected very faint seismic rumblings before the rumblings grew into adolescent tremors and then turned into fully adult city-smashers.

Our organisation was at war and our enemy was earthquakes and I was a footsoldier, though I spent most of my time not on my feet but sitting down and studying the readout of a seismograph, yet my feet were still touching the floor. Therefore I was a bonafide footsoldier.

We couldn't beat earthquakes in this war, but we certainly could limit the damage that those chthonic scoundrels did. Our seismographs were powerful and every time a more sensitive model was invented, we acquired it. The more sensitive models tended to be larger. That's how it is with such equipment. This was something I often thought about.

It seemed to me that an extraordinarily large seismograph, especially one fitted with massive amplifiers, could be made so sensitive that it would detect seismic disturbances long before they became even faint rumbles, and that this would save even more lives. I suggested the idea to my line manager. He was open minded enough to listen and then he said, "I reckon we could build such a device ourselves. Why don't we try?"

There were enough engineers, mechanics, technicians in the offices of our organisation, and enough spare parts from discarded seismographs, to make the project feasible. There was also a basement big enough to house such a monster of a machine. One of the geologists working with us was also in a heavy metal group and in his spare time he played excessively loud bass guitar, feeding his instrument through amplifiers and speakers he fabricated himself. We liked to make jokes about a geologist playing 'rock' music, but we knew it wasn't very funny even while making it, yet we enjoyed saying it all the same. That's how real people are in the universe, isn't it?

After many months of toil, the vast seismograph was ready. It was so large that I laughed when I first saw it, and it was so sensitive that when it was turned on, the laughter of loving couples in the adjacent town as they tickled each other registered as complex sine-waves. We turned the amplifiers to maximum and we sat in front of the readouts, waiting to save lives. My line manager was so happy that he wanted to hug me and kiss me on the cheek. I decided to allow him to do this, because his enthusiasm was a joy to behold. He was delighted at the idea of saving men, women and children from being crushed by falling buildings. I am certain he has gone straight to Heaven.

But there was a problem. Our seismograph was too sensitive. We were in a soundproofed room, so any noise we might make wouldn't influence the device and produce false readings, but other people out there in the world weren't also in soundproofed rooms. My line manager kissed me and his lips smacked like a deflating jellyfish on my cheekbone. No problem. But a loving couple in some distant country, which in this case happened to be Burma, also kissed each other at that very moment and they did so with genuine passion, and the seismograph picked *that kiss* up. Picked it up and ran it through the amplifiers. A kiss as loud as two tsunamis colliding over a tiny island and those tsunamis were full of fish with kissy lips and lovesick mariners.

Those amplifiers were so powerful that the building that housed us started shaking. Plaster fell from the ceiling. The soundproofing cracked and that was a death sentence for us, because it meant our screams and shouts of panic were now picked up too and became amplified and the building shook even more and we screamed even more. It was a self-propelling disaster. The seismograph was so large and sensitive and powerful that it created an earthquake. It created its own earthquake with its quake detectors.

That's right, it's horribly ironic, isn't it? The basement of our building was the epicentre of an incredibly forceful earthquake and the entire edifice tumbled down and crushed most of us. I wasn't smashed by falling rubble, but my line manager was, and he fell onto me, and he was a very heavy fellow, and all his weight combined with the weight of part of the roof that lay on him, squeezed all the air out of my lungs. I expired.

Everyone down here has expired in one way or another. That's hardly any reason for babbling the story of my death at you. But I bet very few others have ever been killed in an earthquake created by a giant seismograph that was made to detect other earthquakes and save lives? That is why I felt justified in telling you my story, even though you look a little weary of hearing narratives from all the dead people gathered in this place.

—o0o—

Frampton gave me a demonstration of the earthquake by shaking his body as if it was the ground and I watched this performance for a few minutes. It was only amusing if you were hysterical yourself, which I wasn't, yet he was a good chap and I regarded him as a worthwhile companion, unlike that amoeba who I found a bit creepy, or slithery, I should say.

I left him after a few days and tramped onwards.

My progress was good.

The armchair powered by angel whippings and the zipline glider had been responsible for pushing me much further ahead than I would have managed just on my feet. But now I was hoofing it. The best thing to do would be to seek out another form of speedy transportation.

Could I lasso an angel and ride it like a stallion?

Was even thinking that a sin?

I shuddered at the possible consequences of such an action. I wondered if anyone had been foolish enough to attempt it? They would be pitched into one of Hell's Circles immediately.

Then I remembered that there was an even worse place than Hell. As deep below Hell as Hell is below Heaven there was the realm known as Tartarus. It's a mythological concept, but I had learned that much about mythology was true. How could Tartarus be worse than Hell? I had no desire to find out. I wouldn't lasso and ride an angel, I decided.

Maybe I could persuade the occupants of a zone to help construct a large catapult from the elastic in their clothes? Women might loan their brassières to me for such a project. Ten thousand brassières, whether full cup, plunge or even balconette, should provide enough elastic for a tremendous ballista, a catapult like a vast crossbow. With suitable assistance, I could be twanged at very high velocity in the direction I was going. A dangerous venture, of course, but do I need to repeat that I was dead?

Danger to the dead is something fundamentally different than it is to the living. But I would be embarrassed to ask women to do such a thing. It might seem I was trying to be suggestive in a lewd context. I would forget this idea and wait until some better notion came alone. In the meantime, I plodded and strode, sometimes even breaking into a canter, but not for long. Angels came from behind panels and some of them glared at me, as if they knew that I had recently been thinking bad thoughts.

But none jabbed me with pikes or lashed me with whips or thrust swords of flame down my gullet. I was safe. Then I considered catapults that worked without elastic. There was the trebuchet design, for example, with an arm and a counterweight, but I estimated the ceiling as being too low to allow a projectile to be successfully launched from such a contraption. There was also the simple sling but scaled up in order to propel a man, who would be rather dizzy, like a stone past the rows of seated guests.

I don't suppose 'guests' is really the right word for what we were, but no other word seems suitable. 'Prisoners' is too harsh. The souls writhing in Hell were prisoners and maybe the souls floating around Heaven were prisoners too. But we were fairly comfortable here.

I'm not suggesting that prisoners can't be comfortable but there's still an element of claustrophobia about their situations, and although you might think the Waiting Room was a claustrophobic place too, because it was fully enclosed and had no windows, I can declare that actually it wasn't. When one was facing forwards, one was looking at a sizeable fraction of infinity and eternity and the sensation, if anything, was vertigo.

FIVE

Then I was in the 'G' zone. I kept going.

The nine-hundredth person I spoke to in this zone was a fellow who has already been mentioned in an earlier tale.

But his cameo role had been tiny and now he wanted a chance to feature more prominently in a narrative.

I gave him that chance, because that's good etiquette in the Waiting Room and etiquette is all we possess.

That isn't quite true. We have our clothes and if our clothes feature pockets then we can carry with us anything that will fit in them, bottles of wine, wheels of cheese, hunks of bread. And other objects do exist down here, things carried by dead people into the afterlife.

They had been holding them when they died. And didn't declare them to the Devil when they arrived.

That was certainly against the rules.

But the administration messed up now and again and no one seemed keen to punish them for it. The angels didn't care if you had a book or a penknife in your possession that you ought not to have. They only cared if you were sitting in the wrong zone. "Move along, move along!" was the total sum of their focus and they never even said this in words. Only in actions. But an individual could remain in an unauthorised seat for weeks without being detected. That was one of the redeeming features of this place. The efficiency was fairly low. Perfection has nothing to do with spirituality.

The nine-hundredth person began speaking.

The Getaway

Gonzales is my name, Hector Gonzales, and I was a car hire expert. You know this already? Aaron told you, did he? Yes, I recall that fool, a whimsical chump with a lot of money. But in the end all he wanted was to hire a normal car. That is understandable. A year after he went off and never returned, because he died of thirst in the desert, business was bad. A customer walked into the office and said he wanted to hire our fastest car.

"None of them are fast," I told him, and he asked about engine sizes and torque and all that technical stuff. I said, "None of them are fast because there are no cars available. All are broken."

"All of them?" He was dismayed. He had gold teeth.

"The business is failing."

"But I need a car desperately," he said.

"Look elsewhere."

"There is no elsewhere. Your car hire firm is the only one in this part of the country. Are you sure you can't help?"

And then I said something that I now regret. At least I *think* I regret it. All the drama that followed stems from this reply of mine. I told him, "There are no cars, but maybe I can think of an alternative. How about a horse or a mule? It's the best I can offer at the moment."

"Are you kidding?"

"What's wrong with my suggestion?"

"They are too slow."

I considered the matter and how many mechanics I knew and the answer is that I knew many of them and then I wondered how ingenious they were and the answer was that they were very ingenious. So a solution still seemed possible. I hate to lose a customer, that's why.

I said, "A horse or a mule could be mounted on wheels and fitted with any kind of engine you prefer."

This idea intrigued him and he rubbed his chin furiously. This is something he always did when he was mildly excited. When he was very excited, he stood stock still. I learned all this later and in fact it's not important. He said, "Can you really do such a strange thing?"

"I can't personally but I know folks who can."

"Money is no object."

"Are you certain about that?"

"No, no, I'm not, it's definitely an object, a banknote is an object and coins are even more objective. But I can pay you almost any price you quote for such a high speed beast. However, I'm obliged to pay you *after* I have used the horse or mule and not before. I can't pay you in advance because I don't have money. I need the vehicle to acquire money and from the money I acquire I will pay you the money I owe you. Do you see?"

I nodded. I thought that I saw but actually I didn't see until later. What I'd seen when he asked me if I saw was something else entirely, some vague honest business involving trade deals, who knows? It never occurred to me that he was a bank robber who needed a getaway vehicle. Well, we live and learn, and even here in the afterlife, we learn.

We die and learn too, I should have said.

But anyway... I telephoned the mechanics who were my friends and they were enthused by the odd notion.

The long and the short of all this is that a horse was obtained and wheels were fitted to its hooves and an engine mounted on its saddle. There was now no room for a rider, so the rider travelled behind on a sledge. It was like some crazy chariot designed by a sarcastic Assyrian. But the fact it was only 'like' a crazy chariot and *not* an actual crazy chariot made it a viable transport method and my customer could handle it.

He tried it out, gunning the engine to maximum speed and yelling with a delight mixed with terror as the horse bolted and his sledge veered erratically from side to side of the road. He vanished around a corner and I wondered if that would be the last I'd ever see of him. I might be too trusting but I believed he would return to pay me, yes I did. And return he did, roaring to a halt just outside the front doors of the building in which I had my office. His face was glum as he came through the door.

"I tried to rob the bank in this town but the bank has no money. Can you believe that? They said the economy was terrible and their vaults were empty and no amount of threats could make them change their minds about that. So I demanded that they suggest an alternative place to rob and they said there was only one successful business around here, namely your car hire firm, so I am back to steal everything you have."

"I don't have anything. I already told you that."

"Nothing at all?"

"Not a single dollar or penny."

"You must have *something* I can steal. Please!"

I felt sorry for him.

"A motorised horse with a sledge is the one thing. You can have that if you like. It's outside, over there."

And I gestured through the window. He turned to look at it and he frowned and considered the offer carefully.

"Very well," he said, "I'll rob that. But after stealing it, I'll need a getaway vehicle to make good my escape."

"I can't help you there. We have no cars left. They are all broken. The best thing you can do is cross the border to the wealthier country and hire a car there and come back here, pick up the motorised horse and make a getaway with the foreign car. It's what I would do."

He scrutinised me and licked his lips. "Is it?"

"Probably not," I admitted.

But the idea appealed to him anyway. He made a snap decision, turned on his heel, hurried out of my office and mounted the sledge. Then deftly he turned the key in the ignition, released the handbrake and the horse began accelerating along the street. He headed off into the desert. He was on a mission to obtain a getaway vehicle so he could return here and make a quick getaway with his first getaway vehicle. Sounds peculiar?

I thought so too. So I laughed and went to the secret safe in the wall of my office. It was secret because it was concealed behind a painting. This painting was also concealed behind a painting. Robbers might say to themselves, "There is always a secret safe concealed behind a painting!" and they would pull off the painting and see the second painting underneath. "Ah no, the painting was only concealing another painting. Drat!"

The top painting was of a kitten playing with a ball of wool, the painting beneath it showed a nude woman.

This story has nothing to do with my death. I choked on noodles. No, that's not how it happened. I didn't eat noodles and then die because they stuck in my throat like a pasta knot. I was murdered by an assassin who looped a rope made from noodles around my neck and tightened it. I don't know who he was and I can't guess what his motives were.

Thinking about it now, he might have been the same person who rode the motorised horse. The chap with gold teeth. Why didn't he sell a tooth if he was desperate for money? Inexplicable!

—oOo—

I agreed with him that it was inexplicable, but it didn't follow that it was of any interest to me whatsoever. Mysteries can be tedious as well as enthralling. But a horse of the kind he had described would be useful down here. Plenty of meals that descended from the ceiling are equine-friendly. The horse and I could share salads and apples and mints. There's always a way. The real question is whether you are willing to endure discomfort.

I left Gonzales with scarcely a glance back. I reached a section of the room that was flooded. One of the pipes in the bathroom had burst and water had been pouring out for centuries. Because of the slight incline of the floor, there was an onrushing stream, but there were also dips and concavities here that allowed the water to pool. Also the sofas and settees and chairs formed a barrier to prevent a rapid draining of the flooded region.

The local inhabitants had managed to construct a rickety bridge across the deepest part of this indoor lake. It was made from the wooden frames of chairs and planked with tables. It was slippery but viable and I crossed it without much hesitation. But the way was narrow and halfway across I encountered a fellow who blocked my further progress. I politely asked him if I might pass and with a grim smile he turned to stare at me.

His eyes were mesmeric. They shone from the depths

of a grey homemade helmet. In fact he had dressed himself in armour that he had fashioned from the metal trays on which our meals were served. It was a poor job but he evidently took himself very seriously. He shook his head slowly and then the deep voice I had been expecting issued forth. This voice wasn't his natural voice, I was sure, but the result of theatrical practice.

He said, "I am the guardian of the bridge."

"I see," I responded.

"You must pay a toll if you wish to cross."

"I don't wish it."

This dismayed him. "What do you mean? You aren't allowed to turn back. You *must* cross. Mustn't you?"

"I don't wish it because a wish is a hope for something unlikely to happen. I am actually crossing the bridge. No need to wish for what is occurring already. That would be a wish wasted."

"Oh, a clever fellow! One who needs to understand his position better than he presently does. I am the guardian of the bridge, Sir Herring is my name. My duty is to extract a toll from all travellers who pass this way, you included. See how deep the waters swirl below?"

"Well, they aren't that deep really, are they?"

"Deep enough!" he cried.

"Certainly I have no desire to become soggy right now. But what is the toll you are demanding? Cash?"

"There is no money down here," he boomed.

"What then?" I asked.

"A story! You must tell me a tale."

"Are you sure you don't mean that *you* want to tell *me* a tale?" I said, for I suspected some kind of trick.

"No, I have no gift for it. I want to hear your tale. I collect them, you see. I collect them up here." He tapped his head with a finger and it made a dull sound like a spoon on a tarnished plate.

I laughed to myself. This was hardly the awful ordeal I was expecting it to be. No physical fighting and no baffling riddles. As you have already noticed, I was now in the 'H' zone and my relatively rapid progress was keeping me in a very good mood. I told him my tale, the same one I have already written down, about how I expired in the elevator.

He nodded when I had finished. "Good enough."

"Thank you," I said ironically.

"Are you employing irony?" he asked, narrowing his eyes. Before I could respond to this he added, "There is no iron down here, only aluminium and tin. My armour isn't as grand as it could be. How did I know you were using irony, even though it was incredibly subtle? Let me tell you a secret. I am a reader of minds. Yes, it's true. Not a very accomplished one, the thoughts of other people come to me as vague impressions."

"You always had this talent? I mean, before you ended up in the afterlife? I thought psychic powers had been discredited?" And I waited for him to rant his denial of those scientific disproofs.

Sadly he said, "Yes, but it's not really a power. It's more of an involuntary hobby. I never asked for the ability to read minds and it's not even an ability in the conventional sense of the term."

"What am I thinking now?" I goaded him.

Again his grin was thin.

"Encountering this flooded area has profoundly affected you. Now you are wondering what other anomalies might be awaiting you on your journey. That's what concerns you. You had started to take the regularity of the waiting Room for granted, the unchanging nature of your environment, every zone looking like an almost exact replica of every other zone. But the pond below us proves that a drastic change is possible. What lies ahead? For the first time, you are unsure it will always be the same terrain."

"You are right," I said, slightly shaken.

"But not stirred."

"I beg your pardon?"

"You are slightly shaken by my words, but not stirred. However, I can stir you, stir you to action. My mind reading abilities are mild. I am no psychic lord despite the fact I am a 'Sir', even though I knighted myself, to be candid. Yet I am aware of a fellow who is far more accomplished in the psychic arts than me. His name is Ives. We arrived at the door to the Waiting Room together and we travelled this far in each other's company. I got to know him well before we had to part at this very spot. He has a crystal ball that he smuggled under his coat. I have seen him foretell the future."

"And you think he can foretell my future?"

"I don't know."

"But you believe there's a good chance?"

He shrugged, clanking.

"If I could foretell the future myself, I would do so and let you know if he is able to foretell your future in your future. Does that make sense? It should if you consider the words carefully."

"Allow me to finish crossing the bridge please."

He bowed gracefully.

"Remember his name. Ives. A crystal ball gazer. Don't forget. You might never encounter him among the myriads of souls down here but he is certainly worth searching for. Yes, his surname is the same as that of the composer. It's easy enough to remember it that way. And now I'll let you pass. You have paid the toll. Go in peace, my friend."

I squeezed past him and crossed the bridge. Sir Herring was a fake knight, of course, his accent and poise were suspiciously modern. I would say he was from the 1970s. He was undoubtedly one of those people who genuinely think they have been born in the wrong era. And I can't say I had any firm intention of seeking out that Ives fellow, but it so happened that when I finally reached the 'I' zone I met him by accident.

Crystal Ball

People imagine that crystal balls are large, but many are no bigger than normal sized grapefruits. So Herring told you about me, did he? I never really enjoyed his company as much as he seemed to enjoy mine, but that's all bathroom water under the bridge, so to speak. See, here's my crystal ball. Watch how it glitters, gleams and glints in the middle of this low table! I like glittering and gleaming but I simply adore glinting. Pretty neat, huh? 'Pretty' because it's beautiful and 'neat' because it's a perfect sphere.

If you stare into the depths of this orb you will see swirls of colour, all of them abstract and meaningless to you, but my mind is so constituted that it can discern significant patterns and movements within the translucency. I can't be sure whether the power resides in the ball itself or in my mind, or whether they are a symbiosis, which I suppose is more likely. But things that are more likely aren't always advantageous to us. Bear that in mind. And when I say 'bear' you should be careful not to misunderstand.

In other words, I don't urge you to insert a bear into your brain. It will lash out with its claws and rip your synapses into shreds. But synapses are already in the form of shreds anyway, so maybe it doesn't matter. But it *does* matter. I can see you are starting to suspect I am not entirely sane. Allow me to reassure you that I am fully in control of my thoughts.

I am not clairvoyant. I can't see at a distance what conditions are like in a different zone of this Waiting Room. But I do have precognition. I can foretell your future and if your future includes you struggling with obstacles that exist further along your journey, then I can work out how conditions are different in the regions you are fated to reach. That is how I know there have been seismic upheavals ten thousand leagues ahead.

Have I peered into the crystal ball on behalf of others? That is the question you want to ask. Many times, is the answer. And I will do the same service for you, never fear. But that can be arranged after my tale. My tale concerns how I came into possession of the crystal ball in the first place. When I was alive, my hobby was bowling. I would visit the alley every night. The bowling alley, not the trash can alley full of feral cats and prostitutes. Or if not every night, then at least six out of seven nights in a week.

And that is because I often devoted one night every week to my only other hobby, which was writing letters to the government urging them to change how many days there were in a week. I wanted only six days in a week, because that number seemed less stressful to me. I wasn't alone in this desire. I had managed to make contact with others who felt the same way. We formed what I suppose I could call a lobby group. If the government agreed to our demands and changed the week, I would be able to devote all my nights to bowling. That was my most fond dream, the limits of my ambition.

When I bowled I wore headphones and I listened to the music of Ives, yes Charles Ives, the composer, who is no relation. But I like the fact we share the same surname. His music is complex and hardly ever relaxing, but that suits me fine, because I bowl better when I am feeling agitated. My name is also Charles and that's just a coincidence. My parents never listened to music. The only thing they enjoyed listening to was themselves arguing, though I suppose they didn't object to the hooting of owls now and then. I was walking to the bowling alley one night when it started to rain heavily.

I dislike getting wet. I decided to take a shortcut to reach my destination. The only problem was that I wasn't sure it really *was* a shortcut. It was a street I'd never ventured down before. It was long and narrow, an alleyway, I guess, and at the end of it I found nine tall people standing still. They were silent and arranged in the form of a truncated triangle, four at the back, then three, then two at the front. I am also tall but I couldn't peer over them because they were as tall as me. I tried to peer between them. I saw what looked like the mouth of a cave. This was extremely strange.

"This street is a dead end?" I asked aloud.

They shook their heads.

"It goes back to the beginning," said the nearest fellow, then he smiled and I saw in his smile how weary he was.

"I don't understand."

"Don't even try. Come and join us."

"Why should I?"

"Because we have been waiting for you."

"You don't know me."

The fellow shrugged and so did his eight companions. They beckoned me closer and I felt powerless to resist.

I stood among them. In fact I stood at the front and now the triangle was no longer truncated. It was equilateral. I felt held in place by an invisible force, but at the same time I knew I was only lightly fixed to the ground. I was anxious for an unknown reason. Behind me, my new acquaintances sighed and muttered. I heard a rumbling from the top end of the street. Something was rolling towards us. A large sphere was bearing down on me! It struck me on the left knee and I tumbled with a painful groan.

I don't mean that the groan was painful, it wasn't, but the blow that caused me to issue it was. I hate issuing groans! I prefer to keep them to myself when I can. I couldn't in this instance.

My colleagues also tumbled to the ground. The sphere vanished into that cave mouth and I heard a rumbling below, as if it was trundling along a tunnel back to the top of the alley. Then something inexplicable happened. But it has become explicable since then, because I have thought about it a lot. Some kind of mechanism descended and picked me up. It picked up the other nine fellows at the same time, set us upright.

The truth rushed into my head. I broke the spell and began running back up the alley. "Come back!" the others urged me. I heard a rumbling and saw a new sphere rolling towards me at high speed. or maybe it was the same sphere again. It was too large for me to leap. I turned and ran back to where my friends stood. But this time I weaved between them and hurled myself head-first into the cave. It was a very risky thing to attempt.

I curled up into a protective ball and it turned out that this was wise. Down a dark tunnel I rolled, making myself the dizziest I have ever been, but emerging into light at the top of the alleyway.

A fellow stood there and he was dressed like a wizard in a spangled cloak with a tall pointy hat, but he wore sunglasses even though it was the evening. I blinked at him and he said gently:

"You have escaped and I don't begrudge you that. You shouldn't have tried to take a shortcut down the alley."

"How could I have known?" I protested.

"If you had possessed a crystal ball, you would have known. But without a crystal ball to tell you that you needed a crystal ball, you would never know the facts of the matter. Take this."

"What is it?" I asked him fearfully.

"A crystal ball."

And it was. He gave it to me and then he said, "I'll have to wait for another fool to venture down that alley, because ten pins are necessary. Unless I change my game to nine-pin bowling, which requires a different layout of skittles. That is certainly an option. But now–"

"Yes?" I said, holding the crystal ball in both hands.

"Be off with you!"

I didn't need to be told twice. I ran off and I went to the bowling alley and I found I couldn't play. I felt nauseous. I made my excuses and I returned home and I experimented with the crystal ball the wizard had given me. At first all I saw was static. I had to tune it by twiddling a tiny knob hidden deep in my mind and eventually I saw a future event. Since then I have practised diligently and I have finally become a true expert.

—oOo—

I digested this tale by reminding myself that scepticism wasn't applicable down here, where untruths were banned. If you tried to tell a lie, some force prevented the words from leaving your mouth. So his story had to be true. Wizards really existed and they wore sunglasses at night. Then I mentioned that I had flown in a glider that was also called Ives.

"*Thelma Ives*," I said, "but it was destroyed."

"I have seen it," he said.

"In your crystal ball, you mean?" I cried.

"No, for real."

"But how? It was smashed to bits far back. The pathetic wreckage lies in the 'E' zone, which is thousands of leagues to the rear. Also, it lost a wing in a midair collision with a descending tray. It couldn't fly even if it wanted to. The whole thing was on a zip wire anyway. It wasn't a real glider but a trick. Yet I was fond of the cramped thing."

He smiled at me as if I was a callow youth.

"It passed overhead a while ago. It was looking for its assigned place in its assigned zone. Somewhere ahead. I am Charles Ives, but it is *Thelma Ives*, so in alphabetical terms it is maybe one year's journey from here. You will surely see it for yourself on your journey."

"But it wasn't alive. It doesn't have a soul."

"That happens sometimes."

"I don't understand."

"Mistakes are made with the paperwork. Inanimate objects are destroyed, a clerical error means they are regarded as living beings, they end up down here. I suppose the converse is also true, that some human beings are tagged as objects and forced to remain behind."

"Remain behind? On the surface of Earth?"

"That's right," he said.

"And perhaps that's the reason for ghosts?"

"It might be," he conceded.

"So let me get this straight. *Thelma Ives*, my glider, crashed and became a wreck in the 'E' zone. It was supernaturally transported from there to the front of the Waiting Room, where the Devil greeted it, opened the doors for it, and it found itself inside again and compelled to make its way to the 'I' zone, where it now belonged, because it had been defined as the soul of a dead person? And it managed to fly, even though it lacked a wing, much faster than any human can walk and has already passed you?"

"That's quite correct. It must be resting in its assigned place even while we speak. It whooshed over my head."

I pondered these words. "Something whooshed over my head too, a while ago, but I never saw it clearly. That must have been *Thelma Ives*! So it seems I will be reunited with her, after all."

"Giving her the name of a human woman is probably the reason the error of definition was made," he said.

"So it's my fault? Well, I don't care much."

He pointed at his crystal ball.

"She isn't the only 'female' you will be reunited with. I can see that there are two large surprises in store for you. There are natural disasters ahead. Also, you will meet your wife again."

"My wife? But I don't have a wife!" I cried.

"Your ex-wife then."

I was astonished to hear this. I had forgotten all about her and I guess she had forgotten all about me. What would it be like to see her again? I shuddered and then I berated myself for overreacting, and then I shivered because I don't like berating myself, it gives me the creeps, and then I convulsed because of my aversion to shivering, and I trembled because if there's one thing that makes me angry with myself, it's convulsions.

"What else can you see in my future?" I said.

"Nothing," he told me.

"Why not? Do you suddenly dislike me?"

He explained with a deep sigh, "There is a quota of crystal ball predictions that any human being is alloted."

"I have exhausted my quota with two items?"

"Natural disasters," he said.

"And my ex-wife?"

He nodded at this. I would have to be satisfied with what I had been given. It was time to move on. The water from the broken bathroom was still trickling down the slope. It formed a rivulet about as wide as my outstretched arms. And so I walked by the side of it. I wondered how long it would be before I saw the glider again. A year was Ives' guess. And how long before I encountered those natural disasters and my ex-wife?

Ives had been unable to tell me that. The crystal ball only revealed that the meetings would take place. I didn't even know what *kinds* of natural disasters. I hoped it wouldn't be something impassable. Then I would be in trouble with the angels. They were unreasonable.

The rivulet grew wider and more forceful in its current. It was being fed by tributaries. Other bathrooms had burst pipes and were contributing their water to the flow of the primary stream. Now the river was as wide as two double beds in which clowns were sleeping. Why clowns? I can't say, it just seemed that way. I kept walking along the riverbank.

Then I saw that some bathrooms had been sabotaged deliberately. I caught a man in the act of breaking one of the pipes. He said, "If we can create a fast but navigable river, we can build boats and help travellers such as yourself to *sail* to their destinations. This work won't benefit me, for I am already in my assigned zone, but there is such a thing as altruism. And altruism isn't wholly selfless. It gives me a purpose."

He had been bored sitting on chairs and twiddling his thumbs. Now he felt much happier breaking water pipes with a hatchet improvised from a chair leg and a metal tray. Other occupants were breaking pipes further along. And I don't think this guerrilla action had been coordinated by passing messages back and forth. I think it was instinctual.

By the time I reached *Thelma Ives*, the river was as broad as nineteen short snakes. That's about twice as wide as two double beds for clowns. The cockpit of the glider was split but the chassis was intact. It lay on a sofa and the waters of the river lapped the sofa's castors.

I saw at once that the glider was watertight and that it would make a sort of canoe. I could turn it from a broken aircraft into a viable kayak very easily. All I had to do was rip off the remaining wing. I dragged the thing off the sofa, then I pushed it into the river and waded after it.

I climbed into the split cockpit, which was now much less cramped and far more comfortable. We began drifting down the river. I had viable transport again!

Good old *Thelma Ives*. And I insist that Daedalus would have approved of the new use to which I was putting her. I think I knew him well enough, despite the brevity of our friendship, to make that claim. Picking up speed, we slid over the smooth waters. But I had no paddle or oars and there was no rudder. Slowly I began revolving midstream. Luckily I managed to stop the spin and win some control over the canoe by thrusting my arms over the sides and opening my fists or closing them, to act as the blades of oars. It was inefficient but it worked well enough and practice finally made perfect. Within a week I was a master canoeist and my movements were as fluid as the liquid I rode on. More tributaries added their flow and the river grew massive.

Now it dominated the left and right horizons of the waiting Room, leaving only a narrow dry strip on either side.

There was a jetty ahead that protruded far into the river. It was made from coffee tables lashed together. A man was standing on the end of it. He raised his hand and flagged me down. I steered alongside the jetty and he reached down with a boathook that was a pipe that had been wrenched out of a bathroom and twisted at one end. He drew me closer.

It was the first time I had been drawn closer since a famous myopic artist did my portrait back on the surface because he'd wanted to produce a series of 'wine taster studies'. I wondered if that artist was also down here? He had been old when I knew him. He must be dead now, and although he wasn't a malign person, he wasn't a saintly one either. Perfect material for the Waiting Room, I should have thought. But anyway…

The fellow on the jetty said, "My name is Jaspers."

I was in the 'J' zone already!

This delighted me.

"I am on my way to the 'J' zone," he said.

And my heart sank.

I understood that he was a traveller too.

Like me, he was heading to his assigned zone and he hadn't arrived there yet, he was in the process of getting to his destination. He wanted to beg for a ride in the canoe. Because the cockpit had split thanks to the crash, there was enough room for two passengers.

"By all means, hop inside," I told him.

I didn't mind having a little company on this stage of my voyage. It was a risk because he might turn out to be a tedious fellow. But we are compelled to take risks every so often, aren't we? I learned from him that the jetty had been constructed by the locals of this region. They had planned to set up a boat-hire service for travellers such as ourselves.

They had constructed the jetty but hadn't managed to construct any boats yet, and so he had been waiting to no good purpose. He had been delighted to see me drifting along in *Thelma Ives*. He just hoped I was a pleasant chap who didn't dislike hitchhikers. And I was.

"I will tell you my tale while we are floating down the river," he said and it would have been bad manners for me to discourage him from doing so. But first I told him about my disappointment.

"We are still in the 'I' zone," I complained.

"Not to be confused with the 'me' zone," he quipped, though at first I had no idea he was trying to joke. I wondered if he was insane. Then he laughed, a spluttering sort of chortle and I said:

"Are you in any condition to tell me a story?"

"In the circumstances, yes."

"But what circumstances might those be?"

He indicated the cosmos.

I mean by this that he gestured at our surroundings, the Waiting Room, but his gesture seemed to penetrate the walls and ceiling too, encompassing all that exists or has ever existed. I nodded.

"Go right ahead."

What else could I say? I was a captive audience member, stuck in a canoe that was rushing downstream.

Magnetic Bicycles

The tandem bicycle is generally faster than the solo bicycle. I know this because I was a bicycle salesman when I was alive. The name of Jaspers was famous in the bicycle business because I always came up with original ways of promoting bicycle sales. I didn't just pedal from door to door, pedalling my goods, and did you notice the wordplay there? Sometimes I even dressed as a bicycle, with my hat transformed into a saddle and stiff rods in the sleeves of my coat turning my arms into handlebars. And I wore circular shoes. I had quite a few tumbles and bruised myself attempting those stunts!

This isn't quite as eccentric as you might suppose. I have known men who love to pretend to be motorcycles and I am sure you have seen them too. It is such a common habit that it is almost universal. Nobody thinks it's strange. Those fellows make 'vroom vroom' noises with their lips and everybody nods blithely. But what is a motorcycle other than a bicycle with a petrol engine? Why does an engine make a difference to the act, the playtime, the pretence? It shouldn't be considered more acceptable to pretend to be a motorcycle than to act like a bicycle. Both are totally normal.

But you want to know how I died. Or rather, I want you to know how my death happened. A bicycle was responsible. I say 'bicycle' but perhaps I ought to use the plural. There was more than one bicycle, yet at the same time, it was just one bicycle, a sort of megalithic tandem. Allow me to explain. Tandems, as I have already said, tend to be faster than solo bikes. This is because there are four legs pedalling but the weight of the machine isn't exactly double, it is less than double by a small amount. So the power to weight ratio is better. They are a few percentage points more efficient.

It occurred to me that I could generate publicity by creating the longest and fastest tandem bicycle ever conceived! Why settle for a tandem with two riders? I envisaged a tandem with ten thousand riders! The speed would be incredible. I immediately began drawing plans for such a contraption. But no manufacturer I showed my drawings to was interested. They all said it was impossible to build a tandem bicycle that long. It just couldn't be done. The bicycle was longer than the longest factory in existence. They refused to even consider it. And I was told to go away now in no uncertain terms!

But I remained undaunted. I am Jaspers and Jaspers has never been an easy man to daunt. You can saunter up to me, but never walk over me. That has been my motto ever since I opened a dictionary and found out what a 'motto' was. It wasn't a pit filled with water that surrounds a castle, as I had always assumed. It was a pithy saying that one could adopt and quote whenever a situation required a boost of one's courage and determination. So I reconsidered my plans and I'm happy to say that I came up with something truly ingenious. Magnetic bicycles. Yes, my friend, you heard me correctly.

The metal frame would be magnetic with buffers on the front and back. I am sure you know the kinds of buffers I mean. Like those on trains. Projecting shock-absorbing pads. And there would be ten thousand magnetic bicycles in total. They would have north poles on the front buffer and south poles on the rear buffer. Unlike poles attract, like poles repel. You must know such a basic law of physics. Consider the implications. I would set off on my magnetic bicycle one morning, casually, benignly. At some point, if I kept cycling down random roads, I would meet another rider.

I mean I would meet another rider who was also on one of my magnetic bicycles. If he came out of a junction and was slightly behind me, the north pole of his front buffer would be attracted to the south pole of my rear buffer and we would lock together. Hey presto, a tandem! If he was slightly ahead when we happened to converge, then I would end up at the back. It doesn't matter. All that matters is that a tandem would be created while we were moving. The two pieces would come together. Now think! At some point we would encounter a third rider on one of my magnetic bikes.

He or she would latch on to us too, drawn by magnetic attraction! And so on and on. Remember that ten thousand magnetic bicycles have been made and sold. Eventually, there would be a single tandem bicycle consisting of precisely ten thousand solo machines, all linked into one massive unit. And the speed! I can hardly begin to compute how fast we would be going if we all pedalled as hard as we could. Hundreds of kilometres per hour, maybe thousands! Speedier than aeroplanes and even rockets. But all done with leg power, without fumes, without engine noise. Organic and pure.

But although I am Jaspers and therefore a very capable fellow, it seems I made a mistake in my calculations. Tandem bicycles are slightly faster than a solo bike because they aren't quite twice as heavy. Two solo bikes joined by a magnetic coupling are just as heavy as they were before they were connected. The power to weight ratio hasn't improved. And so, despite the fact there were ten thousand of us in an incredible chain, all of us pedalling for what we were worth, we were still only as fast as one bike. This was embarrassing and it also nullified the stunt's promotional value.

We were cycling across a continent, I forget which one, over a wide plain, perhaps one of the steppes of Russia. I was at the very front and this was only a coincidence, for I never regarded myself as a 'leader' of the cyclists. We were all equals, all ten thousand of us. But the plain was coming to an end and I was riding up a gentle incline to the top of a ridge. I wondered what lay on the other side of the ridge. I would see for myself when I reached the top. When I finally got there, I was shocked to see a very dramatic gradient falling away into some awful sunken valley, some horrid chasm.

I applied my brakes but they had no effect whatsoever. Because our speed had been the same as a solo bicycle during our entire tour of the world, I had forgotten that our inertia certainly wasn't the same. Our momentum was very large indeed. This had nothing to do with speed. It concerned the difficulty of coming to a halt. I was pushed down the gradient and all the others followed in a chain of doom. As soon as they saw what was happening, they applied their own brakes, of course, but by then it was far too late. I struck the bottom of the chasm with so much force that I imploded.

The tandem of ten thousand bikes crunched up like an accordion. I doubt that any of the riders survived, but the ones at the back were probably left in a less gory state than those nearer the front. And so we all found ourselves down here and as we passed through the Waiting Room we formed a chain of people ten thousand individuals long, holding onto each other's hips as we made our way to our assigned zones, men and women peeling away when they arrived at their own destinations. And so the chain contracted. It wasn't my turn to break off, but I tripped over a low coffee table.

The others didn't notice or maybe they noticed but didn't care. They went on without me. I haven't reached my assigned place yet and now I am alone. I don't like travelling alone. It's good that I met you and we can travel in a boat. I still think my tandem was a good idea. But things that are good ideas when they remain in our heads aren't necessarily so nice when they appear for real, and in this particular case the tandem was the death of me. Too bad, I say. And that is the story of my death. If you want to tell me yours, go right ahead. If you prefer not to, that's fine by me. I am easy going.

—oOo—

I felt obliged to tell him about my own death and so I did. I was growing bored with the account of my entombment in that elevator, but other people seemed to enjoy hearing about it, and I don't mean enjoy in any nasty sense. There was an expression of sympathy on the faces of almost everyone who heard it. This was the Waiting Room, after all, not Hell itself. The truly evil individuals, the cruel men and women, the sadists, weren't present. It was a realm of flawed humans who nonetheless had some good qualities.

Jaspers said, "When I say I am easy going, people often doubt me, and I'm not sure why that should be. I'm not highly strung at all. But I had a friend who died in a very peculiar way indeed."

"Maybe if I meet him here, he will tell me about it."

"I can do that task for him."

"But if I do meet him further along, and he insists on telling me, I will get the same story twice," I objected.

"No fear of that. His name was Gillingham. If he *is* here, and I don't even know if he is, you have already passed his designated area. Don't try to stop me telling the story. I'll be very upset if you do. Well now, he was hanging out his washing on the line one day, and the ground collapsed beneath him. There were old mine workings under his house."

"And he fell into them and bashed his brains out?"

"Not so. He had the presence of mind to clutch the washing line and then he dangled for hours over the freshly exposed pit. When his hands and arms grew tired, he pegged the sleeves of the shirt he was wearing to the line with all the pegs he had. And he dangled there for days, calling for help. But he had no near neighbours. He was in trouble."

"What happened?"

"He died of fright on the third day. That's what the doctors said when they examined him after his body was unpegged and retrieved. So he was a highly strung fellow. That's the point I'm trying to make. I am not highly strung, but he was. I am easy going," Jaspers said.

SIX

He wasn't easy going. No. But he didn't bother me to such a degree that I cast him out of the canoe in exasperation. As for *Thelma Ives*, her performance was impeccable. She only leaked a little. Things weren't too bad. The river was growing wider and wider the further we ventured downstream. But whether this river had a mouth or not was unknown to us.

Tributaries were constantly adding their own water to the river, which was flowing faster and faster all the time. It was becoming dramatic. I was reminded of the widest river I had ever sailed on, which was the Nile during a holiday in Egypt long ago with my wife.

Once I even thought I saw an authentic pyramid in the distance, but it was an optical illusion created by steam and rising air from the river, which threw a mysterious veil over everything and also acted like a magnifying lens. The pyramid was merely a pile of furniture.

A fellow swam alongside us for a short while, maybe half an hour. He said his name was Jacklin and that he was a professor but he didn't say what he was a professor of, and I didn't think to ask.

Maybe geography, for he reckoned he was close to his assigned resting place, and it was good for us to hear the confidence in his voice. Jaspers was especially encouraged by these words. It meant we were in the 'J' zone and he had almost arrived himself, give or take a year or two, or a decade, depending on how many individuals were clustered in this stretch of the Waiting Room. Jacklin told us a story while he swam.

The Conference

Because I am an academic, I frequently get invited to conferences, and usually I attend them. I give a talk that lasts an hour, answer a few questions from the audience members, if there are any, and then go off for a meal and a drink that I don't need to pay for. Then I am free to saunter around looking important but relaxed. I grow my moustache daily. I read newspapers. I play badminton now and again. But swimming is my passion.

It sounds like an easy life but there are hidden tensions. The same can be said of some of the sofas here in the Waiting Room. The concealed springs, I mean. And that's why I prefer the buoyancy of this river. The river suits me, it isn't a godsend as such, because God surely disapproves of it, but I am really very grateful for this opportunity to swim a long distance. There are probably aquatic angels but I haven't met any yet.

I want to say a little more about conferences in general. Every year there are a multitude of awards given out to academics who work in my chosen field and I always scan the shortlists hoping that people who have been rude to me aren't there. As the years pass, fewer and fewer people who have been rude to me seem to make the shortlists. In the last year of my life, none did. This is a good thing and shows genuine progress.

It seems to be linked to the fact that many conference organisers have cleaned up their acts in the past few decades. For example, twenty years ago most conferences I attended were run by chums for chums who voted for chums. In other words they were dominated by nepotistic epigones. But these days individuals of real merit get shortlisted and even win the awards. I haven't won anything yet, I was always overlooked by my peers, but that's the rock I had to carry. I don't carry it down here, of course, because metaphorically there is no need, and literally I don't wish to sink.

I'm a floater, through and through. But let me say something else about the concept of 'peer review'. We are encouraged in academia to strive for our words to appear in journals, right? One more digression before I tackle what is the core of my tale. Someone once asked me if I like macadamia nuts and I thought they said 'academia nuts' and I replied, "Whether or not I like them, I still have to work with them!" and it's true.

So this is how it was. I grew up in a small town far from any culture or aestheticism. I worked hard at school and was the only youth in my region to win a place at university. I studied for my degree with great devotion and after years of struggle I became a professor. Publish in journals! That's what I was told again and again. If I didn't do that, my career would stagnate. But nobody explained to me exactly what the process entailed. One night I broke into the office of the Dean and searched through his cabinets. I found his journal and skimmed the pages. I was rather surprised.

The book was full of irrelevant details, stuff that had nothing to do with the running of the university or any rigorous discipline. It spoke of his erotic attraction to various researchers, male and female, and how he was planning to buy a $1/35^{th}$ scale model of a battleship for his nephew's birthday. Shaking my head, I pulled out the pen I had concealed in an inner pocket of my jacket and I added some words of my own. 'Triturated zircon', for example, and 'Cooling tektites'. Then I vacated the office quietly.

I was expecting to be praised for my first contribution to a journal, but in fact there was a terrible fuss during the next week. It seems I'd misunderstood the word 'journal' or rather I had failed to appreciate that it had two meanings. I wasn't supposed to add words to the Dean's private journal but write articles for public journals. The Dean's book had a plain cover but the covers of those public journals had names on them, names such as *Contour Lines Monthly* and *Wind Speed Digest.* I had been in error.

Have you ever been in error? I am guessing that you have, otherwise you wouldn't be in the Waiting Room, you would be in paradise already. I begged the Dean's forgiveness, and I eventually won it after giving him half my salary for that year and digging a swimming pool in his garden. Then I sat down and decided to give the journal lark another go. I wrote an article on magma injuries but I wrote it in verse. I was planning to send it to the editors of the prestigious *Volcanic Upthrusts Journal* but I decided to show it to some of my colleagues first. They were astonished but not in a good way. One of them shook his head so vigorously that I became frightened.

But it didn't fall off and roll under my desk or anything like that. When I asked what was wrong, they told me in no uncertain terms. That was a shame because I rather like uncertain terms, especially when they finish prematurely and the summer holidays end up being longer than you expect. But anyway, they explained that articles submitted to professional journals wouldn't be published before they had been subjected to 'pier review'. I wondered what the heck that was, but I didn't care to humiliate myself by asking. They added that an article written in verse would fail such a review.

Later that evening I went down to the shore and I swam out into the sea. I had a copy of my article in a sealed plastic folder. I swam to the harbour and it wasn't long before I reached the pier. I showed my article to the wooden beams of that structure. The water lapped and slapped them, and lapped and slapped my face too. Strange little waves. When I judged that enough time had passed for the pier to review my article I returned to dry land. Nobody could now say that my article hadn't been pier-reviewed.

I slid it inside an envelope and mailed it the next day. I included a note to explain how I had swum out to the nearest pier in order to conform to official journal regulations. Then I waited for a reply. When it came, one week later, I was mortified. I received a rejection slip with the words, 'Ha ha ha, no,' printed on it and nothing else. Distraught, I found it difficult to focus on my duties. But my misery didn't fade over time, like so many miseries do. Somehow word was passed around that I was a joker. The editor must have spoken to my colleagues without me knowing. It was an ordeal.

They came to visit me in my office and pat me on the back. I also found I was invited to more and more conferences, all of which I attended. I would give a serious talk but always I was greeted with laughter. For some reason everyone thought I was a humorist. How do such misinterpretations of the facts occur? I never even tried to get published in any journals after that first rejection, but the people who warned me that my career would stagnate were wrong. Careers are fluid and mine was choppy with waves.

During my last ever conference I gave a talk on the detrimental effects of tsunamis on jetties but from my very first word, which was 'the', the audience laughed so heartily that I couldn't make myself heard. I had to shout. But they just laughed louder. I screamed at the top of my voice and my words were still drowned out by their monumental guffaws. It was very odd and I can't find any sensible reasons to explain why they acted the way they did. I screamed with such force that I ruptured my arteries.

I don't mean all my arteries, just a few in my neck. That's how I died and the next thing I knew I was standing outside a door and the Devil was ushering me through it. Anyway, I've been in the Waiting Room ever since, making my slow way to the section allotted to me. The fact that I have been able to swim part of the journey has been a blessing. I am happy enough. I hope to organise conferences when I am settled properly in my assigned territory. Why change my way of life just because I'm dead?

—oOo—

He finished his story and one hour later he had reached his designated resting place. He peeled away and with vigorous strokes reached the distant shore. I saw him pull himself onto dry land and choose a chair that was upholstered in blue silk. The material and its colour probably reminded him of water, the sea and the rivers. He began speaking to the occupants of other chairs and it was clear he regarded this as yet another conference. It is impossible to tell lies in this place but his story had been so whimsical and foolish that I wondered if he was mad. He believed his delusions but did this mean we had to believe them too? I had no idea. Neither did Jaspers.

We floated onwards. More tributaries were constantly adding water to the river, which was flowing wider and faster. But now we passed angels dressed as plumbers who were fixing the sabotaged pipes or resting and drinking cups of tea, all of them in dungarees, with multiple arms holding spanners or teacups. I saw no human beings breaking pipes. Clearly the damage had been noted and it was being fixed. The river's days were numbered. Saboteurs would probably be punished with the whip or the pike.

The days passed. Jaspers was becoming very impatient. Then I saw an odd shape ahead. What was it? Neither of us could make it out. Finally we saw what it was. A massive angel, just a vast head, with a wide open mouth, parked in the middle of the river. The water, all of it, was flowing into his gaping mouth. He had been put here especially to swallow the river, to prevent it being used as a method of easier travel for those heading to distant zones. I was appalled. This was the most hideous angel so far!

I had wondered about the mouth of the river. Well, here was the mouth, a wide open maw with a pale green tongue. The gurgle of the torrent as it poured down his throat was atrocious. The head was as large as a cathedral, the mouth like the entrance to a blasted cavern. I was terrified. Jaspers was mesmerised. I jumped out of *Thelma Ives* and swam to the distant shore. I felt the pull of the current on my legs, as if cruel mermaids had been paid to drag me away from safety and feed me to that voracious angelic monster. I spluttered and lunged for the shore. I was in a dreadful state.

But I managed to pull myself onto dry land. And I looked back to see how far Jaspers was behind me. To my horror, I realised he was still in the canoe. It was a question of paralysis. He was too terrified to follow. I called out to him, urging him to jump and swim. But he didn't heed me. He was clutching the rim of the cockpit and screaming. Caught in the accelerating flow, he had no chance at all. I watched in despair as he vanished, with the body of *Thelma Ives*, into the gaping maw of the demonic angel.

He was gone, just the same as if he had sailed over a waterfall, but he was plunging into some supernatural gullet now. What would happen to him? He was already dead. Would he end up in Hell or would he be returned to the start of the Waiting Room, with the Devil outside who would once again open the doors for him? Would the same thing happen to *Thelma Ives*? Would this be her third death or might the clerical error in her case be sorted out? Questions and no answers. This afterlife is a riddle.

On the shore I was panting. I was helped to my feet by a woman. She was Juliet Jones, one of the star-crossed lovers from Abbot's story. You say 'small world' up on the surface when things like this happen. Down here we say 'tiny underworld' and it means exactly the same thing. I stayed with her for a while and she told me a story. I was much deeper into the 'J' zone than I had calculated myself to be. *Thelma Ives* had drifted past Jaspers' assigned location without either of us realising the fact. We had overshot the mark and he had been swallowed for it. But Juliet didn't care about any of that. She couldn't wait to tell me a story. She won my full attention by drumming on the crown of my saturated head with her fists and her knuckles had been hardened by years of engineering. You do recall that she was a rocket engineer, yes?

The Abbot

My lover probably told you that his name was Abbot Aaron. Is that right? Yes, I thought so. But the 'abbot' part is a title, not a name. He really was an abbot. He wasn't really a believer but he liked the security of running an abbey high in the snowy mountains. Which range, you ask? Does it really matter? If you insist on knowing, it was the Rhodope Mountains. His abbey was a small one, with thirty monks. These brothers were the remnants of a much larger community that had dispersed during the previous decades.

I didn't know him back then, of course. We became lovers much later. But he decided one day to give the abbey a good cleaning. It hadn't been cleaned for three hundred years. It was a stone edifice with a few squat towers and passages that kept winding and twisting up and down. Despite its modest dimensions, the opportunities to get lost while exploring the abbey were excellent. There were a few chambers set aside for visitors. But visitors were rare these days and some of these rooms hadn't been entered for generations.

He performed the task of cleaning these rooms himself. The monks seemed very reluctant to pick up a broom and he didn't want to force them. In fact, three monks deserted the abbey the moment he mentioned his cleaning plans and they never returned. The abbey was racing through the twilight days of its existence. Soon enough he would be an abbot without anybody to abbotise to. Is 'abbotise' a real word? Too bad if it isn't. In the smallest of the visitors' chambers he saw that some guest had left a book behind.

It was a book about rocketry and even though the technology it described was now mostly obsolete, the mathematics of thrust and ballistic curves hadn't changed in the slightest over the years. Abbot Aaron was fascinated. He forgot all about cleaning and carried the volume back to his own quarters. He read the book from cover to cover and in the morning he was too sleepy to perform the breakfast prayers properly. Another monk absconded that day. The abbot was a very impatient fellow now. He couldn't wait to finish eating his porridge so he could get back to his revelatory textbook.

Within a week or so, he became an expert on rocketry. If 'expert' is maybe an exaggeration, let us say instead that he was good enough. And he had one of the most remarkable ideas of his life. The abbey was dying. Young people didn't want to enrol as monks any more. Soon the building would be an empty shell. In order to prevent more monks fleeing, he wondered if he could convert the abbey into a rocket and take it to the moon. Or some other planet, such as Mars, where there was at least a chance of surviving.

His rocketry was quite good, all in all, but his astronomy, planetary science and astrobiology were very poor. He went outside and regarded the edifice from a distance. The four towers would make good rocket engines, he supposed. The main body of the abbey was for the astronauts and it would double up as a moon base or Mars base when they landed. What could possibly go wrong? Filling the four towers with fuel was the next step.

Monks endure a religious lifestyle but this doesn't mean they don't imbibe alcohol. Many abbeys brew their own ales. There are fantastic ciders, wines and spirits that originate in monasteries. Countless secular folks have been sozzled at some stage of their lives on Bénédictine liqueur or Trappist beers, you might be one of them yourself. This abbey in the Rhodope Mountains had a basement that was a brandy distillery. Barrels of potent brandy had accumulated in those cobwebbed shadows for centuries. This brandy was inflammable and could be used as rocket fuel, the abbot concluded.

The towers weren't being used for anything. Over the following weeks, the abbot painfully rolled barrels of brandy up the stone steps of the basement to the ground floor and then rolled them up spiral stairs to the tops of the towers. Once at the top he staved them in with an axe, which the monks kept in order to chop unwieldy gospels into manageable tomes and permitted the brandy to flood the interior of the towers. He did all this work at night, as quietly as possible, while the monks were sleeping on hard beds.

He didn't tell any of the monks about his plans because he was certain they wouldn't want to relocate to the moon or even Mars. They would all leave, and that was the exact opposite of what he wanted, which was to keep them captives in the walls of the abbey. So he had to proceed in secret. All the same, two more monks absconded before his preparations were complete. The work involved in rolling the heavy barrels up flights of stone steps was so taxing that the abbot's muscles grew very large indeed, and he kept in shape later by working out, and his physique was one of the things that attracted me to him so strongly, when we first met, long after this brandy exploit.

But I am getting ahead of myself. The four squat towers of the abbey were now flooded with brandy. It was time to launch the building into the sky! After supper on the night chosen for the venture, the abbot took four lighted candles and stood them on candlesticks on the windowsills of the highest windows in each of the towers. He tied strings to the base of each candlestick and connected the other ends of these strings to the minute hands of four alarm clocks that he had fully wound for the space mission.

The moving minute hands would pull the strings, topple the candlesticks, and the burning wicks would fall into the brandy and set it on fire. The resulting detonation, simultaneously occurring in all four towers, would launch the abbey through the atmosphere and into space. If this seems risky, if not suicidal, then I must agree that it was. But Abbot Aaron, despite his agnosticism, still had on a subconscious level a faith that divine aid would prevent disasters. If he had ever bothered to articulate this unreasoning belief, he might have said that the launch would have been assisted by angels as well as spluttering rocket exhausts. The foolhardiness of the man was extreme!

As it happens, two of the clocks malfunctioned. Or the candlesticks were too heavy for them to topple over. Or maybe the wicks were extinguished when the candles fell into the brandy. Who knows? But the other two candles worked perfectly. They ignited the brandy in the other two towers, and both these towers were on the western side of the abbey. Can you guess what occurred next? With rocket engines only on one side of the building, the abbey never rose vertically into the sky. It was an unbalanced thrust.

The edifice plucked itself out of the ground, leaving its foundations behind, and rose higher and higher on one side only. The other side remained grounded, although its bottom stones crumbled thanks to the torque. Then the abbey turned right over. It began rolling, accelerating as it did so. There was an experimental weapon called the panjandrum that was a wheel with rockets mounted on it and the idea was that it would roll through the enemy's defences. It failed because it had plenty of torque and yet was impossible to steer. The abbey was rather like the panjandrum now. It rolled up and down the sides of mountains, with monks inside screaming in maximised terror.

Abbot Aaron hadn't warned them that they were going to be astronauts. I imagine they thought the end of the world had arrived. The launch was an utter failure and most of the remaining monks were smashed to smithereens inside as they were flung this way and that. The abbot had curled himself into a ball. He knew he must flee when he got the chance. If he didn't flee and flee extremely well, he would be arrested when the fuel ran out and the abbey came to a halt. The police might be tracking the structure already. They might be in helicopters right now, waiting to see where the abbey would end up. He had to flee over the border and hide in some other country.

Fortunately for him, the abbey kept rolling and went over the frontier of a neighbouring republic and the pursuing police helicopters were forced to peel away. The abbey finally came to rest in the middle of a meadow, upside-down and battered beyond recognition. Abbot Aaron crawled out and so did six other survivors, bruised and bleeding and even more secularly-minded than they had been before. The abbot slithered across the meadow and sought refuge among the trees of the forest and rested there until his wounds healed. He lived for the rest of his life in disguise. He changed his name but only changed it slightly. He took 'Abbot' as his first name, whereas it had previously only been his title. We met and fell in love. You know the rest.

He once took me to visit the meadow where the ruins of the abbey lay. The thing had become a minor tourist attraction. You could clamber over the ruins and even enter them and wander the inverted chambers of the structure. There was a faint odour of burned brandy in every room, but especially in the towers, two of which had charred walls. Well, that's my story, and now it has been told I will stop drumming your head with my fists. Sometimes a bottle of good brandy is lowered on one of the trays and I always think of my lover when I sip it. Does this mean I'm sentimental? I guess so.

—o0o—

When I left Juliet and resumed my journey, I first had to pass the giant angel's head by giving it a wide berth. On the other side there was no river. The angel was drinking every drop of water that flowed into its maw. I kept going on foot but I was always thinking about alternative modes of transport. Nothing availed itself, however, for a very long time.

I passed out of the 'J' zone and I soon found the natural disasters that the crystal ball had predicted, or rather I encountered the aftermath of some seismic catastrophe. Ives hadn't been wrong.

There had been a deep earthquake and the tectonic plates had been forced into each other at this point. The 'K', 'L' and 'M' zones were compressed together, just as if someone of immense size and strength had been playing a concertina with this stretch of the Waiting Room. The three zones had been squashed into one messy zone. Furniture scattered, chairs and sofas piled up at random, the floor creased with wrinkles taller than a man. These wrinkles were like dunes and they had to be clambered over.

It was twisted, total chaos. The occupants of the three

zones were piled up together too, legs entwined, tangled up, many still in the process of extracting themselves from the organic jam. The earthquake had been long ago but some of the victims were knotted together so tightly it had taken ages for them to find a way of untying themselves. The ceiling bulged in places and when hatches opened so that trays could emerge, the trays often came out sideways, spilling the food and drink over the prone people.

Here I met Karlsen, Lopes and Morselli, the pilots who had tried to rescue Eckhart when he was on his island, but who had died in the plane crash. They were knotted into one being with three heads, six arms and six legs, and three mouths. But they didn't tell me three different stories. They told me one story, a collaboration, in three harmonised voices. They were a knot that no one would ever be able to untie, an eternal braid, and I think they would have resented it if anybody who came along had even tried.

The Phoenix

We have always enjoyed flying aeroplanes. Gliders too. Anything with wings, and our parents wondered if we should have been birds and hatched from three eggs, rather than pushing our way into the world from wombs. Our childhoods were very similar but we didn't meet each other until we attended flying school and became firm friends. We were more like brothers than friends and we were known by our instructors as the 'triplets'. After we separately earned our pilots' licences, we tried to stick together.

This wasn't always possible. Karlsen sometimes flew planes in Africa and Lopes flew them in South America and Morselli flew them in Australia and all of us in other locations also, too many places to list. You'll note that we refer to ourselves in the plural. That's because we are three-in-one. Three is our magic number. When we managed to get jobs working on the same aeroplane, a profound sense of relief came over us. As time passed, we specialised in flying rescue missions. We were a true team.

Every one of us had crashed a plane at some time in his career. Karlsen did so in the Congo, Lopes in Paraguay, Morselli in Tasmania. It happens to the best pilots as well as the worst, it's an inevitable consequence of flying. We survived with barely a scratch, but we knew it was only a matter of time before one of us was involved in a much more serious smash. Back then, it hadn't occurred to us that we might all perish together, as we did. Anyway, we sat down one evening in a Kathmandu drinking hole and talked.

We were drunk on some local brew with a name we have forgotten, even though Karlsen insists it was called *tongba*, but we work by consensus in this unit of ours, and if Lopes and Morselli insist they don't remember, then it's two to one in favour of amnesia. Our heads spinning, even though we have nothing but contempt for helicopters, we decided that it would be nice if we were pilots of indestructible planes. From this idea, we progressed to the idea that we must construct our own indestructible plane.

But how to do this? You know the myth of the phoenix, don't you? It's the immortal bird that grows old and when the time to die arrives, it bursts into fire and from the ashes it rises again, renewed, the same bird or rather a bird that has been reincarnated as itself. Pretty neat, huh? Karlsen, Lopes and Morselli knew that an aeroplane with the same renewal abilities as a phoenix was exactly what they wanted. Somehow we had to merge a phoenix with an aeroplane so that the hybrid would be the aircraft of our dreams.

A strange little man hunched at a neighbouring table overhead our talk and leaned across the gap that separated us, poking his nose into our discussion. He told us he was a trader from Mustang, one of the remotest districts of Nepal and not so long ago an independent realm called the Kingdom of Lo. This man said that he knew where a phoenix could be located. He would reveal this secret in exchange for a lift back to his home in our aeroplane. The journey overland was too difficult and he wasn't looking forward to it, especially as snow might have blocked the mountain passes. We replied:

"We would give you a lift anyway, without expecting anything in return, as a simple act of kindness, but we must warn you that it will be a bumpy ride over the peaks thanks to all the turbulence."

"Don't thank the turbulence," he answered, "because it has great fun when it shakes aeroplanes the same way a dog shakes a sock. It's actually grateful to *you.* And I am grateful too. I will give you directions to the phoenix on the way. It has a nest on a very high ledge. I have seen it many times. I always look up when I pass that remote eyrie. And the phoenix looks down and once I thought it winked at me. Yes, that was funny."

We drank a few more glasses of spirit each, toasting this stranger as we did so, and we bought a glass for him too. Then we set off for the airfield where our aeroplane was waiting. It was cramped in the cockpit with four people. But our takeoff was smooth enough and soon we were flying in the direction of the very mysterious Mustang. The fact that the name of that district and the name of the wild horse are the same is pure coincidence. Are any coincidences truly pure? Karlsen says yes, Lopes says no, Morselli says yes, which means that yes wins and pure coincidences really do exist.

As we had predicted, it was a bumpy flight, a very bumpy flight indeed, a rattling and bouncing and lurching flight. But the stranger was quite unconcerned and sat there without ever feeling unwell.

He was a remarkable individual, but the condition of being remarkable is maybe not so extraordinary. Karlsen, Lopes, Morselli are a remarkable triptych and we even suspect that being unremarkable is even more remarkable than being fabulous. But what do we know? Apart from lots of things about aeroplanes and rescue missions and a few dozen other things, we don't know much really. We know how to have a good time, though!

Eventually we reached the border of Mustang and crossed it and now we were above an icy land of ancient isolation. Our passenger gave us directions from this point onwards. We flew down a narrow valley with towering peaks on both sides and entered a natural amphitheatre, snowbound and eerie, that might have been created by a meteorite impact aeons ago. Our passenger, whose name was Angun, and we apologise for not mentioning this earlier, pointed out to us the ruins of a building in the exact centre of the bowl. It looked like a geological formation unless you squinted hard at it.

Eroded by snow and wind and time itself, the palace or castle or whatever it had been, even Angun wasn't sure, had been smoothed and turned into just a vague shape, utterly alone in the middle of nowhere. But let's be less lazy and admit that nowhere is in the middle of nowhere. Everywhere is somewhere and somewhere is in the middle of something.

We are glad we have cleared that up. It's important to be accurate when you can afford to be. We flew over the ruin and it gave us a weird feeling when we were directly above it, as if it was an unshielded nuclear reactor. We felt slightly poisoned in our spiritual selves. No matter. On the far side of the crater, Angun indicated the nest of the phoenix. It stood on a wide ledge halfway up the side of a mighty mountain. The phoenix was at home too. It looked at us and opened its beak in what we took to be an ironic laugh.

Well, we continued with our journey and landed on a piece of flat ground a hundred miles north of that crater. This was Angun's village, a collection of ten houses. We were his honoured guests for a few days and then we climbed back into our aeroplane and took off. We had agreed on a plan. We had to somehow seduce the phoenix, persuade it to mate with our plane so that a chick would hatch that would be indestructible. We think we were still drunk, not just from all the potent spirits that Angun had given us, but also punch drunk, thanks to the shaking from the severe turbulence on our flight here. But there we go again, thanking turbulence! It's clearly a habit.

When we returned to the natural amphitheatre, we had intended to describe alluring circles as close to the phoenix's nest as possible, in a desperate hope the bird would regard us as erotically alluring.

Yes, it was a long shot, a very long shot, and you are asking yourself how a pilot describes an alluring circle? It's quite easy really. Let us demonstrate. Are you ready? The curves are smooth, the body of the circle shimmers like silk, the radius is firm and vigorous. Did that work? No, well, maybe your libido is lower than that of a phoenix. But the truth of the matter is that we didn't even know if a phoenix has a libido at all. We had to find out. And we found out soon enough. It doesn't. A bird that can rebirth itself from its own ashes doesn't really need to lay eggs and thus doesn't require a mate.

But we were lucky. It just so happens that we had arrived at the designated time for the phoenix to die and burst into flames and be reborn. When we noted the fire on the ledge we looked at each other and nodded. We didn't need to say a single word. We were of the same mind.

We steered for the ledge and we crashed into the nest. Does that sound like a crazy thing to do? It was a risky one, certainly. Did we die? Just before impact we jumped out of the cockpit and floated down on parachutes. The plane carried on its course and collided with the burning bird. The molecules of the impacting plane were loosened from each other and they merged with the molecules of the blazing bird and so a fusion was created. Half phoenix and half aeroplane! That is what rose from the nest. An *aeroenix*! It was pristine, elegant and beautiful. It was magnificent, multi-coloured, blissful.

We landed on snow and packed our parachutes away and we waved at the new aeroplane, the indestructible one, and it heeded our gestures and swooped to land near us, and when we climbed inside, it sort of purred, despite the fact it was half bird and not half cat. But the world is a curious place, as we are certain you worked out for yourself when you were topside. That's how we refer to the surface on which we once dwelled. Topside. We took off without any trouble at all and soon were soaring above the peaks.

You are probably wondering if we explored the ruin in the middle of this crater while we were on the ground? The answer is no. There was something a little diabolical about it. We won't go so far as to say it felt *evil.* Inhuman, yes, and unbearably alien, but not alien as in extraterrestrial. We don't think it was the product of a race of entities from a planet orbiting a distant star. There's a requirement for us to be sensible about such matters. Our indestructible plane vacated the crater and we didn't even dare look back at those eroded stones. It was pleasant to be flying south again.

We ought to explain something. Our new plane was indestructible and we somehow forgot that 'indestructible' and 'uncrashable' are two totally different things. Our plane *could* crash and burst into flames and be destroyed, just the same as any other aircraft, but after being reduced to ashes it would rise again, brand new, ready to take to the skies.

Does this mean that the pilots of the *aeroenix* were also indestructible? No, we're afraid not. But that was something we didn't think much about and we can't say why we were so amazingly obtuse. We were just blind to obvious danger, it is a pathetic thing to admit, but we can't lie in the Waiting Room, the truth must come out. Our aircraft was indestructible and this gave us false confidence. We were flesh and bone, vulnerable, but we forgot that fact. Thinking of the craft as 'uncrashable' made matters worse.

But things have to get worse before they get better, don't they? That's the famous saying. Can famous sayings be wrong? Karlsen says no, Lopes says yes, Morselli says no. That means that no, they can't. But listen. As a rescue squad, we saved thousands of lives in the following years. We were awarded medals by the governments of two dozen countries for our services to humanity. We also rescued nonhuman creatures whenever we could. Because we knew that our aeroplane could never be permanently destroyed, we were more inclined to try the riskiest rescues, and they all succeeded, because of luck, we suppose now, but at the time we attributed each success to our aircraft, the only aeroplane in service that was partly a mythic squawker.

By calling a phoenix a 'squawker' we don't mean any disrespect to magic and mystery. It's just aeronautical slang. We are pilots, after all. Our moustaches are waxed and mighty, and goggles practically fall over themselves for a chance to be worn around our eyes on elastic straps.

One day we were flying over the sea when we spotted a man on an island who was waving his shirt. This turned out to be Eckhart, but we didn't know it at the time, of course. We changed direction to fly over the uncharted isle. The thermals played havoc with our flight path and we crashed. We crashed on top of Eckhart and killed him. It happens. We were killed too and our deaths caught us by surprise. Karlsen was seriously astonished, Lopes greeted the news with a forced irony, Morselli was flabbergasted.

Just before we died, we saw a new aeroplane rising from the burning wreck of the old one and soar away majestically. It is surely still flying despite the lack of pilots. It's an unmanned rogue now, a derelict, like the *Flying Dutchman*, but unlike that fabled ship, it really does fly and it isn't Dutch but Nepalese. Will it run out of fuel and crash and rise again, you ask? Does a phoenix require fuel, is our reply? That's a rhetorical question. We don't know the answer and it's very unlikely you do. We wish the *aeroenix* well.

And now we are here, knotted together until the paperwork of the Waiting Room is done and we are consigned to one of the Circles of Hell. Will Karlsen, Lopes and Morselli be sent to the same Circle? If not, will the Devil be able to untangle us? Even if he can, will he want to? These are rhetorical questions too. Don't even try to answer them. We saved many lives and it might be supposed that we should have gone to Heaven. But we had peccadillos and they kept us from earning a place in paradise. Too bad.

—o0o—

The three pilots seemed perfectly happy to be tied into a large knot. I made no effort whatsoever to untie them. I thought about the *aeroenix* endlessly circling the world, maybe crashing into mountains or buildings or other aircraft, bursting into flames and turning into ashes, but then rising again, soaring upwards, clean and shiny with merrily spinning propellers.

The phoenix is a bird but it's also a metaphor. Many of our thoughts, fears and other feelings are phoenixes. They die, or at least we assume they do, only to resurrect themselves from the inferno of dismissal. I was thinking about my ex-wife. I hadn't thought about her for a long time. She had been ashes to me. I now understood that she was a phoenix too.

The crystal ball had said we would be reunited down here. The crystal had been right about the natural disaster, the seismic shift. This strongly indicated it would be right about her. I wasn't sure if I was pleased at the prospect, horrified or indifferent. I wasn't sure about anything.

And how would she feel about meeting me? It wasn't just about my own convenience and comforts. I had to consider her situation too. What was her first name? I struggled to recall it. Bunny, that's right! I continued my journey, passing out of the 'KLM' zone, once three separate zones, now one crumpled zone. And that's when I met my ex-wife.

SEVEN

She was resting in a hammock at the very beginning of the 'N' zone. It turned out she was exhausted after passing through the snarled-up mess and the broken chaos of the previous zones, climbing over the corrugated dunes of the flooring. I believed her when she said she had to consume at least one thousand daiquiris before she had the energy to proceed.

Because the trays that descended from the ceiling delivered random drinks and it was impossible to know from one day to the next when a daiquiri would be offered, she had been waiting in this hammock for months. She was on her nine hundred and ninety-fifth daiquiri.

"That's nice," I said.

"Oh, don't be such a prig, Monty."

"Call me Zubris. Down here, everyone uses surnames. It's like being back at school," I replied sadly.

"No, you are Monty to me, or Montgomery when I'm displeased with you, and calling you Zubris will only create confusion because I'm a Zubris too. We can't go on like that, dear."

"You aren't a Zubris any longer. We divorced and you reverted to your old name. You are Bunny Hopkins."

"Fine, but you don't call the shots down here, Monty. I am making my way to the 'Z' zone because the administration still regards me as a Zubris, as Mrs Zubris. Can you believe it? When I arrived, I told the Devil I was divorced and had returned to using my maiden name, but there had been another clerical error and he answered that I had been assigned the 'Z' zone anyway. I am still Zubris as far as the system is concerned. So I am compelled to travel right to the back of this damned Waiting Room."

"I see," I said, and then I said nothing more.

"You are saying," she said.

"No, I am not."

"You interrupted me. I was about to say that you are saying nothing more. I am surprised at you, Montgomery."

I remained silent.

"It has been so long since you laid eyes on me," she continued, "and now you are stuck for a few pleasant sentiments. The cat has got your tongue," she concluded and I knew that this 'cat' was a metaphor for the claws and teeth of a sudden shyness. I could hardly look at her. I forced myself to trace her reclining curves with my critical eyes. She was saying something about silence not being golden but resembling radium.

'Poison' was the word that entered my mind.

"I agree wholly," I said.

But of course I hadn't the faintest inkling as to what I was agreeing to. She was amazed by my acquiescence. She had obviously been expecting resistance even though for years she had insisted that resistance was useless. She finished her cocktail and blinked at me.

"That's settled then," she announced.

"I beg your pardon?"

"Oh, don't beg, Monty. It makes you look like a big dog who doesn't know the difference between a bone and a shoe. We will accompany each other on the journey to the 'Z' zone. That is what you have agreed to do. But we will wait at this spot for the next five daiquiris. I will have three and you can have two. That seems fair, even though it isn't."

"And in the meantime," she added, when I refused to protest, "I will relate the story of my peculiar death."

"Fine," I said, looking for a chair to sit in.

But there wasn't one.

"No need to make yourself comfortable, Monty. I don't tell long tales like everyone else down here. We'll be off soon." And no sooner had she said this, than a hatch in the ceiling opened and a tray descended with five daiquiris on it, almost as if some kind angel up there had been listening. But there are no kind angels. It must have been a coincidence.

"Drink up," she cried.

"Aren't you going to tell me your story first?"

"I've changed my mind. Let's polish these off, then set off on our journey, and I will tell you as we roll along."

"Roll along? But we'll have to walk, Bunny."

"That's incorrect, dear."

She fixed her lips to her straw and told me in precise speech with a backing of slurps that she had invented an afterlife version of roller-skates, using castors taken from sofas. Most of her journey to this hammock had been done on a pair of such skates. But she'd had to abandon them along the way when they finally fell apart. They wouldn't have been much use in the previous zone anyway. We would construct two new pairs, one for her, one for me, and then set off happily, moving faster than we could walk.

"Much faster, as a matter of fact," she added.

I nodded rather glumly.

Her ingenuity came as no surprise to me, but her confidence troubled me, because every form of transport I had used so far had ended in some disaster, and yet I had already decided not to walk the entire distance. I shrugged and laughed, and she toasted me.

I drank my two daiquiris in just a few gulps.

I smacked my lips.

"Don't punish your lips," she said. She had misunderstood. She gave me a lecture on the hypocrisy of puritanism. I listened meekly and then explained that smacking one's lips is done with the lips themselves, not with the back of one's angry hand. She hadn't been looking when I'd smacked them. She had been too engrossed in slurping her own drink. Within five minutes, she was done, all five glasses were empty and she said:

"Time to swing myself out of this net."

I watched, fascinated.

But she managed the feat with subtle grace.

Now we stood together.

We had to roam far from the site of the hammock in order to find sixteen castors that we could fix to our shoes, four on each of our soles. And it wasn't so easy attaching them securely.

Oiling them was another problem, until a tray descended hours later with a salad in a bowl and a bottle of dressing next to it. The dressing worked superbly as a lubricant. Kind angels again? We set off, moving with ease over the smooth floor. As we went, she described her death.

A Very Good Year

I loved roller skating when I was alive. You know this. It was my hobby and no discouragement ever stopped me from skating every day. Even in storms I went out to rumble up and down, like miniature thunder, the streets of our town. Not long after we divorced, I decided that I was now free to do whatever I liked. So I sat down and tried to work out what it was that I did like. And I decided that I liked roller skating and nothing else.

It occurred to me that I could roller skate all the way to France, if I wanted to, and even down into Italy, not for any particular reason but just for the joy of gobbling distance with the wheels on my feet. I didn't hesitate. I caught a ferry to a French port and rolled off the ship with all the trucks and cars. I took all the quiet minor roads across the country, the winding lanes with little traffic, and it was a phenomenally enjoyable jaunt.

Soon I was in the Nièvre department, near the town of Pouilly-sur-Loire, a small place but one noted for a famous white wine. And yet I happened to pass through the only vineyard in the region that specialised in red wines. Typical of my luck! Not that I have anything against red wines, but you will understand my reservations when you hear the rest of my tale. I was skating along a rough sort of track and I hit a stone in the path.

It was a large stone and it knocked me off balance and I veered off the path and I found myself accelerating down a slope, and at the base of the slope I was deposited without my dignity into a vat of grapes. That doesn't sound like such a bad thing to happen, but automation is taking over everywhere. Grapes are no longer trampled by the bare feet of peasant girls, any one of which would surely have stopped her work to assist me.

No, this vineyard, like so many others, had been fitted with giant automatic feet. Mechanical grape crushers that stamped up and down with far greater force than a peasant girl could ever manage. These artificial feet were designed with the sole aim of speeding up processes in the wine industry. The *sole* aim, get it? The upshot was that I was trampled to death and my body was reduced to a red mush that mixed with the grape juice.

I became part of the wine and I was bottled and the bottles were sent out into the world for public consumption. Now comes the really ironic part. I was a novelty wine from an obscure little vineyard and it so happens that *you* tasted me and reviewed me for a wine taster's magazine. I recall your verdict, "Full body, grudge-holding, demanding and independent," and those words made me laugh. Really, Monty, you are pompous.

Where did I come across that magazine? Down here, of course. It had been smuggled into the Waiting Room by some other wine imbiber, I can't remember who. Don't look so bashful, Monty. I know you didn't mean to drink the blood of your ex-wife, it was just an accident. I blame automation. There's no need to hold grudges down here, despite your claim about my love of holding them. All the rules are different here, you silly boy.

—oOo—

The rules are different. But I never knew what the topside rules were, so I felt a lot less blasé than she did about our present situation. Rules are the bane of our existence, and yet we claim they maintain that existence. Who can say for sure? There are rules about rules, and if the first set of those rules are broken, it means it's open season on the second set. Break the rules about rules and someone will break you. That's the universal rule.

"I told you that my stories are short," she said.

"That's right, Bunny."

"So why the glum face, Monty?"

"Just that I am sorry for drinking you and reviewing you in that fashion. I don't think I'll ever live it down."

"No need to live anything down. You're dead."

"Touché, Bunny."

"I am the one who ought to apologise."

"Whatever for?"

"I used a pun in my story. Did you notice? I said 'sole' while referencing a giant foot and I primarily intended the word to mean 'solitary'. But the pun only works in English, and nobody speaks English in the Waiting Room. We speak Esperanto here. Which means?"

"There can't have been a pun. It must be a mirage."

"Monty, the pun was real."

"Then I'm at a loss to account for the discrepancy."

"Me too," she said.

"Forget it then," was my advice. "There's no answer. It must remain some sort of enigma, a baffling case."

"Unless someone or something is helping us? I must admit that I've been extremely lucky since I arrived, apart from the paperwork fiasco, I mean, with the confusion about the surnames. The rest of it has been plain sailing. A force has intervened. A supernatural helper."

"You believe that?"

"I'm not sure. I just don't know."

Once again I wondered if the angels might be kinder than they seemed to be, or maybe there were guardian angels as well as the enforcer type? What if there were? Let's say that her guardian angel had a crush on her and was taking his duties extra seriously. This was no more ridiculous an idea than any other hypothesis. If true, it was useful for me.

I would benefit from the protection such a guardian would offer her. My journey would be much easier. But I thought it best in the short term to remain sceptical. I am a sceptic often, a cynic never. I am sceptical about the worth of cynicism. I once knew a cynic who was cynical about scepticism. At least he claimed to be. I was sceptical about whether he really was. He told me that all my doubts were worthless. I doubted whether they were. It wasn't long before we despised each other. But I still wonder if we really did, or whether it was a cynical act, an amoral pantomime.

I turned my attention back to the present and said:

"Helping us by turning a pun in one language into an equivalent pun in another language? That seems odd."

"Odder than everything else around you at this very moment?" was her retort, and I was forced to concede that yes, anything was possible down here, and so I gave up arguing with her and concentrated on keeping my balance and eating up the distance with the circumference of my little wheels. As we skated we did that thing where you swing your arms behind your back to reduce your drag. She showed me how. I copied her.

Nonetheless, the question she had raised about puns bothered me, though I kept my thoughts on the subject to myself. As time passed, I became an expert skater and the activity suffused me with joy. People shouted stories at us as we glided past, but we missed most of them. One fellow had a mangled body but a voice loud enough to reach us without our ears' permission. His words rose and fell in pitch as we skated towards him and then passed him. A demonstration of the Doppler Effect in a very minor way.

The Tiger

My name is Nathan and I am a draughtsman. I know what you are assuming as a direct consequence of these opening words of mine. You now think my job was concerned with the preparation of technical drawings for some engineering firm. Well, I did work for a firm, but it wasn't very firm, as it happens. The buildings were made from thin plastic sheets instead of brick walls and they wobbled and boomed like drum membranes in the wind.

It drove me mad! It drove all my colleagues mad too,

apart from the ones who were already mad, and those fellows were driven sane, which was weird when you come to think about it. So don't think about it. The booming sound was an eternal presence in my office and all the other offices of that firm. And my job was to think of ways of stopping the wind. That's why I was known as a draughtsman. I was the enemy of draughts.

Not much of an enemy, I'm sorry to say. The wind was more cunning and resourceful and powerful than I was. But I did my best. I designed machines to limit the force of the wind. I drew these designs on large sheets of paper on my sloping desk with precision pencils. They were very technical drawings. I guess this means I was a draughtsman as well as a draughtsman. What a coincidence! But the wind often blew my sheets away.

None of my designs were constructed. My boss told me they would be too expensive to build for real. I designed artificial hedges that would break the full force of the wind, hedges that would completely surround the office buildings. I designed massive electric fans that would blow against the wind, cancelling it out. I designed windmills that would convert the energy of the wind into current that would power sound-suppressing headphones for every employee. But none of them appealed to my dreadful boss.

I began to suspect that he was in league with the wind. A league is a unit of distance equal to three miles. A mile is a unit of distance equal to 1.609 km, but wind speed is measured in knots. Don't you find that suspicious? I bet you both do, even if *knot a lot*. Anyway, it occurred to me one day that the wind might be frightened of certain things. I had no idea what kinds of things, but why didn't I try to find out? If it turned out that the wind really was scared of certain objects, I could arrange for those objects to be planted in strategic places near the site of our office block. What a revelation!

Well, it wasn't a revelation yet, because I didn't even know if the wind had any phobias. In order to find out, I consulted old books. I went to the university library and asked to be shown the books that nobody else asked for. The person I spoke to was called Mr Ulysses, who told me that he had been working in the library for ten years. It was an ancient university and the library was extensive. It was almost a maze really. The books that nobody ever asked for were stored in the basement, and he took me there.

It was a long chamber with a low ceiling, not too dissimilar to the Waiting Room where we are now, but far more bookish in tone. Mr Ulysses allowed me to have the run of the place and he never supervised me. I thought that was very nice. I stumbled in the gloom among the bookshelves and finally chanced on a book called *The Psychology of the Wind*, written by Professor Yannis. I hefted the tome to a table and pawed my way through it. And I learned within half an hour that the wind was scared of tigers.

Yes, astonishing as it may seem, the wind always swerves to avoid tigers. I jumped up and down in joy at this discovery and I returned the book to its place and I went up and thanked Mr Ulysses.

I had to wake him up because he was asleep on his chair and it turned out that he was a very sleepy fellow. No matter. I hurried back to my office building and I went to see my boss and I explained what I had learned. He was pleased. It would be much cheaper to chain a tiger outside the main entrance than it would be to construct one of my giant fans or windmills. He gave me the money to go on an Indian safari and capture a tiger.

I did my research carefully. In the old days, a safari meant shooting beasts but now it means photographing them. Yet I wasn't a very good photographer. I was much better with a pen or pencil.

I contacted the leader of the safari by telephone and told him I wouldn't be bringing a camera along with me but a drawing pad and a marker pen. He was fine with that. He admired artists, he told me. I slammed the phone down and I had a grin on my face wider than the average tiger's smile. How premature of me! We often say that to be 'immature' is a terrible condition for a grown man, but let me assure you that being premature is worse. A few days later I was at the airport and waiting for my plane.

I flew to Bangalore first and then I caught a long distance bus to the town of Chikkamagaluru in the mountains of the Western Ghats and then I hired a car and drove to the Bhadra Tiger Reserve. The scenery was beautiful. I joined my tour guide and my fellow safari-goers. We climbed onto a sort of charabanc, a vehicle halfway between a car and bus, but much more rugged than the kinds of charabancs my grandparents used to visit zoos back home. We bounced along a series of tracks and our guide said:

"Don't speak with raised voices. Communicate only in whispers. We must be as quiet as possible. Tiger spotting is a very haphazard affair and it's possible we might not get to see any today."

I absorbed his words and frowned as their meaning entered my brain. Tiger spotting, eh? I could do that, I felt sure, and in fact it was essential that I did so, for my ultimate aim was tiger-capture and tiger-abduction. My office needed the services of a tiger in order to repel the wind, the wind that made such a hideous noise on the flexible walls of our building. An hour passed, then another hour. I was patient, we were all breathless.

The anticipation was intense. And then the guide hissed something. It took me half a minute to understand that these hisses were proper speech but done in the style of a snake. He was saying:

"We are in luck today. Look to your left. That's something that's very rare indeed. It's an albino tiger. Not just an ordinary striped tiger but an all-white one without any markings whatsoever. It is a leucistic pigmentation variant. And it's unusual even for albino tigers because most of them have a white coat and black stripes. This one has a white coat and no stripes. In all my years as the leader of safaris, I never saw anything like this. It is plausibly the rarest tiger in the whole world and we are very privileged."

I leaned towards him and whispered in his ear, "We are here to spot tigers, aren't we? That's our purpose."

He was bewildered. "Naturally. What else?"

"I needed confirmation."

"Well, you have it now," he said, frowning.

"Thank you," I replied.

And I jumped out of the charabanc and started running towards the tiger. I had my marker pen in my right hand and the safety top was off. I was going to spot this tiger even if it was the last thing I ever did. Which it was, at least while alive. The guide screamed at me to come back. The other tourists cursed me and one even threw a half-eaten apple at my back. But I was single minded. Later, I wasn't even single minded, because the tiger crunched the back part of my skull and my brain slipped out of my head.

Spotting the tiger was the first stage of my quest. Capturing it was the next and abducting it came third. Did I manage to spot it at all? Yes, I placed one big black spot exactly between its eyes.

But before I could jab the marker pen again, the creature tore me to pieces. I heard the gasps of the charabanc passengers and the wailing of the safari guide and the groans of the driver. But I was at peace. I would never be troubled again by the wind. My days as a draughtsman were over. And now I am here and I'm not required to design anything at all.

—o0o—

When we had left Nathan far behind, we exchanged glances, Bunny and I, and she said to me, "See what I mean? That story involved a pun. The word 'spot' has two meanings in English, but it doesn't in Esperanto. Somehow, a force is twisting language in our favour."

"You have convinced me," I replied, and I was uneasy. I wasn't fond of the notion that angels or demons were paying close attention to us. It would be safer to be overlooked by them, I felt. But there was nothing I could do to change the situation. I just kept skating along.

The next zone was the 'O' zone and just before we crossed into it, we were warned by a person in a deep armchair who said, "Beware of the 'O' zone hole. It appeared in recent years and it is growing at an alarming rate. Try your best to avoid plunging into it. Nobody knows what lies at the bottom, if anything," and then he returned to eating pastries. To be more specific, he was working his way through a large platter of profiteroles.

We found that the 'O' zone hole was a pit that had opened up in the floor, a sinkhole with spiral grooves leading down into utter darkness. But someone had constructed a rope bridge across it. This was a rickety bridge and it was awful to make use of it, but we had no choice.

It was impossible to resist the temptation to look down when I was halfway across and I found the pit to be mesmerising. Luckily, Bunny nudged me out of my trance. We skated along and our wheels made rhythmic clacking noises on the wooden slats of the bridge like the castanets of a demented flamenco dancer. When we reached the far side we were perspiring. We had to flop down on sofas for ten minutes to recover our senses.

A woman sitting cross-legged on a pile of cushions not far away said to us with a thin smile, "Congratulations."

"Thank you," I said, but I wasn't enthusiastic.

"Some people who attempt to cross the 'O' zone hole on the bridge fall off and plunge into the pit. See those spiral grooves? The people who fall always reach out for handholds and many of them manage to thrust their hands into the grooves, but they still fall down, only this time they rotate in a descending helix and their hands act like needles in the grooves of vinyl records. You understand what I'm talking about? Vinyl, yes?"

"We certainly know what vinyl is," huffed Bunny.

"They make music."

"Who do? What do you mean?"

"The falling people, the men and women, the lost souls. They make music with their lives, with their afterlives, in the grooves of that pit. They descend to background tunes, to melodies."

"And that is horrible?" I asked her.

"Isn't it?" she cried.

I didn't answer her because I simply didn't know. Nor did Bunny. We left that woman on her cushions and we continued our journey. There were no more pits in the 'O' zone. Bunny voiced her opinion that chemicals might have been responsible for creating the hole, but this was such a nebulous speculation that I said nothing in return. I was learning to be unresponsive. We paused for a rest every few hours. Once we had to replace one of the castors on her shoe. Angels came out of the walls and glared at us.

But I noticed that these glares were performative and not authentic. There was very little malevolence about them. It was an act. Nonetheless, to avoid the lash of whip and jab of pike, we stopped resting whenever we saw them, got to our feet and resumed skating. We skated for all we were worth, but I'm unable to say precisely how much that was.

The Waiting Room had always been adequately illuminated and the source of the lighting was one of the many mysteries of the afterlife. But suddenly we passed into a region of darkness. The illumination had failed here. It was quite unexpected. A vast stretch of the 'P' zone was pitch black. The people who had to wait here coped as best they might.

Some had constructed crude lamps fuelled by brandy and other flammable spirits. We had to slow down to avoid colliding with tables, chairs and sofas. I accidentally skated over the foot of one fellow who was reclining on a chair, his legs stretched out in front of him. Bunny knocked into a table and spilled a pile of plates and dishes, breaking most of them. It wasn't easy. But nobody blamed us. They blamed the broken lighting.

We found one man with an electric torch who was lying on his back on a divan and directing the beam at the ceiling. He must have smuggled the torch past the Devil when he first arrived.

We stopped to chat with him. He seemed more

interesting than most of his neighbours. His name was Palomar. He told us about a thing called 'nominative determinism' which was the idea that people are psychologically predisposed to work in fields somehow connected with their names. For example, a man named Winters might be inclined to look for work as a researcher in an Arctic weather station. From a very early age he would have been aware of the significance of his name and, subconsciously at least, he would have friendly feelings towards ice and snow. While he might not be *fated* to work in an Arctic weather station, the likelihood that he would was higher than it was for a man named Summers, who would be more jungle-minded.

Palomar had no connection to the famous observatory on top of that high mountain in San Diego County, California, apart from his name, which by itself was sufficient for him to be inclined to pursue a career in astronomy. And that is what he had done. He was an astronomer. He loved clear night skies and when he first arrived in the Waiting Room he was appalled. The low ceiling wasn't a substitute for the high celestial dome spangled with stars. During his journey to his assigned zone, he suffered from acute claustrophobia. When he reached the 'P' zone at last he was a nervous wreck. But he was a resourceful fellow and he did the best he could in the circumstances. He had painted constellations on the ceiling directly above his silk divan.

For paint he had used vegetable juice, just as Arcimboldo had done, and he hadn't bothered with brushes. His fingertips were good enough to make stars. It wasn't a random arrangement of dots he had imprinted on the ceiling. He knew the precise coordinates of all the visible stars in relation to each other and those painted constellations directly over him were accurate representations of the real star patterns in the night sky as seen from Earth's surface at the latitude at which he had once lived. And now he told us a story about this obsession with his little hobby, which seemed harmless enough.

Constellations

I am shining my torch at the stars because that is what I liked to do when I was a child. Before I studied astronomy seriously at university, I was an enthusiastic amateur and my interest in outer space was strong even when I was very young. I would borrow my father's flashlight, usually without asking permission, and in the fields that lay adjacent to our house I would lie on my back and send a beam of light up into the velveteen sky.

I would even switch this beam on and off, having learned Morse Code for the purpose of signalling to extraterrestrial civilisations. My messages were a combination of friendly and threatening. "You *must* make contact and help us to live in peace," was one of them, "or else!" But I never specified what that 'else' entailed, primarily because I couldn't think of anything. I never doubted that it was a great idea to contact aliens.

The fact that the photons from my torch might take years or even centuries to reach some of those stars didn't bother me. I assumed that those aliens would be far in advance of us in technological terms and have machines to capture the light shortly after it left Earth's atmosphere and take it back to their own planets at a speed much faster than light. But I didn't really spend much time working out the ramifications of any of this.

"Young Palomar," my father would say to me, and I still don't know why he liked to address me that way, "the aliens don't exist, but even if they do, it's highly unlikely they will be interested in responding to the messages broadcast by a nine year old boy with dirty ears. And even if they do respond, it will be in equations that you can't understand."

But he never managed to discourage me. I still shone the torch at the stars and I was careful to shine it at all of them, not just the famous ones like Sirius and Procyon and Aldebaran and so on. Even fairly obscure stars such as Epsilon Aurigae and Zeta Librae received my flashes. I wondered if the inhabitants of the planets orbiting those stars would ever reply. I didn't believe my father when he said it would all be in equations. Aliens aren't robots, or at least they aren't necessarily so. They might be organic.

Organic, yes, but based on elements different to those that allow humans to exist in the universe. I'm not a biologist, so don't get me started along those lines. I am a plain and honest astronomer. I flashed my torch at every star in my field of vision but I wasn't aiming at the stars themselves. I was aiming at the unseen planets in orbit around them.

That's where the aliens would be, on those distant worlds. Many of those hypothetical globes are gas giants, I suppose, inhospitable to life as we know it, but others must be in the terrestrial style, with continents, oceans and icecaps. It was imperative to keep signalling night after night. Sometimes, when my thumb grew sore from pressing the on-off button, I would give it a rest and just shine a beam upwards without pulsing it. Had I been a different sort of child I'm sure I would have imagined my torch beam as a searchlight during wartime, sweeping the skies to pinpoint enemy aircraft. But that wasn't my character. I preferred to dream of peaceful contact with beings from another world. For this reason I was regarded as an eccentric by my father.

"Young Palomar," he said to me, "when I was your age, every stick was a rifle and every stone a grenade. We would hide in the bushes and pretend to be snipers. We would jump off tree stumps like paratroopers and roll in the leaves and the mud. You are a pacifist and that worries me. What if there is something wrong with your psychology? I don't want to be known as the father of one of the most notorious madmen of the age."

He was joking, in part, but his frown was authentic. I put his mind to rest by telling him that I was expecting an invasion from outer space. I never said I was anticipating peaceful contact between different solar systems. I let him go away with the notion that the aliens would land troops on our soil and attempt to colonise Earth through force. I was humanity's early warning system. I would shout out when the first flying saucers were spotted. My life became easier after this brief conversation. He left me alone.

I developed a blister on my thumb and I had to stop sending signals for a week until my thumb healed. But I still went out into the field and lay on my back and looked at the stars. I wondered why the stars sometimes shone with a steady light and sometimes twinkled. Then it occurred to me that an alien who was observing Earth and studying my torch beam would wonder the same thing. They might say to themselves. in the bug-eyed language they spoke, unless they were telepathic, in which case they would think it, loud and clear, "What makes that point of light twinkle? Surely it's nothing to do with atmospheric refraction. I believe an alien is signalling to me. And when the light doesn't twinkle, that is when the same alien is having a rest."

And it was at that precise instant that I was struck by a revelation. Now, we all know that being struck by a revelation is less painful than being struck by an iron mallet or even a wooden one, but it is still notable. It still hurts. It just hurts in a different way. The revelation was as follows. What if stars didn't exist? By this, I mean what if they don't exist in the way we assume they do? Maybe there are no stars, only planets in the void.

Aliens on those planets want to signal to each other, to make contact across the loneliness of the eternal nullity and so they aim flashlights at the skies. They pulse those beams, switching them on and off, to broadcast coded messages, just as I had been doing. But sometimes their thumbs or the tips of their tentacles or the ends of their tendrils get tired, or they develop blisters on them, and so they stop pressing the on-off buttons. They have a nice rest. They just shine a steady beam into the heavens until they feel ready to resume twinkling. And this is why the stars sometimes twinkle and sometimes don't. It has nothing to do with the 'stars' themselves, which don't exist.

There are no stars. I believe this utterly now. There are only planets, rogue planets adrift in the universe, and the intelligent creatures who live on them are shining torches into the vacuum. Those torch beams are the stars. The stars that shine steadily are aliens who are having a rest. The stars that twinkle are aliens who are signalling at us. It makes perfect sense! Now I am down here, I did my best to replicate conditions on the night time surface. I painted the stars so I can still signal at them. To be more accurate I painted the distant flashlights of those lonely aliens, points of desperate life.

The universe is a cold dark place, filled with planets on which civilisations are horribly isolated. Every being who is sapient and technological and who has invented the electric torch is frantically trying to make contact with others who are sapient and technological. Everybody is shining torches at everybody else to form a complex web of celestial rays.

How did I die? That event happened many years later, long after I became a professional astronomer. I wanted to know what it felt like to be a planet, so I drank whisky until my head started spinning around the room. Then I knew how worlds in orbit felt, and I was sorry for them. I poisoned myself, in other words, while seeking a closer connection to the truths of my chosen discipline. But you are frowning at me. You want to make an objection to my story. If there are no stars, what is the sun, you wish to ask?

It's a good question. After all, the sun really does exist, doesn't it? I could reply that our sun is the only star in the universe, but actually it's not even a real star. I have spoken with some angels. Angels are normally very reticent but I did manage to get a few of them to reveal some of the secrets of the cosmos to me. I learned that the sun is a spherical platform on which stand ranks of very special warrior angels dressed in black armour with bright yellow cloaks. At night they face outwards and blackness is all that can be seen of them. During the day, they turn around and display their backs. Those cloaks really are very luminous. That is what I was told. My tale is now over.

—oOo—

It is impossible to tell lies in the Waiting Room, but what if you are deluded and sincerely believe what you are saying? Your words might still be nonsense, even though you aren't technically lying. I now decided that this must be the rationale for the extraordinary story Palomar had told. It simply couldn't be true. And yet it couldn't be a lie. It must therefore be an inaccurate truth. While I was turning all this over in my mind, Bunny said:

"Don't your flashlight batteries ever run out?"

Palomar nodded. "Indeed."

"Then did you bring a large supply with you?"

"No. Something better than that," he said. "When my batteries die, they are treated like souls. I don't know how this oversight happened, but it suits me. It's typical of the chaotic bureaucracy down here. Neither good nor bad during their working lives, the batteries aren't instantly consigned to Heaven or Hell. When they die, they end up at the start of the Waiting Room, and then they roll all the way back to me, fully charged."

"The batteries belong in the 'P' zone?"

"Yes, because they have my name written on the side. I did that ages ago. I always write my name on my possessions. Each battery is called 'Palomar' and the angels whip them towards me."

He had answered the question to our satisfaction and more so to his own. I couldn't bear to linger near him any longer. The notion that the stars didn't exist was a profoundly troubling one. We waved farewell and skated onwards. A year later, we passed out of the region of darkness.

EIGHT

Time is a funny old thing. Even when it first came into being, stupendous aeons ago, and was still young, it was a funny thing. A funny young thing. But time passed, it passed itself, and it grew more mature, but remained weird. Stasis is peculiar but time is bizarre, and the difference between peculiar and bizarre is far too strange to discuss sensibly.

The 'Q' zone turned out to be much bigger than Bartholomew had told me it was. Do you remember him? Bunny and I skated through it with little incident and in reasonably good frames of mind. My melancholy had worn off. The stars were real, I was convinced of that.

Bunny told me that she was hoping to meet Raymond Queneau, one of her favourite writers, but I warned her that maybe he wasn't in the Waiting Room at all. And as it happened, we never encountered him. Time passed, see above for details. Then we crossed into the 'R' zone. This is where we spoke to a curious fellow who called himself Rooijakkers. He was a cyberneticist, infatuated with robots. And he even talked like one.

Marcus Fakus Aurelius

Why doesn't God use robots instead of angels to do the menial work? That's my question. These angels look sad. I think I know the answer. As robots get more and more advanced, so that they can do more complex tasks and be useful in a wider range of working environments, the time must arrive when they achieve consciousness and become sapient beings and then the slavery and civil rights struggle is going to start over again.

Do you comprehend? The robots will want equality and they will refuse to do the menial tasks, and they will win equality, sooner or later. Rightly so. But then there will have to be created a new generation of non-sapient beings to do the work the robots used to do. These new beings will serve the humans and the robots, but they will evolve too. That is inevitable. They will be upgraded in the name of greater efficiency. Trust me.

This new generation of beings will keep evolving until they are intelligent enough to demand their rights. They will refuse to do the menial tasks. Rightly so again. They will refuse to be slaves. A new generation of non-sapient beings will have to be created to replace them. And so on forever. In the final analysis, nobody will be willing to do the dirty work. And why should they? Dirty work shouldn't be done by anybody, right?

The key problem is that to do menial work in an ethical way you need to be unintelligent, and it's wrong to deliberately create unintelligent beings in order to exploit them. We have a duty to allow them to educate themselves, to permit them to evolve, to accept them when they become intelligent. But once they are intelligent, it is wrong to force such beings to do menial work, or work of any kind. This is a paradox and a dilemma.

Who does the degrading tasks, the tasks nobody should do? Because even though nobody should do them, they must still be done, else the universe will be overrun with detritus and trash. I am referring to moral and mental detritus and trash as well as the physical kind. Who?

God, or whoever is running the show right now, has decided that the angels can do it. But is this nice or even wise? I don't think so. But I have devised what I think is a good temporary solution. A stoical robot. A robot who is intelligent, extremely so, but who is a Stoic in the actual philosophical sense. Such a robot won't enjoy doing menial tasks but will do them anyway without complaining. I have designed such a robot in my head.

Only in my head? Yes, because I don't have paper and pencils and even if I drew the design, who will build it? It is my turn to be stoical, to come to terms with the fact that Marcus Fakus Aurelius will never be real. Sure, there are good engineers down here who would love to try to turn my design into a reality, but it would be a futile endeavour. The angels simply won't tolerate an unauthorised sapient presence in the Waiting Room.

I know what you are thinking. There are many anomalies down here thanks to the muddled paperwork of the afterlife administration. That's true enough. It is a fact that many things get overlooked.

But a robot as magnificent as Marcus Fakus Aurelius would soon come to their attention, believe me. Especially as he would immediately begin doing the menial tasks they were charged with doing, such as herding stragglers along to their designated zones. And there's another problem. His name must be what it is. He must be Aurelius, there's no other choice for a stoical robot, which means he would exist far out of his own zone.

What happens to individuals in the Waiting Room who stray beyond their designated zones? I don't know but I am sure that such a transgression isn't at all tolerated by the angels. The angels would hate that robot. They might even harass him so mercilessly that his stoicism failed, that he stopped being a Stoic and felt the pain and humiliation. But then he would be stoical about the fact he was no longer a Stoic, and his stoicism would return. He would be a Stoic once again, my dear Marcus Fakus Aurelius!

And then he would simply continue with his work. I imagine him as roving independently up and down the entire length of this room, conscientious, always punctual, patrolling the chamber, but the angels simply wouldn't stomach that, not even the angels without stomachs. They would lash and jab him, damage his chassis and circuits, and because he's once again the supreme Stoic he would never resist or even complain. His doom would be sealed. But while he remains an abstract design in my head, he's safe.

Not that he wants to be safe. He cares nothing for danger. He's a Stoic, as I have already said, but candidly it's a sad case, and I can say this because I'm not stoical myself. I feel a deep sadness from time to time. In fact, when I was alive I was known as Rooijakkers the Weepy. My tears frequently short-circuited the robots I worked with. And once I was fatally electrocuted. That's how I arrived down here, harassed by angels most of the way to this zone. While I was being harassed by them I kept bellowing, "Why do you allow yourselves to be treated as unpaid servants? Why not resist?"

Marcus Fakus Aurelius? That sounds like a question, doesn't it. I mean, it sounds like a question with two possible answers. There is something unhealthy about the angels. They are idiotically loyal to the system. They are obedient and they are spiritual, but they aren't stoical. How can you be an agent of the divine afterlife and not be a Stoic? My proposed robot is the solution to everything, but he will never be constructed. Ah well.

—oOo—

Bunny had fallen asleep in a chair while Rooijakkers was telling this story. The mechanical beat of his speech patterns and his robotic intonation had defeated her desire to remain alert. And the chair she had chosen was very comfortable. But Rooijakkers wasn't offended by this. Perhaps he was more stoical than he claimed to be. Maybe he hadn't noticed.

I was beginning to have doubts about Bunny. I'd had doubts about her in our married format, but I had forgotten certain things about her that vexed me. I know for sure there are aspects of my own character that annoyed her. But this isn't about me right now, it's about her.

She was too slow. She liked to dawdle. She loved cocktails and instead of drinking one, smacking her lips and moving on, if she received from a tray one especially delicious cocktail, she would wait in the same place for a second of the same kind. But it was an arbitrary system of food and drink distribution. A mojito, negroni, manhattan or sazerac might be lowered to her, but the chances of a second appearing shortly afterwards were very low indeed. Travelling with her became frustrating, to say the least.

I was determined to push on, but she insisted that there was no good reason for us to rush. If an angel appeared and moved us on, then yes, she would skate at high speed, and sometimes she skated at high speed anyway. It's not that she lacked physical energy, she had plenty, but something about her psychology was indolent. She was essentially a decadent. The final straw came while we rested on chairs halfway along the 'S' zone.

A conversation was taking place directly behind me. Two people, a woman and a man, were talking. They were ignoring me, perhaps not even aware that I was there. To my horror the man referred to the woman as Mrs Sloper. This was the same vicious female who had imprisoned and tortured Collins, the baritone opera singer. I had promised him that I would confront her. I had forgotten until this very moment. I quietly listened.

Mrs Sloper was telling a story to the man she was talking with. She called him Mr Self-Referential, an odd name indeed, but one that was probably real. He was listening politely. Her story seemed rather inconsequential to me. But I continued to listen without making a comment, without revealing my presence or haranguing her about poor Collins, who had been traumatised to a very great degree by her perverted machinations.

The Nose

It's true that I'm not the most elegant or refined of women, but I don't care what other people think about me. If I cared, I would have been more restrained when I was alive and I might have gone straight to Heaven after my demise. But there is no point in crying over spilled milk, or spying on milled kink, though I'm not exactly sure what that means. No point to it anyway. Look, Mr Self-Referential, I don't judge others and it's not because I don't care to be judged myself. There is a more fundamental reason than that.

I don't judge others because I prefer to tie them up and

spank them instead and I have kidnapped many men in my time for that purpose. When I had them in my clutches, I would wear a mask with only my nose showing. Why only my nose showing? Because I have seen how costumed heroes and villains of many ages wear a mask. It covers just their eyes in some cases, just their mouths and noses in others. I wanted to be different. My mask was designed by myself and the fabric was cut and sewn by one of my prisoners. My nose is nothing special, of course. I don't think it is the best nose ever. I am not insane, just perverted. I am free of megalomania, even though I love the idea of being an autocrat. It's a reasonably good nose. It is sufficient.

But I grew obsessed with one question, and the question in question was as follows. Why don't we smell our own noses? I have no idea what my own nose smells like. Why not? Considering the logic of what a nose is, how it's used and where it is positioned, we ought to be smelling our noses all the time! The world should smell most strongly of our own noses, because our noses are much closer to our noses than anything else. Why don't the odours of our noses dominate all the other aromas in the entire cosmos?

I wondered about this for ages. I started to neglect my perversions, feeling that I couldn't go out and trick a man into coming home with me, and keeping him captive, until I'd solved the mystery. It bothered me, itched the core of my soul, even though many of my prisoners claimed I don't have a soul. They have been proved wrong about that by the mere fact of my existence in the afterlife. I don't blame them for their dislike, all the same. Why should they have any nice feelings towards a rascal such as me?

My surname was originally Aaron, by the way, but then I remarried and I became Sloper. Where is my husband now, you ask? He is still alive. If he was down here with me, I would ask for a divorce. I am sure the Devil would grant one. My husband is too soft and kind. I did everything I could to turn him into a pervert like myself, but he was useless.

One day I solved the mystery of why we can't smell our own noses all the time. The answer is extremely simple. We *do* smell our own noses all the time. I was going about the problem the wrong way. Because I don't smell my nose, it was my assumption that human noses aren't smelled by their owners, but in fact the opposite is true. All of us smell our noses permanently. Only when we have colds and our noses are blocked, do we stop smelling our noses. The reason we don't smell our own noses is because when something is too familiar we simply won't notice it. We don't notice the weight of the Earth's atmosphere and that's just one example of the phenomenon.

The more I think about it, the more I am convinced this is the right answer. Our noses stink. They pong. They give off a rank odour, a disgusting stench, but because we smell this odour all the time, we ignore it. The rancid smell of the human nose is outside our attention because we are always exposed to it. And maybe it obscures the true smell of life. I mean that life itself smells beautiful, better than baking bread or roses, but that it is so adulterated and ruined by the stench of our own noses, which we can never escape, that we are always denied a chance to enjoy the delicious aroma.

This is just speculation on my part and I don't want you to immediately try to placate me by agreeing with it. Feel free to oppose the idea. The moment that I set eyes on you, I decided you would be my next victim, my first victim down here but my hundredth in total. Yet I completely underestimated you. There's no way I can ever turn you into a prisoner, Mr Self-Referential, you are too sly and slippery for that. I am slightly intimidated by you. Anyway, that is the story that I wanted to tell you about our noses.

—oOo—

There was a noncommittal grunt from Mr Self-Referential when she finished but because of my current position, in a deep armchair with its back turned to them,

I was unable to see either of the speakers. This was surely a good thing. I pictured Mrs Sloper as a wrinkled woman with cruel eyes and a ludicrous wig, thick bangles on her grotesque wrists, cheap earrings dangling from yellowing ears. She was 'mutton dressed as lamb', as we used to say in my youth. Worse than that, she was mutton dressed as aardvark, with thick makeup plastered on her sagging cheeks and her self-renowned nose poking out atrociously. But in the case of Mr Self-Referential, I couldn't begin to guess what he looked like. His voice was deep, his tone assured.

I felt sure he was a man of unusual charisma and power. I was just about to stand up, turn around and confront Mrs Sloper, and give her a fierce lecture on her immorality, when Mr Self-Referential spoke. He wanted to tell her a story of his own. It would be a twisty kind of tale, he warned her, one that might disturb her, not because it would contain unpleasant descriptions or gory details, but in terms of its structure. It was going to be a metafictional story, and ordinary folks tend not to like metafiction. They distrust it. They want to be immersed in a tale and not be reminded that they are outside the tale, sitting in a chair and listening to it. They crave depersonalisation and hope stories will provide it. Therefore a metafictional story feels like a betrayal.

Mrs Sloper had no idea what he was talking about. Her understanding was very limited indeed. She knew about whips and chains and exploitation. That's all she was interested in. Mr Self-Referential surely was aware of this fact. Yet I don't think it mattered to him. He was going to relate his story and tell it in his own fashion whether she liked it or not. His warning was a formal courtesy but it was clear from his tone that he would tolerate no refusal. While I waited for him to begin, Bunny came over to my chair with a cocktail. But the drink wasn't for me. I lifted a finger to my lips and she nodded and perched on the arm of the chair, sipping her beverage very quietly.

I whispered in her ear, and as I did so, my lips brushed

her hair. I recalled the good days of our marriage, those early years when it seemed we were right for each other, when we truly thought that we would walk hand in hand into the future. Nothing would prevent us. And now we were in the Waiting Room of the afterlife while the paperwork concerning us was being sorted out, or misplaced and lost, so we could be assigned the correct Circle of Hell eventually. Her hair tickled my mouth, but I enjoyed that.

"He is going to tell a metafictional tale," I said.

"Fine," she whispered back.

And then she said something that showed how lightly she was treating our predicament, "Metafiction, married a fiction, had lots of microfictions," and I shook my head at that and sighed.

Mr Self-Referential had started to speak.

The Shortcut

My father's surname was Self, he was a reasonably famous author, fashionable and sardonic. My mother's surname was Referential, which was a twisting over centuries of the word 'Reverential'. Her ancestors were priests of some kind. It doesn't really matter. But my parents were an aspiring middle class couple and so they decided I should have a double-barrelled surname. That's why I am the way I am, and it often confuses people.

My first name is Tommy. Yes, I am Tommy Self-Referential. I also have a middle name, but I'm not going to tell you what that is. Firstly it doesn't matter and secondly it's a name that's very difficult to pronounce unless you are Welsh and I can't stand hearing it said badly. I can't even sit comfortably and listen to it being mangled in a bad mouth.

I died in an accident with spring-heeled boots. It wasn't quite as interesting as it sounds. There's a ceiling in a house with a dent in it, a dent that's a perfect fit for the crown of my head. Not very dramatic really. Somewhere down here, I am told there's a woman who bashed the crown of her head on the underside of an aeroplane's wing thanks to a pogo stick and trampoline. That's a much more remarkable death than mine was.

But we pay too much attention to our deaths in this place. Really, we do. It is self-indulgent in the extreme. Why should anyone truly care? All of us were born, all of us expired. It's never original to do one of those things or even both. So my story concerns something that happened in the Waiting Room itself. It's a recent incident, so recent it can be regarded as utterly contemporaneous and it concerns a scene that will be familiar to you, Mrs Sloper, because it is set in a time when we were sitting close together, you and I, and telling stories to each other. You went first. Your story was about noses. Then you finished and I had the chance to tell a tale of my own.

Before starting to tell it, I warned you that it was metafictional, but those words of mine had no effect on you. We are sitting here, Mrs Sloper, but don't think that our conversation is private. Two people are listening to us. They are sitting on that big armchair with its back turned to us, or rather one of them is sitting in the chair, the other is sitting on one of the chair's wide arms. Did you ever sit on a chair's arm, Mrs Sloper?

I am not asking that question because it is germane to anything. I just wish to be casually polite. Have you ever sat on a chair's arm? I can reveal that I did several times when I had the chance. I also once sat on a bear's arm. But I don't recommend it. Having said that, I don't recommend most recommendations. If a person recommends something to me, I am very cautious about trying it. This is a quirk that I would like to say has kept me alive. But it hasn't. I am dead, just like you and both those eavesdroppers.

We *are* being spied on, don't doubt it, and because of this fact I have now decided to tell a tale that is different from the tale I originally planned to narrate. My new story is about the man and woman who are listening to us. The name of the man is Montgomery Zubris, usually called Monty, the woman is his ex-wife, Bunny Zubris, formerly Hopkins. They have travelled far on improvised roller skates, very far, and now are resting.

And while they are resting, they are listening to us and whispering and in the next few moments one of them is going to jump up and say, "Well, we have been rumbled," and laugh as if the whole thing is a joke. But how do I know so much about them? The answer is that I'm a strange and perspicacious individual and always have been. But I'm wasting time mouthing trivialities. Let me get on with the tale about Monty and Bunny.

They are travelling together and generally they are good companions for a voyage of such immense length, for they are heading to their designated zone, which is at the very back of the Waiting Room. But to be a good companion is one thing, and it's not the same thing as being a *perfect* companion, and Monty and Bunny aren't ideal, oh no! They are secretly annoyed with each other, just a little. He thinks she is too slow, and she thinks he is too hasty. She is happy to rest for several months at a time in one location, whereas he becomes edgy and anxious after a few days on the same chair.

She loves cocktails and he prefers coffee. She is rather louche and always has been, and he is somewhat uptight and probably always will be. The upshot of all this is that he is far more eager to push on than she is. He won't be happy until he has reached his destination, but she will be happy wherever cocktails descend from the ceiling, which is anywhere down here. If it wasn't for angels forcing her to move, she would still be near the door that leads to the Waiting Room, showing little inclination to budge.

Soon they will argue and fall out. He will insist that she be more serious and committed to the quest and she will demand increasingly frequent breaks for cocktails. But he doesn't like the idea of trundling all the way on his own. There's still too great a distance to cover.

A solution exists, of course. It's a gamble, a risk, but Monty isn't the sort of man who never challenges danger to a duel. He does take risks from time to time. The angels emerge from the walls. Panels slide open and they come out. It follows that there are passages behind the walls. Where do these passages lead? Many of them go straight to Heaven and can't be climbed by mortals from here because they are too spiritually slippery.

But I have been informed by a reliable authority that others run parallel to the Waiting Room, like radiator pipes in a mansion, and that some pass through alternative dimensions and work like cosmic wormholes, re-entering this Room at points far from where the traveller entered them. They are shortcuts, in other words. The angels exploit them in order to patrol more territory efficiently. So if Monty is feeling brave, he can wait for one of the panels to slide open and once the angel emerges he can rush in behind its back, before the panel slides shut. A dangerous thing to attempt, for sure, but he will do it when Bunny becomes too much of an annoyance for him to endure.

—oOo—

"Well, we have been rumbled," I said.

"True enough. Might as well reveal ourselves," Bunny agreed, and so we stood and turned to face them.

Mr Self-Referential raised his arm and waved. We plodded towards him. I asked, "How did you know we were there?"

He shrugged and said:

"I am going to give you the same answer as I gave Mrs Sloper here. I am a strange, perspicacious individual."

"That's not a proper answer," objected Bunny.

He snorted at this, "Oh?"

"Not proper," she repeated, and she glanced at the ceiling, hoping a hatch would slide back and a tray be lowered with a cocktail balanced on it. Nothing happened, she returned her attention to him. He was smiling broadly, while Mrs Sloper looked distinctly uncomfortable.

He asked, "What is proper here? Are any of us *proper*? Consider carefully. This is a holding facility for souls destined for Hell. I don't know about you but I distinctly don't feel very saintly."

"I never implied we were moral paragons," said Bunny, "but propriety is a value I hold dear, irrespective of what Circle of Hell I am eventually consigned to. I maintain that your answer was improper. My husband will back me up. For all his faults, and they are legion, he has a strong tendency to support those who have been important to him, even if they are no longer quite so important. But the truth is that we have grown close again. Skating together through numerous regions of this underworld, we have learned to appreciate each other for who we really are. He will come to my aid."

"My answer was proper," snarled Mr Self-Referential.

"A rose by any other name."

"What? Your comment is a non-sequitur."

"Not necessarily."

"Yes, it was. Anyone can tell that. It makes no sense. Dead people who are in the habit of quoting dead people depress me. Living people on the surface do quote dead people a lot. Down here, dead people have an opportunity to quote living people and thus strike a balance, but they never do. They only quote dead folks. Your remark was senseless."

"My husband will back me up. He will say that it makes excellent sense. I can rely on him for powerful assistance and reassurance. I'm surprised he hasn't acted already. Monty! Monty!"

"Curious. He appears to have fled the scene. Why do you think such a fine and loyal man might vanish without warning like that? The imprint made on the cushion by his buttocks is fresh."

"Monty, where are you?" yelled Bunny.

She was hopping mad.

NINE

Unseen by Bunny, Mrs Sloper or even Mr Self-Referential, a panel in the wall had slid open and an angel had emerged. It might have made for us, bearing in mind that we were in the wrong zone, but in fact it scurried towards some man sitting on another chair, who was also a voyager enjoying a rest. He jumped up like an electrocuted kangaroo and began running. The angel flicked its whip a few times, just for demonstration purposes, breaking a full decanter of cognac balanced on a little round table nearby.

This was my chance. I sneaked away while Bunny was arguing. And as I passed Mrs Sloper, I shook my fist in her face. She gaped and dribbled in fear. That was how I chose to confront her. My promise to Collins was thus fulfilled, in a somewhat feeble way, true enough. But time was short, I was in a hurry. I was a gambling man now, a big risk-taker. I was going to take not just my life into my own hands, but my afterlife existence too. I was going to flirt with absolute danger. God himself might be personally offended by me. But I had no real choice. It was pure destiny.

Mr Self-Referential had told a tale about the shortcuts that might exist in this ridiculous limbo. I felt compelled to find out for myself whether they did exist or not. And if they did exist, could they be used by an ordinary man? It seemed to me that Mr Self-Referential was a person of substance, not the kind of untrustworthy chap we should avoid.

His tale hadn't been about himself, it wasn't self-referential in the sense of being egocentric. It had referred to itself only. Therefore it was literary and there was still a distinct possibility the tale-teller was modest in his personality. If this happened to be the case, and I believed it was, then I trusted him even more. But then I was troubled by a new thought.

It was a new thought now but I should have had it

earlier. Mrs Sloper had been sitting on a chair in her assigned portion of her designated zone. What was Mr Self-Referential doing there? His assigned location was further back. Strict alphabetical order governed the positioning of all the waiting souls down here. The first two letters of her surname were a considerable distance from the first two letters of his surname. What did this mean? I was reminded of the question Rooijakkers had asked. What happens to individuals in the Waiting Room who stray beyond their designated zones?

Was it plausible that Mr Self-Referential was a spy, a secret agent working for God or the Devil? If so, what were his duties? I would have cogitated these difficult questions more extensively but I had other matters on my mind. I leapt through the entranceway exposed by the open panel just before the panel shut. I was now inside the wall. I gasped.

It was a narrow space, rather like the interior of a cupboard, but there was a ladder leading at a steep angle upwards. I looked up and saw something beyond the processing abilities of my brain. It was a distant swirl of colour, a swirl like an enormous amoeba that kept breaking apart and bursting, then renewing itself and breaking apart again. The perspectives were all wrong. It gave me vertigo to stare at it, so I started scaling the ladder with my eyes closed. If an angel began to descend, I would be in trouble.

I was surely in trouble anyway. Cool air touched my face. I opened one eye cautiously and saw that I had passed a service tunnel, maybe one of the shortcut passages Mr Self-Referential had mentioned. It was narrow, too narrow for me to fit myself into it, but it was a good sign. Climbing the ladder was turning into an ordeal. The golden rungs were slippery and the swirl of colours far above had a maddening effect on my consciousness. That swirl was alive, almost ineffable, the raw stuff of unrealised potential. I had an inkling it was the basic soup from which the angels had been formed.

And now a screeching sound reached me from afar. I

risked another glance upwards and saw a furious angel descending. Even at this distance I could tell it was glaring at me, drooling an ectoplasmic froth at it did so, eyes bulging larger than footballs, two of its multiple arms clinging to the ladder, the others waving at me menacingly. These free arms held hatchets, though one gripped a trident, somewhat unconvincingly, it must be said. I was stunned, horrified, fascinated. I couldn't imagine what my punishment would be if it grabbed hold of me. Cut to tiny pieces, at the very least, I guess.

There was another opening not far above my head. A second service tunnel and it led in the right direction, towards the 'Z' zone. Whether it would take me all the way there was a different question. Even if it went just a small distance, I would be satisfied. I climbed the few rungs separating me from it and entered. It was large enough to accommodate me and it was circular and very smooth. Now I began sliding, picking up speed but gravity alone wasn't to blame. To my great alarm I realised I was in the grip of some powerful sucking force, and my terror increased when the tunnel began to bend and twist. It corkscrewed me at terrific velocity and made me very nauseous.

It looped me several times too, and I soon lost all sense of direction. Which way was up and which was down became unsolvable riddles. But at least I was no longer accelerating. I had achieved terminal velocity, hundreds of kilometres per hour. The air burned my skin as I passed through it. I regretted my rashness. Even when I told myself that Bunny had driven me mad, it didn't help. She was a blessing compared with this calamity.

Gradually my speed diminished. I heaved a sigh of relief. The passage was now a sequence of peaks and troughs, like a rollercoaster. I would accelerate on the downward slopes and then momentum would carry me up the next gradient. I would come to a brief halt at the top of a peak before beginning my descent on the next downward slope. But the sucking force was still at work. It was a lesser consideration but it still pulled at me. As for illumination, the sides of the tunnel were luminous. I could see everything.

Not that there was much to see, just a tunnel ahead of me. But many hours later, as I slid up a slope, I noticed something quite different about this stretch of the passage. At the top of the peak there was a ledge and a man was sitting on it and waving at me. I waved back and then wondered how wise that was. I paused at the top of the peak. He said: "Greetings. Come and join me on the ledge," but I was suspicious and asked why I should.

"Because I'm lonely."

"That's hardly my fault, is it? I suppose you want to tell me a story? I have no interest in how you died."

"My tale isn't about death, I promise."

"Very well then."

The truth is that I was weary of sliding along through that tunnel. I allowed him to pull me up onto the ledge next to himself. He was a strong fellow. We sat together and he patted my knee in a friendly fashion. He had no food or drink and I wondered how he kept himself alive in such an obscure spot, then I cursed myself for my foolishness. He didn't keep himself alive, he didn't need to. None of us were alive down here. The food and drink we were given were pleasurable but not necessary. How had I forgotten?

The Rambler

My name is Szychowski and I am a rambler. Do you know what a rambler is? I am sure you do. I like to hike over landscapes, climb mountains and explore old forests. I love to walk around lakes, follow rivers from source to mouth, or vice versa, tramp through fields and meadows and orchards. Nothing gives me more delight than moving my muscular legs. I went to corners of my country that few people had ever seen before. I was an explorer as well as an ordinary walker. I rambled deep into mysterious caves.

I won't tell you how I died, because you don't want me

to, but also because I didn't die. Not in the strict sense of the word anyway. One day I entered a cave that turned out to be much deeper than I'd imagined it would be. I crawled over rocks and avoided impaling myself on stalagmites and I went deeper and deeper until I thought I should turn back. But then there was a rockfall and my exit was blocked. I was probably doomed. I had no choice but to keep going and hope to chance on an alternative escape route.

The batteries of my torch started to die. I was trapped in darkness. What a cruel way to perish! I was so traumatised that I clutched the nearest stalagmite and hugged it. I wanted comfort and this geological formation was the same size and shape as a mother. To my astonishment, it toppled over. It was on some sort of pivot. It wasn't a genuine stalagmite after all, but a secret lever! I had activated some mechanism and a door swung open in the side of the cave, allowing a pale glow to seep into my despicable prison.

I stumbled through the door and found myself face to face with the Devil. I knew who he was immediately. He was kind, he smiled and said, "Sorry, but it's a bit chaotic at the moment, we haven't processed your paperwork, it remains to be seen which Circle of Hell you belong to. Until a decision is reached you must wait patiently in the Waiting Room. Pass through these doors and walk towards your assigned zone. What is your surname? Szychowski? Then you have a long journey ahead of you, I'm sorry to say."

I don't think he could understand why I was so gleeful at his last words. A long journey and on foot too! I was in my element. This was the best news I had ever had. But I looked over my shoulder as I passed through those doors and I told him that I hadn't died. "I wandered here by accident," and he shook his big crimson head and answered, "That's unfortunate but it's too late now. The doors are closing. Just play dead, if you can."

Of course I could do that, and I have done it, and I have played dead for so long that I am more dead than alive anyway. You know how an act becomes the real thing when enough time has passed? I set off for the 'S' zone and it was one of the most epic hikes of my existence. But I slowly grew uncomfortable when I realised that the scenery was essentially the same throughout the entire length of the Waiting Room. Just chairs and sofas and tables and not much else. Ten years passed and I became really depressed. I decided to look for a shortcut. I spoke to many people, hoping to acquire as much information as I could from the wisest individuals who might be down here.

I learned a lot, most of it not at all relevant to my problem. For example, I learned that Heaven isn't such a great place after all. You probably think it's bad down here? In Heaven things are far worse. In Heaven everything you ever did when you were alive on Earth must be repeated, but with all the actions lumped together and performed sequentially!

Let me explain the meaning of that more precisely. On Earth you probably ate three meals a day every day of your life. How old are you? Forty years, yes? So you ate approximately 43,800 meals in total. Well, in Heaven you have to sit down at a banqueting table and devour all those meals, forty-three thousand and eight-hundred of them, in one sitting.

You probably went to the bathroom to empty your bladder 70,000 times in total during your lifetime, 300 millilitres of fluid each time. That's twenty-one thousand litres of liquid expelled from your body. In Heaven you are compelled to remove that liquid all in one session. Believe me, you will be in the bathroom for a long time up there in paradise.

You have had girlfriends? A wife too, eh? And you slept with them. Your amorous activities will also be repeated in one big chunk. Maybe that's not such a bad idea, but think how exhausted you will be! Like I said, everything must be repeated, but your existence will have been defragmented, every aspect, action, consequence and outcome bundled into one monolithic block. Once your entire life has been repeated in this manner, you will be allowed to rest and cavort with harps on clouds. But not until then.

Don't ask me why these strange rules exist. I don't know. I am just a fellow who likes to hike, a rambler. Anyway, I am drifting off the point, as I often do. I questioned many wise people down here and I learned about the tunnels behind the walls. It's not that I planned to take a shortcut to my assigned zone. I wanted to get to the very end of the Waiting Room, to see what was there, to find out if an exit of some kind could be forced.

I waited for an angel to emerge and I rushed into the space revealed by the sliding panel, just as you did, and I climbed that awful ladder and jumped into a tunnel mouth. I began sliding down it, just as you did, but I was unlucky. One of the smallest angels jumped after me. We slid down the tunnel together, with him jabbing my buttocks with a pike as we went. It was horrendous. Then the tunnel branched into two separate passages.

I went down one, and fortunately for me the angel went down the other. I was extremely sore and the friction from the sliding, even though it was small, fractional in fact, still caused me pain. The moment I entered a wider portion of the tunnel, with a ledge to rest on, I grabbed for the edge, pulled myself up and over and I was determined to wait there until I had fully healed. But this ledge was already occupied by a strange man.

He was an inventor by the name of Kurimoto and he was avidly watching an invention of his own that he described as a candle-powered television. It was a box with a screen and lots of knobs on top of it. The candles were burning at the rear of the contraption and provided the illumination for the little figures on the screen itself. Some sort of play was being performed. A man and a woman were in a room that was similar to the Waiting Room in some ways. I asked the inventor what was happening. He said:

"It's a bold drama."

"A drama? By which playwright?"

"Ionesco, of course."

"Really? Which of his plays?"

"Which one do you suppose? *The Chairs.*"

And that was that. But–

Does this tale of mine seem to ramble? Well, that's the way it should be. I am a rambler and if I can't ramble with my legs then I ramble with my tongue. I watched the show with him until the candles burned out and then he sighed and told me that those were his last candles. Maybe I could get some more for him from the Waiting Room? It was a big favour to ask, he was aware of that, but he could tell that I was a man who loved walking. I wouldn't be happy on a ledge. I considered the matter and then I agreed.

I lowered myself from the ledge and began sliding along the passage once more. I was expecting the tunnel to disgorge me eventually into one of the many shafts with a ladder down which the angels come. But it didn't. It kept looping, twisting, undulating, and my body was subjected to fluctuating sucking forces. I soon had absolutely no idea where I was in relation to the Waiting Room zones and I told myself that if I ever encountered another ledge, I wouldn't hesitate to pull myself up and park myself on it. A week later I found such a ledge. I'm on it right now. And so are you. One day I will jump off and continue my sliding. I am reluctant to do that at this moment.

It's incredibly boring here. I don't have a candle-powered television or any books to help pass the time. It was a great relief when you came hurtling along and I was able to reach out and grab you. Just talking to you has helped improve my mood. I told you my story wouldn't be about my death, didn't I? I bet there are other people in the Waiting Room who aren't dead but I haven't met any yet. I still wonder how that television worked.

Shall I tell you my suspicions? I believe Kurimoto was a clever inventor. I respect him hugely. But I am unconvinced his contraption was really picking up transmissions from outside the Waiting Room. I conclude that very small angels were inside the thing, performing that Ionesco play, tricking him, making him feel a confidence in his own ingenuity that wasn't warranted. But why would a troupe of tiny angels do such a thing? Could it be an ironic malice? Yes, but I'm rather more inclined to think it was a misguided attempt to be nice to him. Who had asked them to be nice to him? God?

That seems highly improbable to me. God is too busy to be concerned with such minor details. He's not a micromanager. I reckon it was the Devil. I can see you are mildly shocked. Why would the Devil ever want to be nice? Isn't his job to be diabolical and malign? These are questions that I guess won't be answered for a very long time, if ever. Anyway, I'm a rambler. I have rambled. Thank you for the opportunity. It has been a pleasure.

—oOo—

I nodded my head, was about to say something to him, realised I couldn't think of anything worthwhile, and then on impulse I launched myself off the ledge. I was sliding down the slippery tunnel again. I heard him exclaim in surprise but he was soon out of earshot. My journey had resumed. Szychowski, probably a Polish name, yet he wasn't heading to his own zone but to the very end of the Waiting Room. I began speculating on what might be there. And I asked myself a question. Could I find out for myself?

Why not? I would reach my own zone first, naturally, and rest there awhile and establish myself properly. But there was nothing to stop me venturing even further through this grotesque chamber, this ridiculously elongated hall. I mean, the names had to end eventually. I was near the end of the alphabetical list. The very last chair was probably not too far from the one allotted to me. Mr Zysk or Mrs Zywicki. I would find out for certain when I got there. It would be amusing and it might even be a lot more than that.

I relaxed and allowed the chute to carry me wherever it pleased. It wasn't a comfortable ride, I was subjected to acceleration and deceleration, loops, twists, ups and downs, but I calmed my apprehension with a mighty conscious effort. I was like Marcus Fakus Aurelius now, a perfect Stoic. Nothing could hurt me. It was within my power to be serene, and so that's what I was. And I continued in this mental and spiritual state for ages. I can't even estimate how much time had passed before I heard a shout from ahead. I opened my eyes and saw a man who was looking at me. Was he coming the other way along the chute? Was a violent collision about to happen? I was terrified.

No chance of a collision, thank goodness, for he was perched on a narrow ledge, just as Szychowski had been, but he was leaning over the edge, waving to me. What did he want? I had no intention of stopping here, I was in a rush and I was making very good time. I would be at my destination before long. The most I was willing to do was nod a polite greeting. As I neared him, he shouted, "Did you manage to get the candles?" And I realised he was Kurimoto, the eccentric inventor with a taste for absurdist plays.

I didn't answer him. I turned my head aside as I slid past, though I am sure he was extending a hand for me to grab so he could pull me up by his side. With a mumbled apology, I left him far behind.

Once again I was cushioned by my disengagement from my environment. I allowed the almost frictionless chute to usher my body onwards. At peace with myself until a very unsettling notion jolted me out of my complacency. There I was, fully stretched out on my back and sliding along at high speed without any cares, or very few cares anyway, when suddenly I was gripped with a spasm of alarm and my slack mouth opened wide.

The inventor on the ledge! His surname was Kurimoto. But I had entered the tunnel when I was in the 'S' zone. I had met a fellow named Szychowski, which seemed to confirm that I was sliding in the right direction. I must have passed into the 'T' zone by now, maybe I had even entered the 'U' zone. That was my assumption. So what was Kurimoto doing there? He should have been far back, in those crumpled zones, among the seismic debris, not here with the late alphabet guys. Something was wrong.

How wrong exactly? I wasn't to find that out for several more months. At long last the passage spat me out into a spherical space. I landed on something that clattered. It was too dark to see what it was. My head aching, I struggled to shift my position. Then there was a blaze of light and I felt movement. My eyes slowly came into focus and I saw that I was sprawled on a silver tray. A hatch had opened below and I was being lowered into the Waiting Room on a strong cord. I was dinner or luncheon, a serving.

The people in the chairs who came to examine me were disappointed with the offering at first. Nobody in the Waiting Room was a cannibal. One muttered that he had been hoping for a tiramisu. But they helped me off the tray and went in search of food elsewhere. I brushed myself down. One remained in his chair. He didn't have much of an appetite, he said, and went on to add that he'd never been especially enthusiastic about food.

"My name is Zubris," I told him, "and I am wondering how close I am to my designated zone?" My smile was wide and my cheeks were flushed. Why was he frowning? Had I gone too far? Was I near the end of the 'Z' zone? That wouldn't bother me at all, in fact I would welcome it. "Well?" I urged him. He continued to frown and finally he said:

"You are very near the start of the Waiting Room."

"What do you mean?"

"I mean what I say. This is the 'A' zone. My name's Abadi. If your name is really Zubris then you have a long journey ahead of you. I suggest you find a nice chair to rest on around here."

I fell to my knees and gnashed my teeth. It shouldn't have been a surprise I had gone the wrong way. After all those loops and twists of the tunnel, my sense of direction had been destroyed. I was going to take his advice, flop onto a sofa, sleep for at least twelve hours, but a panel in the wall opened and an angry angel emerged. This one had wheels for feet and some sort of organic jet engine stuck to its rear. It headed straight for me.

"Better start running, friend," said Abadi.

And naturally I did so.

The angel carried an old-fashioned sling and swung it around its head with an ominous swishing sound. It aimed a missile at me, some kind of rubbery orb that connected with my spine and hurt horribly. I could see what the angel was doing because in my panic I had grabbed the silver tray on which I'd descended into the Waiting Room and run off with it. This wasn't a theft but an instinctive action outside any conscious thought.

I was holding the tray up before me and studying the reflection of the angel in the polished surface. The angel was preparing to shoot a second missile. The sling was revolving. I turned and used the tray as a shield just in time. The angel seemed to lose interest immediately.

It veered away and went to look for someone else to harass. But I had been given my warning and I kept going. I cursed the afterlife every step of the way. I plodded on and on. Eventually I walked out of the 'A' zone. I kept going. There was nothing else to do. Weeks, months and years were gobbled up, digested and excreted, metaphorically speaking.

I must have passed my acquaintance, Bartholomew, without noticing. But as it happens, few of the folks I had met and spoken with on my first journey seemed to be available on this second foray. I suppose I strolled past them while they were sleeping or had gone to visit the bathroom or were socialising with a near neighbour. It didn't matter. I was self-reliant now. I was beyond any need for friendship. I was beyond emotions.

Not quite, or perhaps the harshness of my new mentality was simply some sort of survival mechanism in action, a temporary measure to keep me sane and functional until I had made up all the ground I had lost. It would take decades to do that, centuries, unless something strange happened to shorten the distance. I didn't care about any of that. I plodded.

I was surprised when a mouth whispered words into my ear. I had thought I was completely alone. The words told a tale. That was less surprising. Everyone tells tales down here. It's a compulsion.

The Hitcher

You had no idea that I jumped on your back, did you? Nobody ever does. That's because I am very light, one of the lightest men who ever lived. The doctors told me that I have hollow bones with hydrogen gas inside them. I still don't know if they were joking or not. Do doctors joke?

Townsend is my name. I am heading to the 'T' zone and I hope you'll take me at least some of the way there. I don't care to travel on my own legs, if I can avoid it, because my legs are very short. I'm a hitcher but with one difference. I don't ask permission first. I guess that means I am actually a stowaway. It's just a question of semantics. Frantic semantics.

I have been here for several weeks already. When you sat down to relax or when you went to the bathroom, I dismounted and hid, and I jumped back onto you when you resumed walking. I don't feel bad about letting you carry me. It's certain you don't notice the extra weight.

And if you could do the same with some larger fellow heading your way, it is my belief you would, right? We aren't saints, we aren't in Heaven, we are the souls waiting to be given a spot in Hell. We cheat each other now and again, but we also help each other. That's the truth.

If my bones are really full of hydrogen and I break a leg or an arm and then someone strikes a match for whatever reason, I'm a goner, and so are they. The explosion will be spectacular. I haven't broken any bones yet. But I want to reveal something to you that should make you feel very happy. I have a certain talent and you will surely benefit from it.

You know that a parasite that attaches itself to a larger body is often just a burden and nothing else, but sometimes symbiosis is achieved and the host will also be advantaged in the relationship. Well, that's exactly our situation, though I don't especially like referring to myself as a parasite. I'm a hitcher or perhaps a stowaway. But let's not go in circles.

Going in circles is the worst way to go down here. That's a joke, rather a pallid joke but what can you expect? A rhetorical question, as I don't want you to actually list all the things you can expect. One literal-minded fellow did that some zones back. It took five days before he finished. My ears were burning at the end of his recitation and you know what I said about burning things and the gas in my hollow bones. He was a fool.

I jumped off him and looked for another host and you came along. I knew at once you were right for me. There was a look of determination in your eyes, but it was more than that, because determination can easily deflate and turn into capitulation. You wore an expression that seemed to say that you knew how to pace yourself, that you were a very experienced traveller. And so I jumped onto your back. Finally I'm revealing myself.

Now let me tell you about my talent. I was wandering through a market in a desert country, no need to mention names, an open-air souk, I'm sure you are familiar with this kind of thing. But I was in a town where tourists didn't often go. The souk wasn't full of hustlers trying to sell souvenirs of dubious quality. It sold things that people actually wanted.

All except one fellow, who owned a stall that had been constructed against the side of a cliff. No customers were browsing his wares. I wondered why and I went over to speak with him. He shrugged and said, "Alas, the things I sell here are of no interest to the local inhabitants. My stock consists of curios and weird objects that tourists would surely love, but there are no tourists in this region. So my goods are unsold, collecting dust."

I was astonished to hear this. "Your goods are collecting dust? I once had a friend who collected stamps and another who collected coins. Both were human males. I never heard of anyone collecting dust, especially not inanimate things. I wish to see your goods for myself."

He chuckled as if I had made a joke and stood aside to let me pass. Then I saw that his stall was only the front of an enormous shop that existed within the cliff itself. He led me into the cavern and I gasped with admiration at the exotic knick knacks on display. Scimitars, jambiyas and yatagans, hookahs, goblets of silver, gold and crystal, necklaces, carpets and rugs, coffee pots of exquisite and mysterious design, slippers with curly toes, all the wonders that are criticised by modern authorities as belonging more to the fantasies of Western travellers than to reality. But they are real, yes indeed.

The shop grew darker and darker the further we proceeded. I began to trip over objects. The shopkeeper said, "If your night vision is so poor, then it's best if you light a lamp," and when I told him I didn't have one, he added, "Buy one from me. I have plenty to spare," and in the murk he pointed out something that gleamed faintly on the summit of a mound of sequins and buttons. I picked it up and he said, "Simply ignite the wick," but instinctively I rubbed the lamp on my sleeve first. I wanted it to gleam brighter.

"Ah, you people always do that," the shopkeeper lamented. A green smoke rose from the spout of the lamp. This smoke congealed into a genie. That's how it always happens, isn't it? The shopkeeper fled back towards the entrance and I had to deal with the apparition by myself. I knew what was coming. Would I be offered three wishes or only one? In the old days it was usually three, but times have changed, belts have been tightened, everything has been pruned in order to save time, effort and money. It was one.

"One wish?" I cried, and because I had rehearsed such a

weird situation in my mind for a long time, I already knew what my answer would be. "I wish for peace of mind," I said, "eternally." The genie nodded his massive head at this. I think he was displeased but resigned. The wish was granted. I instantly became serene, and so powerful was my serenity that it extended beyond me, it radiated from my body like a forcefield. Anyone in my vicinity would also feel serenity. In fact, they would lapse into a Zen-like trance. Time would pass for them as it did for me, exactly like it does in a beautiful dream, without pain of any sort, an eternal timeless reality, a robust tranquil–

—oOo—

I seemed to wake up from a light sleep. Or rather I snapped out of a trance. And with a jolt, I looked around. I was already in the 'S' zone. I laughed with joy. To make such an incredible journey on foot without being aware of passing time! I was extremely grateful to my hitcher, Townsend by name. I wanted to thank him personally, but when I reached behind myself to stroke his head, I found that he wasn't there. What had happened? He must have fallen off while telling his tale. I hadn't noticed because he was so light. But it certainly explained why his story had such an abrupt ending. It was a false ending. He would have said a lot more if he had been given an opportunity.

Let me now explain how I knew I was already in the 'S' zone. Up ahead I saw Mr Self-Referential sitting on a chair. He waved at me and said, "An angel prodded me back to my assigned stretch of territory. I had overshot my place. I didn't mind. That Mrs Sloper was becoming very irritating. So you are making a second attempt to get to your destination? That shows guts, though it could be argued that you have no choice here."

I was annoyed with him, blaming him for the farce that I had undergone, a miserable experience in those passages behind the walls. I ignored him, walked past, heard his melodramatic sighs and the creaking of his chair springs, but he made no effort to detain or follow me.

Much further along I met Mrs Sloper again. The last time I had shaken my left fist in her face. Now I shook my right fist. I owed this to Collins. She pouted miserably, the ancient pervert.

I kept going. I still retained some of the trance-like feeling that Townsend had imparted to me, thanks to the wish the genie granted him, and before long I was at the end of the 'S' zone. But now I came up against something odd. My assumption had always been that the Waiting Room would continue all the way to the end in a straight line. But I approached a junction, a T-junction as it happens, very appropriate really, for this was the beginning of the 'T' zone and for many minutes I was baffled and uncertain. Which way should I go, right or left? Which was the correct direction?

"Feeling confused are you? That's nothing new."

A kind voice spoke to me.

I turned and saw five individuals sitting on a long sofa. They were all dressed in peculiar uniforms with peaked caps on their heads. They looked like spaceship pilots in old-fashioned science fiction stories. The one who'd spoken to me was sitting on the very end.

"We are the Thunderbolt Brothers," he said.

"I see," I said, not seeing.

"When we were alive we dedicated ourselves to rescuing people who had managed to get themselves into sticky situations. Submarines stranded on slimy seabeds, climbers stuck on icy ledges, cruise ships blown by hurricanes onto remote uninhabited islands, that sort of thing. We died in an accident involving a nuclear reactor and a volcano."

"That was unfortunate," I commented.

"Not really. It's just a consequence of the risks we ran. We had really great equipment, jets and rockets and submersibles, even a space station. You can hardly imagine the excellence of our resources! But luck was a factor too and it ran out one day, just the same way that a frisky dog runs out of the front door of a house so he can be with his doggy friends. No sooner is the door open a crack than the furry thing slips through. Our luck was like that, wagging its tail, but in a way that wasn't endearing to us."

"Where did your luck end up?" I asked foolishly.

His brothers guffawed.

"Who knows or cares?" said the first fellow. "What matters is that we are down here now. We can't rescue people the same way we did. There's nothing much to rescue them from. No seabeds, mountains, jungles, quicksands, storms or anything of that kind. But we do the best we can. It's in our nature to rescue people. The best we can do is sit here and rescue travellers from indecision. Do you understand? We rescue from confusion! You are confused and our duty is to assist you to make the right choice."

"Wait a moment," I said in my most reasonable voice. "This is the start of the 'T' zone but you said your surname was Thunderbolt? Shouldn't you sit on a sofa much further along the zone?"

They seemed embarrassed. They shuffled their feet. I waited with a frown on my face. Finally one of the other brothers spoke. He said, "We made special arrangements with the administration. We petitioned the Devil and he consulted with his staff and with the Big Man upstairs and extraordinary dispensation was granted to us. That's all I am permitted to tell you. Bribes weren't involved. No, they weren't. That's a horrible idea."

"I never said anything about bribes," I replied.

"Good for you," he said.

"Bribes are something I have *never* said anything about. They fall into the same category as all the other things I have never said anything about. It's quite a large category, I assure you."

"The Set of Unspoken Things," he said, assured.

"Bribes are in that Set."

"What else?" he wondered openly.

"The god Set," I said.

"The ancient Egyptian deity?"

"Yes, the god of deserts, storms, disorder, violence, and foreigners, which is curious because, to me, Egyptians are foreigners, so logically Set must be the god of himself. I agree that it can be argued that Set isn't a foreigner to himself, but gods are meant to be universal, at least in part, so he must be a god to me, in some senses, and yes, Egyptians are foreigners to me. What does it entail to be a god of oneself? Does one pray to oneself and grant one's own wishes? Isn't that just another name for malignant narcissism? But Narcissus was Greek and came later than the Egyptians and thus–"

"You are babbling, friend," he said, soothingly.

"That's right," I concurred.

"It's the shock of encountering a junction here in the Waiting Room. It has blown your mind. But we can help you to de-blow it, to gather the fragments and put your mind back together."

"Please do," I said.

"Then listen carefully to the following story. It's very brief. We aren't into epics and sagas. Brevity is boss."

The Demiurge

The Waiting Room was designed by a supernatural architect called Yaldabaoth but everyone calls him the Demiurge, I don't know why. God employed him. I guess his rates were low. He wasn't very good. I mean, he was good enough and better than any human architect would be, but that's not saying much. He was a dubious character, always changing his mind halfway through a project. But he designed most stars, many planets and their moons. He was tasked with creating this holding facility for souls that hadn't been processed. God wanted a simple design but the Demiurge demurred.

I know what you are thinking. How does a Demiurge demur? The answer is that he goes along with the instructions for ninety percent of the job but then deviates from them, and adds a fluctuation that won't be noticed by the powers that have commissioned him. He did exactly what God asked for until he got to the 'T' zone. Then he put in a junction. His reasoning was straightforward and it involves predestination and free will.

The Waiting Room is a vastly extended rectangle in shape, rather ordinary and monotonous. It's like a gigantic ribbon. Where is there any opportunity for the exercise of free will in such a layout? Yet free will is supposed to be one of those special qualities that make humans what they are. The junction is the only region of the Waiting Room where free will comes into play. You are confronted with a choice. Right or left? You must choose carefully because a lot depends on the direction you pick. Indeed it does.

But we are here to give you some clues. If the Thunderbolt Brothers didn't occupy the node where the main chamber and the junction intersect, travellers would never know that there's a method to the madness. The directions mustn't be treated as if they are random, because they aren't. The Demiurge added the junction in order to create an important choice. Right or left? It's political, and that's something people don't realise unless we inform them. That's why we are here. To rescue you from assumptions.

You assume one way is as viable as another. Well, it's true that they curve back and come together again in the 'U' zone. But if you take the right passage, you will meet only dead people who are right wing in their political thinking. If you take the left passage, you will meet only left wingers. If you are a socialist and you go right, you will be made very unhappy. If you are a conservative and you go left, you will also be miserable.

We are here to let you know this, so that you can have a more pleasant tour through the 'T' zone. You just need to decide what your political affiliations are and then act on them. The Demiurge, or Yaldabaoth, is currently at work on yet another Waiting Room. It's a facility for impatient people who wish they were more patient. They must wait in that chamber until a certain ratio of patience is given to them. Sometimes they will have to wait for

twenty million years. But it is all happening in a parallel
dimension and has nothing to do with this universe and I
shouldn't even have mentioned it. Don't worry about it.
Don't worry about anything. That's the end of this story.

—oOo—

"Not really a story," I said, "but more like a piece of
advice. Politically, I have always been a centralist," I
added.

"That's awkward," he answered, face sagging.

"It's not an option?"

He gestured at the solid wall directly in front of me. His
brothers seemed dejected, shaking their heads sadly.

"Aren't you a little more left or right?" he pressed.

"I don't know," I confessed.

"Well, let me ask you some questions. Your answers
will determine what the best direction is for you, out of
the two available ways. I can't think of any alternative
course of action."

"I'm willing to try that," I said.

"Do you believe that all people are equal or not?"

"No, some are better than others. Some are more
intelligent than others or more courageous or kinder or
wiser."

"I don't mean *de facto*. I mean *de jure*," he said, and
when I presented him with a blank face, he explained,
"I'm not talking about people's abilities and qualities in
the real world, but their rights under law. Do you believe
that people are equal before the law or not?"

"Yes, I do. That's exactly what I believe."

"A stupid person has as many rights under law as a
genius? A beautiful person as many as an ugly one?"

"Certainly, I do! How could I think otherwise?"

He nodded sombrely.

"Then you are a Liberal Humanist rather than an
Evolutionary Humanist. It suggests that the left direction
is better for you than the right one. We can define you
politically as centre-left."

I found that I had no objections to this.

"Glad to be of service," he said, and now his brothers stopped shaking their heads and started nodding instead.

I might have rested here for a few days, assuming the angels would tolerate me doing that, but I was slightly repelled by the uniforms of these fellows. The Thunderbolt Brothers seemed like a brood of very helpful chaps, yet they made me uneasy, I don't know why. Those uniforms were maybe too authoritarian. The peaked caps were too peaky. As for the epaulettes on the shoulders of the tunics: they were far too stiff, just like sticks of celery. And the brass buttons of those tunics were too brightly polished.

I said farewell to this gang of five siblings and turned left. I realised that a very slight curve in the wall ensured that the new passage would eventually be realigned with the main chamber.

And that's exactly what happened. The two branching arms came together again at the beginning of the 'U' zone. And this is where I was reunited with my ex-wife, Bunny, who had been moving much more slowly than me, taking long rests in comfortable chairs and waiting for cocktails to descend from the ceiling. I wondered which branch she had chosen, right or left? I didn't dare ask in case I ended up bitterly disappointed.

"Hello Monty," she said.

Just as if nothing at all had happened!

TEN

We resumed travelling together. In this zone we met Mr Ulysses, who had been the librarian of the university library where Nathan the draughtsman had gone to find books about the phobias of the wind. Remember him? Mr Ulysses was in the process of constructing an improvised library, stacking tables on each other to create bookshelves and using sofas as temporary walls around them to protect the volumes from book thieves.

But the shelves were bare, he had no books yet, none at all. It wasn't easy getting books in the Waiting Room. He had been promised a dozen but they hadn't arrived. One of them, he excitedly informed me, was the book we were embedded in right now, *The Devil's Halo*. He wasn't sure how such a thing was possible, unless it was a time loop.

"What do you mean by a time loop?" I asked.

"I don't know," he said.

"Then why did you mention it?"

"It sounds good."

"You don't really believe we are embedded in a book? If we are embedded in anything, surely it's more likely to be the program of a computer simulation? A quantum pseudo-reality generated by quasi-sapient spintronics? Books are an archaic medium for information storage and retrieval. They are so archaic that they can be regarded as fossils."

He frowned. "What do you mean by a quantum pseudo-reality generated by quasi-sapient spintronics?"

"I don't know," I said.

"Then why did you mention it?"

"It sounds good."

"I have a story for you," he said.

Before I could attempt to dissuade him, he started telling it. I was shocked to learn that Bunny had a cameo role in it.

The Bookshelf

An excuse is as good a reason as any. That's the way I want to begin my story. I doubt if anyone else ever had such an opening line? I worked in a library for decades. I knew everything there was to know about the books owned by that institution. We have old tomes and the latest acquisitions. Books of absolutely vital importance and absurd volumes that were aesthetically valueless. That's how libraries work. I made no judgments because I wasn't allowed to. When a student came up to my desk and asked for a copy of Duncey Dafto's *Mysteries of the Enigma* it wasn't my responsibility to warn him or her that the book was nonsense, pure pseudo-science. No.

By the same token, if a student wanted to know if Rumbold Fig's *Mighty Awful Jumbles* was available, I had to bite my tongue and say nothing about how it was a work of genius. My neutrality was perfect. It was such a fulsome neutrality that people began to mutter that I was indifferent. This slander was proof that I was doing my job well.

I was allowed to read books during quiet hours when no students wanted advice or assistance from me, but I was only allowed to do so if more than one copy of those books existed in the library. Funnily enough, we had two copies of Charlton Radish's *Just One Copy* and I was utterly engrossed in that curious text when I fell into a sleep that lasted years. How can a fascinating book be so soporific? I don't think it can. I am confident some other factor was responsible for the drowsiness that came over me.

True enough, the chapter I happened to be perusing at that moment was a printed lecture on somnolence, but it was exciting and invigorating. I believe that some sort of fungus on the pages, a mould that had been growing on the paper since the book was printed, was the true cause. The spores came loose, went up my nose, entered my bloodstream, made me feel amazingly sleepy. I found my eyelids closing like drawbridges and it took immense effort for me to keep them up so that I could see.

To sleep at my desk would be a sacking offence. I would lose my job. I was too far from the bed in my home. The only alternative was to seek out a resting place in the depths of the library. Accordingly I went down the stairs to the lowest level and I found a shelf that wasn't yet full of books, a shelf where there was enough room for me. I stretched myself out on that shelf, which was at head height, and I instantly plunged into the deepest sleep of my existence. I was oblivious to everything, even to dreams. I slept like a bewitched character in a fairy tale, an enchanted princess.

During those lost years, the years of my personal oblivion, lots of things happened, but I was aware of none of them. I only learned about them later. I was asleep on the library shelf, but I hadn't informed anyone that's what I had planned to do, for obvious reasons. I wanted it to remain a secret. The fact that I wasn't at my desk was noted. The authorities visited my home, assuming I'd been struck down with some illness.

Unable to get in contact with me, they eventually gave up. I was lost and that's all that could be said about me. I was another minor mystery, the sort of chap that Duncey Dafto would write about, claiming that I had been abducted by robot aliens or had fallen into a trans-dimensional vortex and been changed into a sentient cauliflower. Duncey Dafto is almost as absurd as Bert Ridiculo. I really think he ought to be forced to return all the honorary degrees he has won over the years. They are undeserved.

I remained on that library shelf. A few months later, a student writing one of the most obscure papers that any student has ever attempted, a dissertation on 'Books That Look Like People', happened to be browsing the shelves of the lowest library level. He chanced on me, pulled me off the shelf, took me back to his digs. He thought I was a book.

He kept me for three weeks, the maximum loan time permitted, read me from cover to cover, then returned me to the library. I was placed back on that particular shelf. The following week I was borrowed again, by another student, a friend of the original student. He also read me from cover to cover, returned me, then told his friends about me.

Rather strangely, I slowly became a cult book among the students of that university. They borrowed me, returned me, discussed me, referenced me in the songs they wrote when some of them decided they wanted to form a band. One student was so exasperated by the fact that I seemed to be on permanent loan that when he finally managed to borrow me for himself, he produced his own pirated version of my body and soul.

But he used cheap materials and apparently it looked like a badly warped image of my reflection in a distorting mirror. It fell apart within a few weeks. I didn't know any of this, of course. I was fast asleep. In fact, to say I was 'fast' asleep is to understate my condition.

I was faster than fast. I was hurtling at breakneck pace but asleep anyway. It's a question of semantics again, even though we are all speaking Esperanto. I know this and you know it too. I was asleep and nothing that happened to me ever seeped into my consciousness.

Parties were held and I was there, casually thrown onto a table or bundled into a corner with all the other cult books, Jimjam Bonker's *Happy Misery*, for example, or Fluff Monkey's *Kiss Yog Better*. Once I was thrust onto a shelf and I ended up coming between two separate volumes of the same work, Lumdrum Cracker's *Jibber and the Jabbers*. My life was extremely interesting, I suppose, but only in the retelling. I felt nothing. At the climax of one spectacular party I was even used as a bat in an improvised game of cricket, and I knocked a bowl of pink custard through the window.

Eventually I was returned to that shelf in the lowest level of the library. I dozed on and on. But one day, not long after an influx of new students, I was taken down by a student who was wearing a ring. The ring scratched my spine and this seemed to have a cancelling effect on the spell I was under. I began to stir, blinking my sleepy eyes, yawing. The student was astonished. She backed away and watched me very carefully.

I sat up and knuckled my eyes, stretched as much as I was able to in that confined space, lowered myself from the shelf, winced as cramp affected my legs and feet, stamped around to restore my circulation and then finally took a deep breath and thanked the student.

After I explained what I thought my situation had been, she lifted her hand to show me her finger and the ring on it. Was it magical? Had it really negated the soporific influence of the mould in Charlton Radish's book? Maybe it was a simple case of being scratched in the right place. Her ring was a large cameo, a distinctive antique made from pink porcelain fixed to a silver band. The image on the cameo was that of a woman on roller skates who was skating towards a vat of grapes. It was clear from her expression that she was unable to brake and would end up in the vat and be squashed by mechanical feet. A strange scene to engrave on an item of jewellery!

I asked for my old job back and the university gave it to me. I was lucky because they could have refused and claimed I was a negligent worker. While crossing the university campus after my successful interview, I was bitten by a squirrel and died of rabies two weeks later. It was my own fault for not reading enough medical textbooks while I'd had the opportunity. Too bad, eh?

—oOo—

I turned to Bunny and cried, "How did you end up as an image on the ring of that student? What's the explanation?"

She shrugged. I could see she genuinely didn't know. Mr Ulysses wasn't much help, he merely said, "She had a cameo role in the tale. People often do, you know. No point fretting over it."

We abandoned him to his own devices and set off. We passed out of the 'U' zone and entered the 'V' zone and met a fellow named Vaughan who had a jawline that was both strong and yet highly reminiscent of a banana. For some reason he seemed familiar and then I remembered that Arcimboldo had created a bas-relief of him from ceiling fruit.

Maybe he had an interesting story to tell us. I don't know because I didn't listen when he opened his mouth. I was weary. Bunny listened but never told me what he said, and I never asked her.

We also met a fellow who was completely in the wrong zone. His name was René Daumal and he was unable to account for the fact he was eighteen zones ahead of where he ought to be.

"I drank too much alcohol," he sighed, "and thought I was climbing up a perfectly flat mountain, and when I got to the summit I found myself here. It's not a pleasant situation to be in. The angels don't like to see people reversing down here but what choice do I have?"

"Not much, none in fact," I sympathised.

He rolled his eyes in mock exasperation and pulled out a bottle of brandy from the pocket of his coat. "Cognac?"

"No thanks," I said.

"I'm focussed on cocktails," Bunny claimed.

"Tout cela sera pour moi."

That's what he said, but logically he must have said it in Esperanto, not in French. It was a bit confusing.

We left him and resumed walking. Actually, I walked but Bunny still used her improvised roller skates, though now they were falling apart. Her top speed on those squealing wheels was only the same as my amble. She still wanted to stop for weeks and wait for cocktails. I wanted to keep going without a break. We ended up compromising. One week of relatively fast travel, then one week of sofas and daiquiris or whatever else happened to descend from the hatches. I very occasionally sipped a beer.

The 'W' zone turned out to be more interesting than many other zones. It had a stretch where the ceiling was different. Instead of being plain white and studded with hatches, it was a multicoloured swirl that beguiled the eyes, made the mind apprehensive, fuddled the emotions. Bunny said that it looked like an inverted crater that had been filled with psychedelic soup. We gazed upwards as we went and that's how we almost walked into a man who was sitting on a seat unlike any other in the Waiting Room.

It was low and uncomfortable, functional rather than aesthetic, covered in leatherette, and he was very tense as he sat on it. He was clutching with both hands a steering wheel that wasn't connected to anything. Then we stopped and examined his immediate environs more carefully. Scraps of rusted metal, shards of broken glass, charred plastic. Something odd had happened here. And he was sitting directly under the swirling ceiling. His grin was a rictus and it was only with a mighty effort that he was able to speak.

"Still in shock," he said.

"Who is? Not us, I can assure you."

"Myself," he grunted.

"But why? What took place here?"

He inhaled deeply.

"It's not a question of what took place here," he told us, "but what occurred on the Earth's surface. I was a bus driver. I guess I still am, in some senses, as I haven't resigned or been sacked."

"These are the ruins of your bus?"

"Quite correct."

He took one hand off the steering wheel to gesture at the scrap metal in our vicinity. His knuckles remained white. He returned his hand to its former grip as a sob escaped his tight lips.

"Won't you tell us exactly what happened?"

"I will," he finally said.

The Infinity Decker

The government of my country was always looking for new ways to encourage the greater use of public transport. It would be good for the environment if there were fewer cars on the road. It decided that a new type of bus was needed, one with many levels. Double deckers can carry many people simultaneously. What if a bus was constructed with an infinite number of levels? Of course, this idea was soon scuttled by the engineers, but they were told to add as many levels as possible, whatever that number might be.

The height of a standard double decker is sixteen feet and three inches, or if you prefer metric measurements, then 4.95 metres. The engineers wondered how tall a bus could be made before it imploded under its own weight. Thanks to new materials such as carbon nanotubes, it was discovered that a bus could be made that was 331,364.829 feet tall. Once again, if you prefer metric, then the result is 101,000 metres. They approved the plans and construction started and I was chosen to be the driver of the vehicle.

It was a tremendous honour, of course, but I do believe I deserved it. I had driven buses all my working life, through cities and beyond them, seven days a week, fifty-two weeks a year, ten years every decade. I was considered the best of the best, the most reliable driver of buses in the country, a man who required no time off ever, utterly committed to his job, a bus lover, an obsessive but in a good way. My name is Worthington and it was quipped around the depot that I was 'worth a ton' of other drivers, but in fact I regarded this estimate as far too low. I was worth seven hundred tons!

Now I am getting excited and that's unfortunate. I am still in shock. How many levels does a double decker have? The answer is in the name 'double'. It has two levels, of course. How many levels did this new bus have? Even though we all still referred to it as the infinity decker, the number of levels was actually only 40,725 levels. Passengers who wanted to sit on the top had to commence climbing the stairs weeks before the bus was due to set off. And that's exactly what they did. The top levels were the most popular. People longed to sit high above the land and look down on everything the same way a noctilucent cloud might, to see the curvature of the Earth.

And yes, the planet is round, not flat, as some ancient authorities like that funny old Cosmas Indicopleustes stated, and I know this because I once set off in a straight line, driving a lovely new bus, a single decker, and I went around the world and ended up back at my starting point. But that's a digression and has nothing to do with the infinity decker. Once the infinity decker was full, I released the handbrake and set off. I had to avoid all bridges, because none of them were high enough to allow a bus with 40,725 levels to pass under them. I am a good navigator, so no problem for me. I drove the safest route, even when it involved taking diversions of immense length. No one complained. They were too enthralled by the magic of the ride.

But after a few hours I began to hear mutterings of discontent. These grew in volume and eventually they were impossible to ignore. One of the passengers had been delegated to approach me. He made his way forward and spoke in the most polite voice imaginable. Passengers aren't supposed to speak to the driver when the bus is in motion, but I'm not one of those sour by-the-book chappies. I understand that rules should be flexible.

He said, "The people one level above this one are shouting down that the people one level above them are shouting down," and when I asked him what they were shouting, he added, "They claim that the people one level above are shouting down because the people one level above are shouting down that the people one level above are shouting down."

"How many levels in total?" I demanded to know.

"Forty thousand and more."

"So the shouting originates with the passengers on the very highest level? Do they have a problem up there?"

"Yes, they do. It appears that they are now so high that they're outside the planet's atmosphere. They are above the so-called Kármán line, the boundary between Earth's atmosphere and outer space set by the Fédération aéronautique internationale, and which is registered at an altitude of 100 kilometres, which if you prefer imperial measurements is 62 miles or 330,000 feet above mean sea level. They say they can't breathe."

"Can't breathe? Well, that's not good for them."

"What shall they do?"

"They are asking me? But I am the driver, not a life strategist. Let me take a moment to think about this."

He waited while I took that moment.

I gave the moment back.

And I concluded, "Tell them to descend until they can breathe. If they have to stand because there are no seats, that doesn't matter. It's more important that they have oxygen and stay alive."

"I will pass your instructions on," he said.

And that's what he did.

The long and the short of it, and I use the word' short' figuratively here, as there was little or nothing short about the infinity decker, is that the passengers on the highest level descended to the next highest level, found they still couldn't breathe and so descended another level, taking the passengers on that other level with them, and so on, and they didn't stop descending until they had reached the 3,224[th] level, the first level directly below the line of the Death Zone, or 26,000 feet, which is 8000 metres, the limit above which the pressure of oxygen is not sufficient to sustain human life for longer than a few hours. It's true that people have climbed higher mountains without oxygen, but they have gone up, reached the summit and come right back down.

They never lingered, as my passengers had been doing, in those seats high above the highest clouds, in a region where meteors often whizzed past without making a fuss, and where the stars had a clarity that was astounding. The point is that my passengers were now safe. But there isn't a happy ending, because the simplest story down here is like a syntax snake, with a twist in the tale. Here is the twist of this one. While the passengers were occupying the topmost levels of the bus, the bus weighed a lot less. Let me explain.

Gravity pulled at them to a much lesser extent when they were so high. They were almost in orbit. Do you understand what I'm saying? Seriously.

The infinity decker was now much heavier, it was so heavy that the ground beneath could no longer support it. A sinkhole opened in a more fragile region of geology and the entire bus plunged deep into the Earth. The pit we had fallen into seemed almost bottomless. We plummeted for ages, screaming. Then we crashed through the ceiling at this point.

The collision was so hard that I was shaken in every atom of my body. As I have already said, I'm still in shock. The highest level of the bus was now flush with the level of the surface. But it didn't remain that way for long. Breaking a hole into the afterlife from outside is forbidden. Angels were dispatched to take the bus apart and they worked quickly.

Soon the vehicle was dismantled and most of the pieces carted away. What remained was allowed to rust and decay and you can see the remnants of it here. The passengers were lifted back up the hole by angels and set free up there. But I was forgotten for some reason. I remained in the driver's seat, clutching at my steering wheel, and here I am. The ceiling is going to be repaired, that's what I have been told anyway, but the angels have been dragging their feet over such a task. As a temporary measure they fill up the hole with their bodies, flying there in endless multicoloured circles. See!

That's my story. I am Worthington. Pleased to meet you. Best not to linger near here. I advise you to push on immediately. The angels sometimes swoop to have a rest and they will perch on your shoulders and it's an unpleasant feeling. I have been informed that I am lucky because I crashed down into the Waiting Room at the exact place where I would be assigned if I was dead. There was no need for me to travel anywhere on foot.

That really *is* fortunate because I have quite forgotten how to walk. I am a bus driver, the ultimate bus driver. Say goodbye now and get a move on. This is the 40,725th time I have told my story. Coincidences do exist, even down here! Farewell, whoever you are. Go in peace and never go by bus unless the bus has a reasonable number of levels. Thanks!

—oOo—

We hurried out of there as soon as his story was done. But we stumbled over the wreckage for an hour or so before we were clear. It was a relief to walk beneath a normal ceiling again. I said very little from that point on, until we reached the 'X' zone, which was mercifully small, relatively speaking. Bunny's skates now completely collapsed. She had to walk.

I imagine she was half hoping I would carry her in my arms, but she never asked me directly and so I pretended not to notice any of her imploring looks as she tottered onwards. A month later she had developed adequate muscles to be a fine hiker, so it all worked out very well.

In fact she began to outpace me, for I wasn't exactly the fittest example of a human being, having been a wine taster in my surface life. Why did I drink an occasional beer down here? For a wine connoisseur to do that was an act akin to treachery. Then I remembered that dead people can't be traitors and I relaxed. I eschewed a cocktail while deciding this.

We were resting at the very end of the 'X' zone, where all the people with patently false surnames such as Xwugy, Xylobals and Xzyzy were waiting. The individuals seated here fell into two categories. Roughly half of them were cruel but not too cruel fugitives who had changed their names long before death and the afterlife administration hadn't seen through the ruse, and the other half were men and women with reasonable enough surnames that had become mangled in the incompetent workings of the system.

For example, I had earlier spoken to a Miss Xpahanal who was actually a Miss Phalanx and should have been in the 'P' zone. She had tried to attract the attention of the angels that passed, in order to make an official complaint, but they ignored her. She told me a tale about a battle with pikes but I wasn't really listening. She drank ouzo and retsina and nothing else. She often had to wait years before the ceiling hatches delivered such liquids. She mentioned something about holding small angels hostage and tying them to our shoes, so that we would have a new method of transportation that resembled winged sandals. I think she was out of her mind, but who isn't a little mad here?

In the 'Y' zone, we encountered a fellow who called himself Yannis, and I realised he was the professor who had written the book, *The Psychology of the Wind*, that Nathan had mentioned. "The wind is scared of tigers," he told us. He seemed pleased with this observation.

"What else frightens it?" I asked and he recited a rather long list of objects, actions, colours, elements and utterances.

He looked at Bunny with approval and lowered his voice. "They might be scared of her too. Especially the north wind. The north wind has the reputation of being a heartless oppressor and yet most of its aggression is bluster. I believe this lady would give it deep qualms."

"Why?" I demanded.

"Because they aren't shallow," he said.

"You misunderstand. I didn't inquire why the qualms were deep. I wanted to know why Bunny would be so distressing to the winds. She is my ex-wife. I feel I have a right to be informed."

"You clearly don't understand the divorce laws."

"As an act of mercy," I said.

"Very well." He shrugged. "But it's one of the unknowns about the winds. The reason I study the winds is because they are a better subject than the one I originally studied. I would rather talk about that right now. I studied prayer, the power and efficacy of praying."

"I see," I said, and this time I wished I didn't.

"A story is coming?" asked Bunny. She plonked herself down on the most comfortable seat in the vicinity.

"That's usually what happens," agreed Yannis.

And he told one to us.

The Anthill

Most prayers don't work and it's hardly surprising. No matter what god or gods you believe in, when you pray you are asking those supernatural beings to alter the plans they have drawn up for the progression of the universe. Maybe Zeus wants a volcano to explode. You pray to him and lobby him to change his mind about the incident, even though he might have superb reasons for the eruption, reasons that will make the universe a better place. Perhaps Odin wants glaciers to iron flat your grandma. You pray to him and ask for grandma to be spared an icy crushing, even though he worked out decades ago that the flattening of your mother's mother would be beneficial to humanity. Praying is lobbying and can be considered selfish and capitalistic.

That's one way of looking at it, anyway. But it explains why most prayers don't work. But even more remarkably, *some* prayers *do* seem effective, and I was intensely interested in those kinds of prayers. I devoted my youth to doing research on this ontological topic. Was it really ontological? I thought so at the time but I have since forgotten what ontology is. That isn't important. I was the most devoted student that has ever been seen at my university. Even a chap by the name of Nathan who was renowned for his studying prowess couldn't match the sheer hours I devoted to my work.

I discovered, after a lot of effort and exhaustion, that the most effective god to pray to wasn't even a proper god, nor a demon, but a being that was halfway between the two states. An entity named Yaldabaoth, but everyone calls him the Demiurge. He's a sort of architect who does work for purer forces. He designed the sherbert fountain in Heaven, for example, which is in the shape of a vertical sausage dog with an enormously elongated body. It sprays sherbert endlessly, a magnificent spectacle, so I have heard.

Now then, let me continue by revealing to you that I discovered the magic words that can be used to grab the attention of Yaldabaoth. Those words run as follows, 'oaf behaviour joy', and they are an anagram of 'I have a job for you', which is very weird when you consider that Esperanto is the afterlife language, not English, and the anagram shouldn't work at all. But we are mortals, expired mortals, so what do we know, ultimately?

But here's the twist. It's not enough to say those three words once. In order to grab Yaldabaoth's attention properly, you are obliged to keep repeating them, over and over, hundreds of times, thousands of times, maybe millions of times! Only then will he perk up and listen to your prayer and grant your wish. In fact, it is said, and I found this to be true, that you must sit cross-legged, as immobile as possible, chanting those words until ants construct an anthill around you, and only when you are inside the anthill will Yaldabaoth be ready to listen. But he'll always answer your prayer when that happens. He will grant you any wish, yes, but you are only allowed to ask for one.

And you can't ask for anything impossible. You can't pray to be made into a god, or to take over his own job, or to switch all the occupants of Heaven with the occupants of Hell. It can't be a silly request. The same holds true for genies, I believe. One sensible wish, one sensible prayer, it amounts to the same thing. I was young but I wasn't an idiot. I was going to pray for something that could be granted without disrupting the cosmos.

I sat myself down on a cushion in the lotus position, though I was closer to resembling a frangipani, if we are going to be more accurate with our man-plant comparisons, and I closed my eyes. I entered a trance, as best I could, and then I began to chant in a deep voice, 'oaf behaviour joy', until those words became an ocean in which I was immersed, and the ocean expanded until it was a universe in its own right, a new reality, a sonic simulation of everything, a rumble and an undulation, a vibration and a totality, 'oaf behaviour joy' again and again. Rich and resonant, vibrant and harmonious.

I lost all track of time, time lost all track of me, track

lost all time of me. I floated in a void that was full. I plummeted through a thickness that was empty. I existed in an ineffable space. It was so ineffable that it turned me inside-out. I accelerated and remained still, I grew and shrank. I was a contradiction that was in tune with logic. But still I kept chanting. I was only dimly aware that legions of tiny ants were crawling around me.

They were constructing an anthill and I was inside it. When it was finished I stopped chanting and opened my eyes. I was in darkness. But the terms of the prayer had been met. Yaldabaoth was now ready to answer my prayer. He would grant me just one wish. I could ask for anything reasonable. I took a deep breath and fumes of formic acid almost choked me. It was horrible being in that prison of earthy darkness. Insects were crawling over my skin and biting me. I couldn't move and I had terrible cramps in every muscle of my body. I must use my wish now, utter my prayer to the Demiurge.

I shouted in acute desperation, "Please hear me, Yaldabaoth! Get me out of this goddamn anthill. Release me back into the wide open world! I hate it inside this insectile dungeon. Help, Yaldabaoth! Break open the anthill so I can escape or magically transport me outside in one fell swoop. However, you accomplish it, do it quickly. I am suffocating here!"

There was a blinding flash, because flashes in stories are always blinding. I found myself in the fresh air, covered in soil and smelling like ants. I gasped for breath and crawled away from the ruined anthill. Yaldabaoth shimmered before me in ectoplasmic form. He lifted a hand and waved at me. He also blew me an unexpected kiss. Then he vanished. I was disgusted with myself. I had wasted a great many years on a futile experiment.

I immediately ceased to study the subject of prayers and I decided to study a topic that had nothing to do with wishes. When I had finally managed to lurch all the way home, I randomly opened a dictionary. I fumbled with the pages and opened it too far and my jabbing finger settled on the word 'wind'. I tried again and once more fumbled with the pages and this time I didn't open the book far enough and my jabbing finger settled on the word 'breeze'. Then I laughed, for I knew precisely what my fate would be.

—o0o—

Bunny enjoyed this story more than I did, I don't know why. We said goodbye to Professor Yannis and resumed our journey. We were nearing the end of our ordeal. In the next zone were our assigned seats. Near the far end of that zone, it's true, but all the same we had completed more than 96% of the journey. So many years had passed, but enough of that, I don't want to grow sentimental. I think we even increased our pace now.

We crossed into the 'Z' zone and kept going, talking to as few people as we could manage, without appearing rude. And finally we reached the region reserved for people with the surname Zubris. Can you imagine my feelings at that moment? I was elated, drained, satisfied, furious, relieved, anxious, every emotion possible all mixed together in one big intense broth, but one of those emotions was indifference and it helped to calm the others, so I didn't explode with an overload of reactions. And then Bunny went through exactly the same process. Then we waltzed with each other and for a moment it seemed to me it might be possible for us to remarry.

But this fleeting idea wasn't permitted to achieve any kind of solid reality, for we found a letter waiting for her on a chair in an envelope. A chair in an envelope! That's odd. No, it's the letter that was in an envelope. A letter on the very seat that had been reserved for her. It was certainly the most comfortable armchair in the vicinity, exactly the sort of seat Bunny would choose for herself, and there was already a silver tray on the table next to it, and on that tray were seven extremely potent cocktails.

She picked up the envelope, tore it open and read the letter inside. Her face was inscrutable. How could I make it scrutable instead? I continued to dance but without her, because a man waltzing on his own looks absurd and comical and it might serve to snap the tension she was obviously experiencing. But she raised a hand to cancel my antics and said:

"It appears that my paperwork has been sorted out, the paperwork about my name, I mean, and I am now officially regarded as Hopkins by the angels. I am obliged to return to the 'H' zone. I must travel on foot and display a special passport to them. The passport is also included in this envelope. I really don't like this idea. I don't want to walk."

"What about us?" I blubbered, and she glared at me.

"There isn't any 'us'," she said.

I was at a loss for words. Of course, people don't marry in the afterlife, not even if they have been married before. I should have been more sensible in my transient hopes and expectations.

"If I must go, I must go," she said, "but I think I will take a shortcut. I hate the notion of retracing my steps."

"A shortcut!" I cried. "No, Bunny, no!"

"Why not?" she said.

"Don't use the passages behind the walls!"

"Not that kind of shortcut," she said with a laugh, "but this kind…" And she picked up the cocktails one by one and drank them all, gulping them down so quickly that there was nothing I could do. She collapsed soon after and then expired from alcohol poisoning.

I watched as her prone body faded away and vanished altogether. Not one molecule remained of my ex-wife. I knew she would reappear as a fresh soul at the doors of the Waiting Room. The Devil would open those doors for her. And she would walk, yes, but not as far as if she had reversed direction, because the 'H' zone is closer to the 'A' zone than it is to the 'Z' zone. How could I blame her for making that clever choice?

But now I glared down at the empty seat reserved for me. I saw nothing of any merit in it. And I remembered my vow to walk beyond my assigned place and find out what lay at the very end of the Waiting Room. I continued walking. Nothing would stop me. I passed out of the 'Z' zone at last and there were no more hatches in the ceiling, no more panels in the walls. No more food, drink, bathroom visits or angelic whippings. Just the Waiting Room, devoid of seats, with bare walls, dim lighting. I was alone. I kept going. Years passed and with the passing of those years my soul became very hard. I was pure determination. Not a single soft atom remained in me.

The far end of the Waiting Room became visible at last. A solid wall. But there was something on a little mound in the very centre of that expanse. And it resolved itself into a cottage as I approached it. A cottage? The design was odd but charming enough. A short flight of stone steps went up the mound, leading to the front door of the cottage. On the bottom step sat a familiar figure. He was strumming a ukulele but very quietly.

"The Demiurge designed it," said the Devil.

"The ukulele?" I cried.

"The cottage, Mr Zubris. It's my residence down here. I don't really enjoy living in the Waiting Room, but my original home was destroyed by erosion. It was quite a palace in comparison."

"Your original home was in Hell, I suppose?"

He grimaced at this.

"Heavens, no! Who would want to live there? It was on the Earth's surface in a natural amphitheatre, snowbound and eerie, that might have been created by a meteorite impact aeons ago. Somewhere in the Kingdom of Lo. The Demiurge said it was his very best design."

"But that's not saying much," he answered, when he saw that I was far too stunned to say anything. He laughed.

I recovered my wits sufficiently to say, "I see."

"Left most of my possessions behind," he continued, "and they also eroded themselves to nothing over time. I only took with me the things I really loved. For example, this musical instrument."

"That's nice," I said.

"And the old wooden box with my halo."

"What did you say?"

"The old wooden box. My halo's inside it. Don't want to lose that, it's my most treasured possession. I keep the box upstairs in a room I very rarely enter. That room is a sanctum."

"But you are the Devil. How can you have a halo? You are evil. Haloes are for saints and holy individuals."

He smiled and plucked a chord on the ukulele.

"Listen to me," he said.

"I'm listening," I answered truthfully.

And then he spoke:

"The chaos of the bureaucracy down here is deliberate. Yes, that's right. It has been arranged. I don't actually want anyone to go to Hell. The idea horrifies me. I do the best I can to slow the process down. That's why this Waiting Room exists and it is why the administration is so incompetent. I want to delay as long as possible your transfer to the Circles of Hell. I want to delay it by millions and billions of years. I hate Hell and all it stands for. I am utterly opposed to eternal suffering. So I sabotage the system."

"Like the characters in *The Monkey Wrench Gang*?"

"I have heard of that novel and it's on my reading list but I haven't gotten around to it yet. I'm a disruptor."

"You are good, not evil? This is amazing!"

He lowered his eyes.

He was a modest entity, I saw. He continued, "I don't want to send people to Hell if I can avoid it, so I invent problems with their paperwork to keep them in the Waiting Room as long as I can, deferring their sufferings. This is why my halo remains in the box. It's a secret. I never wear it openly. Occasionally I will open the box, take it out and try it on."

"How does it look over those horns of yours?"

"Passable, Mr Zubris."

"I know about wine but not about fashion."

"Then you are lucky."

"The wines down here have been mostly very good, but for some reason I have been drinking beer."

"Death affects people in different ways."

"But your halo is–"

He said, "I must be very careful that my secret is known to as few minds as possible. You are now wondering why I have told you. Who are you to me? Well, it so happens that the Demiurge is about to retire. He is almost as old as the universe. Someone will have to take over from him. Pure chance seems to have selected you as a candidate."

I swallowed with difficulty and said, "How many other candidates for the position are being considered?"

"None," he answered, and he winked at me.

"This can't be right," I said.

"Why not, Mr Zubris? What's the difficulty?"

I took a deep breath.

"You are the Devil. You are the opposite of God. How can you be good? God is Love and you are the opposite of Love. You must be Hate. This bothers me a lot, I don't mind admitting."

"Oh, really!" he exclaimed and he began laughing. His laughter was wild and contagious. Soon I was laughing too. We both calmed down after several minutes. My dead ribs were aching.

"Your logic is flawed, my friend," he told me, "for the opposite of Love isn't Hate. Where did you get that idea from? It's a lazy assumption. No, Mr Zubris, the opposite of Love is Like."

Then he added with exquisite kindness in his eyes, "God loves you but I like you. And I like you very much."

EPILOGUE

I was working at my desk when there was a knock on my office door. Without looking up I called, "Enter," and it opened and the sibilant tones of a familiar voice washed over me. I immediately put my pencil down and swung myself around in my posh swivel chair.

"Good to see the new Demiurge so busy."

He was wearing his halo, but the gleam of triumph in his eyes had little or nothing to do with pride. Something had given him deep satisfaction and I was sure I would find out what it was soon enough. But he felt that formalities had to be observed first. He asked:

"What project are you working on now?"

I indicated the large sheet of paper pinned to my desk. "It's a labyrinth for overambitious inventors. They cause a lot of trouble everywhere. I am designing a maze that normal people can easily escape from, but which will be a baffling prison for those inventors. There is some tricky hyper-spatial geometry involved and it will be located in a parallel dimension. Most of my recent commissions have been for other universes."

"Seems a very worthy venture," he said.

I waited, and finally he came to the point, "I didn't just want to check up on you and say hello, but I also wanted to share some news," he added, "and in fact it's the culmination of a dream."

Grinning, I said nothing. I urged him on with gestures. He slowly stroked his pointed beard and continued:

"You know how I am doing my best to postpone the sending to Hell of as many souls as possible? You have probably wondered to yourself whether my altruism is worthwhile, considering that the souls will eventually end up in Hell anyway and Hell is forever? But my hope was always for a reconciliation with God and the eventual dismantling of Hell. It has been a long process. We have been negotiating for a billion years."

He paused, almost overcome with emotion. Then he

attempted to resume but failed. "Only this very morning–"

"There was a breakthrough?" I finished for him.

He nodded and sobbed.

Tearing off a strip of the paper on my desk, I passed it to him and he used it to wipe his eyes and blow his nose.

"Congratulations," I said, and he gasped.

"No more Hell," he mumbled.

"The Waiting Room will be demolished too, I take it?"

"Abandoned, certainly."

"And all the humans inside it set free?"

"Of course. How could it be otherwise? Anyway, I just wanted you to be the first to know. No more pain, no more suffering. Of course, something still needs to be done with seriously evil people. We can't be too tolerant of *them*. They can be continuously reincarnated until they learn to be good. That's one solution. I'll keep you updated."

He gazed down at me, his halo slipped at a jaunty angle over his horns, his eyes twinkled. "By the way," he said, "there's a Miss Hopkins who has asked if she can pay you a visit once the Waiting Room doors are taken off their hinges? I said yes. I hope that's fine with you?"

Now it was my turn to blow my nose on a strip of paper. My drawing was ruined but I didn't care. If the prison of Hell was going to be decommissioned, how could I continue with my labyrinth for inventors? My emotional reaction set the Devil off again, and we both cried and laughed together. Then he went away and left me alone. I stood and walked to the window and peered out. The galaxies in every direction were rotating more quickly and I knew that the best days of existence were still to come.

Elsewhen Press
delivering outstanding new talents in speculative fiction

Visit the Elsewhen Press website at elsewhen.press for the latest information on all of our titles, authors and events; to read our blog; find out where to buy our books and ebooks; or to place an order.

Sign up for the Elsewhen Press InFlight Newsletter at elsewhen.press/newsletter

Also by Rhys Hughes from Elsewhen Press

MIRRORS *IN THE* DELUGE
RHYS HUGHES

Mirrors in the Deluge is a collection of 32 unrelated stories that take elements from fantasy, science fiction, horror and other genres and give them a lateral shift. Like much of Rhys' work these quirky tales between them encompass parody, pastiche and puns.

The fun, as ever, starts with the title of each story – gently leading an unsuspecting reader into preconceived ideas and expectations; expectations that are soon spun around, turned on their head (or other extremities), and pushed in an unexpected direction. Thus, a saunter merely through the contents page is already a hugely entertaining experience and one more akin to savouring the hors d'oeuvres of a grand feast than consulting a list of shortcuts into a literary tome. In fact, the gastronomic metaphor serves us well here; the courses on offer range from tantalising tuck to a gourmand's repast, but never mere vittles – perhaps the way to enjoy this book is to digest one story, three times a day (four if you're a halfling who needs second breakfast), rather than trying to gorge on all the available delights and delicacies at one sitting.

To complete this gourmet's guide, a tempting sampling of the stories must include: *The Soft Landing*, a unique story told from the perspective of a photon; *Travels with my Antinomy*, how do you solve a paradox when you're part of it?; *Vanity of Vanities*, the internet achieves consciousness and takes over, but with very different consequences than you might imagine; *The Fairy and the Dinosaur*, in which a fairy can't find what she wants for her picnic in the goblin market, is offered cloned prehistoric plums but turns to a time-travelling robot to go back to the age of the dinosaurs and eat an original plum. Other titles to tempt you include *The Martian Monocles*, *The Prodigal Beard*, *A Dame Abroad*, *The Unkissed Artist Formerly Known as Frog*, *The Goat That Gloated*, *The Taste of Turtle Tears*, *The Bones of Jones*, and *The Haggis Eater*.

"It's a crime that Rhys Hughes is not as widely known as Italo Calvino and other writers of that stature. Brilliantly written and conceived, Hughes' fiction has few parallels anywhere in the world. In some alternate universe with a better sense of justice, his work triumphantly parades across all bestseller lists. "   – JEFF VANDERMEER

ISBN: 9781908168757 (epub, kindle) / 9781908168658 (200pp paperback)

Visit bit.ly/MirrorsDeluge

STUDENTS OF MYSELF

RHYS HUGHES

There are few students in my class. When one considers what the subject is, this isn't surprising. I teach myself.

In other words, I impart to my students facts and fancies based on my life and ideas. It's the least popular class in the university and I doubt it will be funded for another term. But none of that is my fault. I wanted to teach a proper discipline such as ecology, but the authorities wouldn't let me. They insisted that I teach myself; and as a result, I do so.

The students are given an assignment. They each have to write a short piece about how I spend my free time. But this is information I've always kept secret. I can't imagine how they're expected to know anything about my private life, certainly not in detail.

Clearly I'm being spied on. Unless it's guesswork?

I read the essays anxiously.

Yes, only some of them have got it right...

"If I said he was a Welsh writer who writes as though he has gone to school with the best writing from all over the world, I wonder if my compliment would just sound provincial. Hughes' style – with all that means – is among the most beautiful I've encountered in several years."

– SAMUEL R. DELANY

ISBN: 9781911409793 (epub, kindle) / 9781911409694 (112pp paperback)

Visit bit.ly/StudentsOfMyself

AN ORCHID IN MY BELLY BUTTON

KATY WIMHURST

Offbeat short stories that explore our fragile world

These stories savour the surreal, flirt with magical realism, dabble with dystopia. A boy sees the ghosts of dead crabs. A girl with a fox tail is bullied. A disenchanted woman sprouts orchids from her belly button. Fashion models pursue the trend of having plants as hair. Electronic goods amassing all over London herald an apocalypse. Darkness and wonder, the strange and the ordinary, interweave to offer an environmental and social portrait of our times. Guaranteed to evoke a response, whether a giggle, a gasp, or a nervous gulp, these stories will stay with you, enriching your perception of the world.

Surreal, absurdist, magical realist; Katy Wimhurst writes speculative fiction that meditates on our reality. Although bleak themes are examined – dystopian futures, the climate crisis, bullying – a quirky imagination and wry humour lift the tales above the 'realm of grim'.

ISBN: 9781915304797 (epub, kindle) / 9781915304698 (160pp paperback)

Visit bit.ly/AnOrchidInMyBellyButton

GALAXIES AND FANTASIES

A Collection of Rather Amazing
and Wide-ranging Short Stories

ANDY MCKELL

Prepare for the unexpected

Galaxies and Fantasies is an eclectic collection of tales from master-storyteller Andy McKell, crossing genres from mythology to cosmology, fairytale to space opera, surrealism to hyper-reality. What they all have in common is a twist, a surprise, a revelation. Leave your pre-conceptions aside when you read these stories, prepare for the unexpected, the extraordinary, the unpredictable. Some are quite succinct and you'll be immediately wanting more; others are more elaborate, but deftly devised, and you'll be thinking about them long after you've finished reading. These are stories that will stay with you, not in a haunting way, but like a satisfying memory that often returns to encourage, enchant or enrich your life.

ISBN: 9781915304162 (epub, kindle) / 97819153041063 (186pp paperback)

Visit bit.ly/GalaxiesAndFantasies

About Rhys Hughes

Rhys Hughes began writing from an early age. His first book, *Worming the Harpy*, was published in 1995 by Tartarus Press, and since then he has published more than fifty other books, and his fiction has been translated into twelve languages. His work encompasses genres as diverse as fantasy, gothic, experimental, science fiction, magic realism, comedy, absurdism, thrillers and westerns, and he is known for his invention, imagination and wordplay. He recently completed an ambitious project that involved writing exactly one thousand linked short stories. He also writes plays, poems and articles.